Stealing Home

Stealing Home

A Diamonds and Dugouts Novel

JENNIFER SEASONS

AVONIMPULSE
An Imprint of HarperCollins Publishers

Excerpt from *Playing the Field* copyright © 2013 by Candice Wakoff.

Excerpt from *All or Nothing* copyright © 2013 by Dixie Brown.

EPub Edition APRIL 2013 ISBN: 9780062271440

Print Edition ISBN: 9780062271457

10 9 8 7 6 5 4 3 2 1

For Brad:
Because when I met you I found home.

Chapter 1

DESPERATION WAS A funny thing. Everybody thought they knew themselves until it crept into their subconscious like a stealth ninja. Perfectly logical, intelligent people scoffed at the idea that a single emotion could override all rational thought. To them, irrational behavior was for the weak-minded.

But raw desperation didn't discriminate.

It changed a person.

Made them do things that in their normal, everyday lives they'd be appalled to even consider.

Raking a shaky hand through her long dark hair, Lorelei Littleton gave herself a mental kick to get on with it. Procrastination wasted precious minutes she couldn't afford to lose.

A well of emotion rose in her throat at the thought and she felt the inappropriate urge to giggle. She did that when she was freaked out. If she gave in to the urge she'd probably just end up crying and that wouldn't solve anything, either. Action was the only solution.

As she took a deep breath, her green eyes shifted over the crowd in the dimly lit blues bar. Nobody noticed her sitting at the back table by herself.

Not that she was dressed to command attention. That wasn't her style. She was more of a casual girl. Other women in the bar were sleek in designer clothes with professionally highlighted hair done just so in typical man-bait fashion. Lorelei, on the other hand, slumped in her seat sans makeup, with old jeans and a faded yellow T-shirt from REI that read "I Dig Everything." Since she was a writer for a gardening magazine, it had tickled her funny bone.

She wasn't dressed to get a man, even though she was there *for* a man. She'd spent the past hour in her little dark corner watching and observing him. But he wasn't just anyone.

He was *the* one. The antidote to her break from sanity.

The display on her cell phone began flashing, signaling she'd received a new text message. Picking it up off the table, Lorelei flipped it open. The text was from Dina Andrews, the woman who'd started her down this road of shady behavior. Well, no, that wasn't exactly true. She'd started down that road all by herself, and tripped over Dina in the process. No use blaming somebody else for her long slide down from the moral high ground. She'd made that choice and could at least be big enough to admit it. Squaring her shoulders, Lorelei ignored the trail of unease skittering down her spine and quickly scanned the message.

To anyone else it would have looked like nothing but a bunch of numbers, but she knew better. It was the security code to a posh condo in downtown Denver that belonged to the man she had been watching—Dina's ex-husband, major league baseball's hottest catcher, Mark "The Wall" Cutter.

Snapping the phone shut, Lorelei glanced up and across the room toward the Denver Rush player. It didn't surprise her in the least to see a big-breasted blond flirting and batting her eyelashes at the infamous ballplayer. Women had been trying since she'd arrived at seven to score a seat at his table. And why not? He was known not to discriminate. Even she, who rarely paid attention to the media, had heard of his playboy ways.

She was surprised that none of them had succeeded in landing a spot, however. It had been her impression that he was pretty notorious with the ladies. But if that was the case, she wasn't seeing it tonight. Not that it mattered, or changed the plan either way.

The fact was he had something she needed. And she was going to get it.

Unexpected amusement filled her as the blond stalked off in a huff, her attempts to charm the catcher unproductive. It seemed that no sooner had the blond left than a brunette slithered her way over to him. Lorelei shook her head and adjusted in her seat, bumping her knee on the underside of the table as she crossed her legs.

Watching Mark Cutter get hit on was almost more entertaining than going to the movies.

Not that she could really blame the women. His team profile picture didn't do him justice at all. The man was gorgeous. Dark blond hair, tan, tall, and powerfully built. He had delicious dimples in his lean cheeks when he smiled.

Boy, was that grin of his potent. Lorelei could feel the power of it in the pit of her stomach every time it flashed. Thank goodness he didn't seem to be much in the smiling mood tonight. She didn't need to be sidetracked and lose focus. Dina had concocted a plan that was simple and straightforward, but she didn't want to risk screwing it up by being stupid.

The house band kicked into a new set just as the brunette stomped away in a pout, making Lorelei chuckle under her breath. Sultry blues filled the bar, all guitar and moody sax. Her gaze shifted from the catcher to the two other men sitting at the table with him. Both she recognized from the Denver Rush Web site. Even if she hadn't seen their pictures there was no mistaking them for anything but baseball players. They had that rough-and-cocky quality about them.

All three of them had been drinking steadily since they'd arrived. Fabulous. It was going to make her job that much easier. Mark Cutter wouldn't even know he'd been robbed until it was too late.

Shame echoed in the recesses of her mind at the word "robbed," but she shoved it away.

Tapping a foot with nervous energy, Lorelei thought back to the night she'd met Dina Andrews. She'd painted the picture of a womanizing, alcohol-chugging, drug-abusing jerk. But her conscience had nagged at her to rate the guy for herself and not go on faith alone. Which explained why she was currently running surveillance and being all inconspicuous in her little corner.

Dina's description wasn't quite jiving with what she'd been observing the past hour, but it'd been enough at the time to get her to agree to the deal. Now it was too late to back out and she was caught between the proverbial rock and hard place.

She and her brother had tried everything under the sun to get the money to pay for the surgery that would save her niece's life. Nothing had worked and now their backs were to the wall. Everybody understood the state of national health care these days, and its shortcomings. Her brother made too much money for government assistance, but couldn't afford health insurance on his own, being self-employed. Plus, with her niece's congenital condition, no private insurance would touch them.

They were stuck. Michelle had been given six months to live if the hole in her heart wasn't repaired soon.

That's where the desperation came into play. Every legitimate avenue had been exhausted in search of money, and as the clock ticked down and panic ratcheted up, that line between right and wrong had become increasingly easy to cross.

The way Lorelei saw it she had two options.

Option A: Watch a two-year-old die while secure in the knowledge that her own moral purity had been maintained.

Or Option B: Break into the home of a man at the request of his bitter ex-wife to steal his good luck charm for a whole lot of money.

Sign her up for a trip to purgatory and stamp her passport. It wasn't even a competition.

People might disagree, but it wasn't their precious family member on the line. Let them judge. She was past caring.

What she did care about was the money, its implications, and the bailout in place if she got caught. Dina had put some serious thought into this plan. If there was any trouble at all, Lorelei was covered.

They'd planned out all the scenarios and set up escape routes. The operation was foolproof. All she had to do was slip into the catcher's condo, swipe the gold chain he kept in his nightstand drawer when he wasn't playing, and slide right back out.

Thirty seconds max. Easy as pie. If she did get caught, Dina said her name was still on the lease. Lorelei would simply say that she was there at the request of her friend to pick up a few items, and that if they'd like to call Ms. Andrews she could corroborate her story in full. Then Lorelei would meet up with her and she'd exchange the charm for a hundred grand.

Over and done. What Dina planned to do with the necklace after that, Lorelei didn't know and didn't care.

She'd hightail it back to Loveland and Michelle would have her surgery. Life would get back to normal—whatever that was. It'd been so long since she'd known anything close to normalcy that Lorelei sometimes wondered if she'd even be able to recognize it. For two years her life had been put on hold while she helped her brother. Not that she was complaining. Family was family, and with it came certain obligations.

She hadn't minded giving up her apartment and moving back to the ranch. That old farmhouse was the perfect place for a writer to gain inspiration. It was also the perfect place for her niece to grow up.

That thought brought her right back around to the present. Lorelei signaled a waitress as she hurried past. "Excuse me. I'd like to order a drink."

The redhead gave her a slightly harried smile. "Sure thing. What can I get for ya?"

Usually she'd go for an ale—good ol' Guinness. Hard liquor wasn't on her regular drink menu. But, with what she was about to do, tonight definitely called for a shot or two of liquid courage. "I'll take two Forest Fires. And if you can tell me what that man across the room in the dark gray sweater is drinking, I'd appreciate it."

The waitress didn't even have to look. "Oh, you must mean Mark Cutter, the Rush's catcher."

Lorelei nodded and watched Mark toss back the rest of his glass out of the corner of her eye. "That's the one." Too bad it appeared he was drinking pints instead of shots. She'd have preferred him to be downing Crown or something. It would make her feel even more secure about tonight going off without a hitch.

Then again, if she wanted him drinking whiskey, all she had to do was send it to him. Before the waitress left, Lorelei added, "Actually, I'd like to send him a double of your finest Scotch." She wanted to ensure he got sloshed.

"No problem. I'll be right back with your Forest Fires."

Turning her attention once again to the ballplayer, Lorelei jolted when her gaze landed on him, and anxiety slithered up her back. Had he just been staring at her? It sure as heck felt like it, even though he wasn't looking now. She was almost positive he'd just been watching her.

That wasn't part of the plan. She was supposed to be invisible. She'd chosen the darkest corner in the already dim bar for her concealment. The guy had so many cleat chasers flaunting and traipsing around in front of him that they practically made a moving screen, shielding her from view. Besides, dark hair, dim corner, boring clothing. She'd been positive she could see him, but that he wouldn't notice her. Surely she wasn't wrong?

Lorelei was there only to get a measure of the man who had reportedly caused such pain and suffering to his ex-wife. Something about the way Dina had described him that fortuitous night had picked at her. Something didn't square. It wasn't that she didn't believe Dina, precisely. It was just that she trusted her own eyes and judgment more.

Well that, and because there was a tiny cynical part of her that had been worried the plan seemed a little too pat and cozy, for all she tried to convince herself otherwise. She wanted to make sure that things would go smoothly and that he would be drunk and possibly high out of his mind on prescription narcotics as Dina had said he would be by the time he got home.

Insurance was what she'd been after, but now instinct told her that looking for it had been a bad idea. Typical.

The waitress arrived with her shots and set them neatly in front of her on the small black lacquered table. Over the wail of saxophone Lorelei heard the woman ask if she wanted to start a tab. She shook her head and declined the offer. After these drinks she'd need to be leaving if everything was going to go as planned. Reaching inside the front pocket of her worn jeans, she retrieved a twenty from its recesses and handed it to the redhead. "Keep the change."

The young woman smirked and pocketed the cash. Then she melted into the crowd and began making her way with the last drink to the Rush player.

Butterflies started fluttering in her stomach unexpectedly, so Lorelei reached for a drink and watched the Tabasco bleed red as it mixed with the Everclear. Now she wasn't so certain sending him a drink was the wisest move. Especially since she'd just realized that she'd forgotten to mention to the waitress to keep her anonymous when she delivered the drink.

Crap.

Lifting the glass to her lips, Lorelei took a deep breath and tossed back the shot. Fire burned a wicked path down her throat as she slapped the glass back down on the table. Her lips tingled from the Tabasco and felt two sizes too big. Blowing out a rush of air, she blinked back tears and focused her gaze across the room just as her waitress reached the blond catcher.

Still feeling the heat, Lorelei braced herself for the second dose as she watched the waitress serve Mark. He was shaking his head at her and frowning, like he hadn't ordered the drink, when she smiled and pointed in Lorelei's direction.

His head whipped around and his focus snapped to her instantly, his gaze penetrating even from the distance across the room. She could feel it clear down to her toes, and suddenly blood pounded hard in her ears. No way had she expected such intensity. It made her feel like throwing her hands in the air and shrieking, *The jig is up!*

She needed that other shot.

He was still staring at her like she was a bug under a microscope, so Lorelei grabbed up that second shot with a shaky hand. Being zoned in on like that was damn disconcerting. Understanding of what made him such a famously fierce baseball player instantly dawned. Nobody in their right mind would want to be opposite that gaze on the field. It was lethal.

Good thing she wasn't in her right mind.

What was she going to do now? Should she act nonchalant? Should she acknowledge him? Obviously, playing the Invisible Woman wasn't going to work anymore. She forced a smile and met his unblinking stare with her own. Then she raised her glass in a silent toast.

She saw his eyebrow shoot up in surprise at the salute and watched him reach for his drink. But then his brows pulled down into a frown. Lorelei felt her stomach sink as he pushed the drink away from him—very slowly, very deliberately. His eyes never left hers.

Okay, so no, she wasn't dolled up like the other women in the bar, and she knew she wasn't gorgeous by any means. She was average. Average height, average curves, average weight.

Sigh. Fine, so a few pounds beyond that. She liked food. Sue her. But seriously, she had her redeeming qualities, and the sting still hurt, damn it. He'd sent a message and it was brutally clear.

She'd been rejected.

Chapter 2

MARK PUSHED THE drink away and shook his head. He'd wondered how long it would take the brunette to make a move. For the past hour he'd watched her out of the corner of his eye. And for that hour, her eyes had been fixed on him.

It was something he'd become used to over the years—having ladies stare at him. Most of the time he enjoyed it as a major perk of being a professional athlete. Lately, for whatever reason, not so much. And he really wasn't in the mood tonight to analyze why. Or really ever. He considered it a momentary glitch in his programming and nothing more.

So why was he vaguely disappointed that the brunette was making a move? And just what had that salute meant? It was such an odd gesture from a woman hiding in the corner. A salute was something that belonged at a wedding—charming and full of goodwill.

The woman looked anything but full of goodwill. In fact, she looked somewhere between scared shitless and royally pissed. How she managed to pull off those two emotions at the same time was oddly fascinating to him. She wasn't his usual type, so why he was so intrigued beat the hell outta him. He usually preferred his women fake on the inside and out. It was safer that way.

Raking his hair back with a hand, Mark watched her and waited for her reaction. When it came, his eyebrows shot up and he felt a chuckle rise in his chest. It was the complete opposite of what he would have assumed she'd do.

In his experience, natural women like her had major attitude. It was that whole liberated feminist schtick. He'd more than half expected her to march over to him and demand to know what was wrong with her and her drink. Instead, she looked confused; she frowned and shook her head.

Then she stood up clumsily from the table, wobbled a bit, and began glancing around like she was looking for a purse or something. Apparently she couldn't find it, or didn't have one, because she threw her hands up and headed for the exit.

It was the oddest reaction Mark had ever seen.

And because it was so odd and unexpected, he was even more intrigued. Keeping his eyes on her retreating back, he pushed away from the table and stood. Then he whipped out his wallet and threw a twenty down.

Peter Kowalskin—Denver Rush's ace pitcher—eyed Mark and asked, "Where you off to in such a hurry? The night's still young and so are the women here tonight, bro."

The team's newest rookie, JP Trudeau, piped up, "Yeah, where are you going?"

Mark glanced down at the young Iowan and grinned. The kid was shaved bald as a cue ball from a bout of rookie initiation, but was sporting a black ski cap to cover up that fact. It didn't help. At the ripe old age of twenty-five he looked like a boy band member, even with the nasty shiner.

Man, had he ever been that fresh-faced and innocent-looking?

Yeah, maybe. Back in the day before the major leagues when he couldn't get play with a girl to save his life. But one good luck charm and a contract with the Toronto Blue Jays had changed all that. Now those days seemed almost surreal. Women weren't hard to come by anymore, and hadn't been for years.

Mark glanced at the rookie again, his thoughts turning back to the brunette. Hell, maybe he was becoming jaded in his old age. There'd been a time when a drink from any woman would have sent him to the moon and back. And it kind of sucked that he hadn't felt that excitement in a very long time.

Turning his gaze just in time, he caught sight of her as she slipped out the back door. He needed to catch up to her before she got away. "I'm curious about something. I may or may not be back. Either way, don't wait up."

Kowalskin grinned. "Ah, the cute brunette that just left. Good choice, brother."

JP's eyes went huge. "I saw her, too. Great ass."

Suddenly impatient, Mark tucked his wallet away and said, "If you boys don't stop yapping, I'll miss her."

Why did it even matter?

Making his way through the bar with long, purposeful strides, Mark hit the back door and stepped out into the chilly Colorado night. As he scanned the parking lot, anxiety quickened his pulse when at first he didn't see her. Then his eyes fell on her curvy figure near a small red car and he smiled. Anticipation and curiosity quickened his pace as he headed across the parking lot toward her.

A crowd exited the bar, their laughter and loud voices muffling his footsteps as he approached. "So, what? You buy me a drink and then skip out before introducing yourself?"

The brunette spun toward him on a gasp, one hand flying to her throat.

Biting back a laugh at her reaction, Mark crossed his arms over his chest and raised an eyebrow. "The logic of that is all wrong."

He had to give her points. Even though she was obviously off balance, she rallied and replied, "Is that so? Just what would the logical step have been for me then, being as you rejected my drink?"

Good question. What had he really wanted her to do? Damned if he knew. Apparently tonight he was a bundle of contradictions. So he settled for an easy answer. "Come over and down the shot yourself. No need to waste good booze."

"And then what? You would have been overcome with

desire and whisked me back to your place?" The expression on her face told him clearly that she had her doubts.

So did he. "I might have. But the night's young. It's still a possibility." And why in the *hell* had he just said that? She wasn't even his type! He'd meant to deny her suggestion, not proposition her. Shit.

Obviously he'd had one too many drinks and his ability to reason was impaired. That, or he'd taken one too many balls upside the head in his career and it was finally catching up with him.

LORELEI PAUSED AND narrowed her eyes at the catcher. Had he just hit on her? It sounded suspiciously like the guy was inviting her back to his place. Lordy, she'd never had a one-night stand in her life. Wasn't her style.

Her first instinct was to laugh at the thought of going home with a strange man. Especially since the man suggesting the tryst was the very one she planned on stealing from.

She opened her mouth to blow off the invite, but something occurred to her and she snapped it closed again.

Fate was handing her a cookie. And now she felt like smacking her forehead at her denseness. Why break in and steal from him when she could simply get invited back to his place as a one-night stand? Was it a viable alternative?

It was an even better idea than the original plan and with less guilt on her part. Besides, what was the point of big breasts if they couldn't be put to good use at a time like this? Why not act like a tease and take advantage of the opportunity being presented to her?

Lorelei contemplated all her choices for a moment, turned them over in her mind to see all the angles. Pondered briefly which approach would make her feel less deceitful and guilty in the morning. Then she came to a conclusion: It was time to get her slut on.

Pasting a hopefully sultry smile on her face, she placed her hands on her waist and cocked her hip. "You're right. The night is still so full of possibilities. It'd be a shame to waste it. What do you say we make it one to remember?"

Flat-footed in her sneakers, she had to tilt her head back to look into his eyes. Mark Cutter was an imposing man. But he wasn't so imposing at the moment with that mildly shocked expression he wore. Obviously he hadn't expected her to take him up on the offer. Well, too bad for him. The man should have kept his sexy mouth shut. Because now that she'd been presented with this avenue of attack, she was darn well going to take it.

Lorelei stared leisurely down his body and back up again. Even in the dark sweater and jeans she could tell he was all muscle and fit, gorgeous body. It wasn't hard to appear appreciative—she most definitely was. A woman would have to be dead not to feel a temperature spike at what he had.

Bringing her eyes back up to meet his, she waited for him to respond to her boldness. It didn't take long.

"By the way you bailed out of the bar I wouldn't have guessed you for that type of woman."

She wasn't that type of woman, but she sure as hell was going to act like it tonight. "I'm complex."

"Is that so?"

His gaze had dropped to her hands. Good. It meant she had his attention. Sliding them slowly over the soft cotton of her shirt, she moved them down her hips, then up to her ribs and back. "What do you think of my T-shirt? Do you like it?"

She felt a bit ridiculous saying that, but she was trying to be provocative. She had her slut on, darn it. They said things like that—all kinds of trashy pickup lines. And she had some good ones stored up.

Lorelei watched his gaze follow her hands before they broke contact. The corner of his mouth lifted and he smirked as he stared at the slogan smeared across her chest.

"Makes me wonder if you're the kinda girl who really digs *everything*."

Nice. Now she was a naughty slut. "Yeah? You think?"

He raked a hand through his hair and nodded. "It's kinda hot."

Lorelei smiled at him through her lashes and tossed out another line. "Take me back to your place, darlin', and I'll show you hot."

His stare was amused and speculative at the same time. "Oh yeah?"

She had a killer comeback for that and pushed her chest out a little more, let her voice go all soft and husky. "I'll ride you so hard you'll walk bowlegged for a week."

Mark Cutter's smile was lightning-quick, twice as

wicked, and she felt those darn butterflies in her stomach again.

"Wow. I thought only guys had cheesy pickup lines like that. Does that one ever work for you?"

They were cheesy lines, for sure. Velveeta-style, smooth and creamy. "You'll have to let me know in the morning."

His eyebrow lifted and he took a step closer to her. The butterflies turned into grasshoppers on crack and Lorelei had to fight the urge to scramble backward.

A big, warm hand cupped her chin and he said, "Is that so?"

A tremble vibrated down her spine at his touch, but she stood her ground. "By the way, I take my coffee with sugar." Not that she had any intention of being there in the morning, but that one was true.

Heck no, she planned on being on her way home to Loveland with the money she was going to earn tonight. And she *was* earning it. It wasn't so easy playing the tramp.

Mark tilted his head to the side and laughed as he studied her. "Okay, Ms. Rodeo. What's your name?"

Lorelei took a deep breath. "I'm Fonda."

"Fonda what?"

She looked him square in the eye and lied. "Fonda Peters."

His hand dropped and so did his jaw. "You've got to be kidding me. You're Fonda Peters?"

How she found the audacity to wink at him, she'd never know. "I am tonight."

Mark shook his head and grinned as he took a step back. His voice sounded both exasperated and intrigued, if that was possible. "You're too much. All right, you win. Get in the car, Fonda Peters. I'm taking you home with me."

She shot him a smile and released a tiny squeal of delight. "Oh goodie." Actually, she was delighted. Such a perfect opportunity. And it was so much better than breaking and entering—even if she did have a key. A little more law-abiding. Now all she had to do was figure out how to swipe his good luck charm without *actually* sleeping with him.

Good thing she had a car ride to figure that one out.

Chapter 3

THE DOOR TO Mark's condo shut with a muffled thud and Lorelei had to fight the urge to jump. Her nerves were too close to the surface and it was taking some major concentration not to start biting her nails—she'd quit that awful habit two years ago. Instead, she curled her fingers into her palms and let the nails dig into them.

Stepping farther into the spacious condo, Lorelei replayed in her mind the new plan she'd concocted on the ride over. But before she could put it into action Mark grabbed her. His deep voice carried easily through the quiet.

"Well, Fonda Peters, now that I have you here, whatever *am* I going to do with you?"

Not what he was hoping, that's for sure. With any luck she'd be out of there before he'd even taken off his shoes.

But she hadn't forgotten the role she was playing. "You

tell me, catcher. Now that you have me here, what *are* you going to do with me?"

She stopped in the center of the vast living room after dropping on the counter the purse she'd kept in her car. Lorelei turned her head and looked over her shoulder at Mark. She shouldn't have. He'd left a light on in the kitchen and it pooled across him, casting his face into beautiful rugged angles. When he began walking toward her with a long, loose-hipped stride, her stomach dipped low and she could practically feel her knees turning to liquid.

This was not good.

Tonight was supposed to be nothing more than a quick and easy illegal dealing: swipe his good luck charm for a boatload of cash. It had seemed so simple, practically elementary, when she and Dina had cooked up the scheme the other night. She'd take something from a no-good baseball jerk, his ex-wife would have her revenge for his foul behavior, and she'd save a little girl's life. Win-win situation.

Only now that she was actually standing in Mark Cutter's condo it didn't seem quite so simple. And he didn't seem quite so bad after all. But a deal was a deal and she wasn't about to back out now.

It would just be easier if he was sloppy drunk and butt-ugly. Then she wouldn't be having these infuriating twinges of attraction and excitement. All she'd feel was repulsed. Instead, the man was sinfully gorgeous and too darn sober. And if she didn't do something about that soon, she'd find herself flat on her back with her feet in the air. Not that she had any real moral objection to that. Heck, from the looks of him, she'd more than enjoy it. But it wasn't on her to-do list for the night.

It was almost a shame, really. *Almost*. But not quite.

Mark stopped when he was only a foot away, and she eyed him warily as he reached for her hand, tugged her flush against him. Her body shivered at the contact.

"I'm going to see what secrets you've got hidden beneath your clothes, Ms. Rodeo. Are you a satin or lace girl?"

Neither. She was a good ol' cotton kind of girl. But she didn't think that was the right answer for a lady of the night to give, so she said, "Why don't we have a drink and then you can find out for yourself, pretty boy?"

Dimples creased his lean cheeks at that remark and Lorelei had to look away when he smiled. Mark was male sexiness personified. And to think that Dina had told her he was a busted-up baseball pro. Sure his nose was slightly crooked from being broken a time or two, but oddly enough that only added to his appeal.

Since Lorelei had only heard of him, but never seen him, she'd believed Dina. Now she was beginning to think the woman must have downed one too many of those prescription drugs she'd thrust on her. Briefly she pondered what else Dina might have been wrong about. Was he really such a lousy cheating husband? An emotional abuser? A user and a horrible human being?

Good God, was Dina's name even really on the lease? Nothing was turning out to be what it seemed. She just hoped to hell that his good luck charm was in the spot

Dina had sworn it would be. To get to it, Lorelei needed to be in his bedroom. She was suddenly very glad for those prescription pills now in her purse.

The night she'd met up with Dina to finalize plans, she'd had an attack of conscience. That's when Dina had whipped open her purse and shoved the bottle of muscle relaxers into her hand, insisting that they'd help calm her anxiety. Good heavens, that woman had been a walking pharmacy. Lorelei must have seen at least half a dozen prescription bottles lining the Gucci bag. She'd commented on the amount, and Dina had said they were all for a bulging disk in her neck.

She'd refused at first, but the ex-Mrs. Cutter had persisted, assuring her that she took them all the time and that they were perfectly harmless. In the end, Lorelei had wound up with them just to hush the woman up. Now she felt like kissing her for them.

They were going to save her behind.

"If you want a drink, then by all means. What's mine is yours tonight."

Lorelei glanced up and looked into Mark's pale gray eyes. "You're going to have a drink, too, sugar, to make up for refusing mine at the bar."

He smirked down at her. "Is that so? And what if I refuse a second time?"

Lorelei raised her hand and cupped his cheek, feeling the day's growth of stubble beneath her palm. "You wouldn't do that, darlin'."

His voice went soft and seductive as he lowered his face closer to hers. "And why is that?"

When his mouth was mere inches from hers he stopped and she could feel his breath whisper across her lips. Desire sparked between them, tangible and hot. "Because you want to see me naked."

Before he could respond, Lorelei slipped out of his embrace, letting her hand trail down his neck and across his chest as she strode away. She heard his slow exhale and felt his hand cover hers briefly before she broke contact.

"I do. I really do."

Lorelei believed him. His voice had sounded completely sincere and it made her insides shaky. And *that* made her frown. Being attracted to Mark Cutter was not an option.

Without a backward glance, she strolled leisurely toward the kitchen, aware that his eyes were on her the whole time. Thank goodness she'd had the foresight to set her purse on the kitchen counter when she'd walked in, because she'd never have been able to reach in and grab the bottle otherwise.

To cover the noise of the lid popping, Lorelei asked, "Where do you keep your liquor, cowboy?"

"In the cabinet above the microwave."

Fabulous. She palmed some pills. "Do you take your whiskey straight up or on the rocks?"

"I'll take it neat, beautiful."

Fine with her. Spotting snifters through the glass door cabinet to her right, Lorelei got them down and reached above the microwave for the liquor. Quickly pouring the amber liquid into the cut crystal snifter, she dropped the pills in and willed them to dissolve in record time. She hurried the process along by mixing with her finger, then wiped it on a dish towel hanging off the fridge door.

When they'd disappeared fully into the drink, she picked up the glasses, mindful of the drugged one, and went back into the living room. She found Mark standing in front of the open floor-to-ceiling windows, the lights from downtown Denver playing shadows across his sculpted body. Hair the color of old gold in the dim light curled lazily over the collar of his sweater. He stood there, broad shouldered, with his muscular legs spread, looking ready to do battle until he saw her. Though his face smoothed into a smile meant to charm her, Lorelei could still sense the tension in his body by the way his hands curled into fists at his sides.

"Let's try this again." Lorelei held the glass out to him and said a quick prayer for forgiveness. "Don't disappoint me a second time, handsome."

MARK REACHED FOR the glass and let his hand skim across her wrist before taking it. Her stunning green eyes grew round at the touch, but she only smiled. It was obvious that she was nervous—he'd felt the way her pulse raced when he'd touched her wrist. And her hand wasn't quite steady as he took the glass from her.

It charmed the hell out of him.

He couldn't remember the last time he'd been with a shy woman. And that in itself told him it'd been way too long. Vacant minds, vapid personalities, and silicone had been his norm for more than five years, and he'd gone through them like water. It meant no surprises and no complications, but he realized now he was so burnt out by it that his rejection of her at the bar had been knee-jerk. He'd thought it was the same old dance. Call him jaded, but he was sick of it. He wanted to *want* a woman—really want her. Wanted something . . . Well, he wasn't quite sure what. *More.* Just something more.

With her wide eyes and delectable curves, she was a breath of fresh air. The little vixen that dug everything still had a wholesomeness about her he hadn't even realized he'd been missing until just now. No wonder he'd been intrigued by her.

It suddenly made sense to him why he'd invited her home with him—it'd just taken him a while to recognize the feeling.

Maybe she was that *more.*

"It's been a very long time since I've wanted to see any woman undressed and underneath me the way I do you."

She bit her bottom lip and glanced down at her glass, tucked a strand of hair behind her ear. "Soon."

If she needed a shot of liquor to bolster her confidence, he'd give her whatever she needed. And since his earlier rejection of her drink had bothered her, Mark figured he'd make it up to her, starting with a toast. Raising his glass, he smiled and said, "To the rodeo. May you ride your bronc well."

Color singed her cheeks as they tapped their glasses. But her eyes remained on his while he took a long pull of smooth, aged whiskey.

Then she spoke, her voice low. "I'll make your head spin, cowboy. That I promise."

That surprised a laugh out of him, even as heat began to pool heavy in his groin. "I'll drink to that." And he did. He lifted the glass and drained it, suddenly anxious to get on to the next stage. A drop of liquid shimmered on her full bottom lip and it beckoned him. Reaching an arm out, Mark pulled her close and leaned down. With his eyes on hers, he slowly licked the drop off, his tongue teasing her pouty mouth until she released a soft moan.

Arousal coursed through him at the provocative sound. Pulling her more fully against him, Mark deepened the kiss. Her lush little body fit perfectly against him and her lips melted under the heat of his. He slid a hand up her back and fisted the dark, thick mass of her long hair. He loved the feel of the cool, silky strands against his skin.

He wanted more.

Tugging gently, Mark encouraged her mouth to open for him. When she did, his tongue slid inside and tasted, explored the exotic flavor of her. Hunger spiked inside him and he took the kiss deeper. Hotter. She whimpered into his mouth and dug her fingers into his hair, pulled. Her body began pushing against his, restless and searching.

Mark felt like he'd been tossed into an incinerator when he pushed a thigh between her long, shapely legs and discovered the heat there. He groaned and rubbed his thigh against her, feeling her tremble in response.

Suddenly she broke the kiss and pushed out of his arms. Her breathing was ragged, her lips red and swollen from his kiss. Confusion and desire mixed like a heady concoction in his blood, but before he could say anything she turned and began walking toward the hallway to his bedroom.

At the entrance she stopped and beckoned to him. "Come and get me, catcher."

So she wanted to play did she? Hell yeah. Games were his life.

Mark toed off his shoes as he yanked his sweater over his head and tossed it on the floor. He began working the button of his fly and strode after her. He was a little unsteady on his feet, but he didn't care. He just wanted to catch her. When he entered his room he found her by the bed. She'd turned on the bedside lamp, and the light illuminated every gorgeous inch of her curvaceous body.

He started toward her, but she shook her head. "I want you to sit on the bed."

Mark walked to her anyway and gave her a deep, hungry kiss before he sat on the edge of the bed. He wondered what she had in store for him and felt his gut tighten in anticipation. "Are you going to put on a show for me?" God, that'd be so hot if she did.

All she said was "Mmm hmm," and turned her back to him. Mark let his eyes wander over her body and decided her tight round ass in denim was just about the sexiest thing he'd ever seen.

When his gaze rose back up he found her smiling over her shoulder at him. "Are you ready for the ride of your life, cowboy?"

Hell yes he was. "Bring it, baby. Show me what you've got."

Her smile grew sultry with unspoken promise as she reached for the hem of her T-shirt. She pulled it up leisurely while she kept eye contact with him. All he could hear was the soft sound of fabric rustling, but it fueled him—this seductively slow striptease she was giving him.

He wanted to see her. "Turn around."

As she turned she continued to pull it up until she was facing him with the yellow cotton dangling loosely from her fingertips. A black, lacy bra barely covered the most voluptuous, gorgeous pair of breasts he'd ever laid eyes on. He couldn't stop staring.

"Do you like what you see?"

Good God, yes. The woman was a goddess. He nodded, a little harder than he meant because he almost fell forward. He started to tell her how sexy she was when suddenly a full-blown wave of dizziness hit him and he shook his head to clear it. What the hell?

"Is everything all right, Mark?"

The room started spinning and he tried to stand, but couldn't. It felt like the world had been tipped sideways and his body was sliding onto the floor. He tried to stand again, but fell backward onto the bed instead. He stared up at her as he tried to right himself and couldn't.

Fonda stood there like a siren, dark hair tousled around her head, breasts barely contained—guilt plastered across her stunning face.

Before he fell unconscious on the bed, he knew. Knew it with gut certainty. He tried to tell her, but his mouth wouldn't move. Son of a bitch.

Fonda Peters had drugged him.

Chapter 4

LORELEI DIDN'T WASTE any time. As soon as Mark hit the bed she stepped over to him and cringed, feeling momentarily rotten. Thank goodness he'd fallen on the bed and not on the floor. No way could she have lifted all of Mark Cutter and his muscles up onto the bed.

After she pulled the comforter over him, she went to the kitchen and filled a glass with water. She rifled through her purse until she found ibuprofen and grabbed three . . . no, better make that four. With them in hand she hurried back to his bedroom and set them on the nightstand.

She wiped her palms on her thighs and opened the drawer.

There it was, right where Dina had said it would be. Nothing like an ex-wife to know such things.

Reaching for it, she stole a quick sideways glance at

Mark. His good luck charm wasn't what she'd expected. It was nothing more than a gold braided necklace and a simple small cross. Nothing exciting, nothing flashy. No fancy embellishments. It was rather boring, actually.

But, boring or not, it was very, very valuable. It was going to save Michelle's life.

Lorelei curled her fingers around it and grimaced.

Mark was going to hurt like hell when he woke up. But then again, he was a professional baseball player. He was used to getting bowled over and feeling crappy the next morning, so she shouldn't feel too bad about it.

It was such an odd sensation standing over a virile, unconscious male. Disconcerting, but in a strange way empowering. Especially when that unconscious male was one of the MLB's toughest men and its most notorious womanizer.

And *wow*, he had a body. Seriously fabulous. Even out cold he looked hard and dangerous. Lorelei let her eyes roam over his naked body as she palmed his necklace. Well-developed muscles rippled over his wide shoulders and down his chest to a lean, corded waist.

She couldn't resist running her free hand lightly over his amazingly flat stomach for a brief second. Mark Cutter had a stomach worthy of framing and hanging on her wall.

She removed her hand and raked her gaze down the rest of his body. Distressed jeans covered his sculpted legs, and Lorelei let out a low whistle at the slight bulge she saw between his heavy thighs. Lord have mercy.

The clock on the nightstand by the bed caught her attention as it clicked over a new hour. Two A.M. Definitely time to go.

Just as she was about to turn, she thought better of it. Leaning over him instead, Lorelei placed a tender kiss on his hair. "Thanks for the necklace, catcher."

Then she straightened, put her shirt back on, and left the room without glancing around. Just grabbed her purse off the counter and went straight for the exit. Lorelei shoved his good luck charm in the bag and stepped through the door. Sighing, she closed it quietly behind her, firmly shutting the image of his perfect body out of her head. It wasn't like she hadn't seen a hot body or had good sex before. She was a liberated woman of the twenty-first century. A modern-day woman. Of course she'd had good sex before.

As she walked down the hall to the elevator, she remembered their kiss, could still feel his lips hot and demanding on hers. When she stepped inside the empty lift and punched the lobby button, she melted against the arm rail and sighed.

Who was she trying to kid?

MARK WOKE TO the sound of a whole construction crew hammering in his head. As he rolled onto his back with a groan, it took him a minute to realize where he was.

His first clue was the soft, plush mattress beneath his bare back. The second was the comforter tangled around his legs. He was obviously in a bed. But, why was he still wearing his pants?

Moaning, his mouth full of sand, he lifted a shaky hand to his face and rubbed his scruffy cheek. Shit, he felt weak as a newborn.

Mark painstakingly pried one gritty eye open. Sunlight streamed through the bedroom's massive windows, making his head pound furiously. Why weren't the drapes closed? Couldn't they see he was in agony? He closed his eye again and tried to swear. His parched mouth and sore throat wouldn't comply. A pathetic whimper came out instead. He tried again and barely managed a sound.

It must have been one wild time last night. His head hurt damn bad. It really sucked to wake up to the worst hangover of his life. Not that hangovers were ever fun. But this one really blew. Plain and simple.

Mustering up the courage, Mark pried his eyes open and slowly rolled to a sitting position. He had to grab hold of his head to keep it from falling off. The comforter wedged tightly between his thighs, royally pissing him off.

Holding his head steady with a hand, he reached between his legs and yanked out the offender. The comforter fell to the floor as he swore a blue streak in the quiet condo.

He wanted to know what had gone on last night, because he couldn't remember a thing. Other than the best breasts he'd ever seen. Those he remembered with crystal clarity. It was everything else that was blurrier than a Colorado blizzard.

Groaning his way to his feet, he stumbled toward the hallway and tripped over his discarded shoes from the night before. He kicked them out of the way with another curse and went in search of Fonda Peters. He was in a real foul mood by the time he'd wandered throughout his condo and come up empty. A pair of his crystal snifters on the glass table, his clothes strung all over the place— but no sign of the delectable temptress.

Mother Nature called and Mark wandered back down the hall to the bathroom to take a leak. Had Fonda up and left last night afterward? If she had, she'd be the first. Apparently she was different from all the rest. And that was odd, because in his pretty extensive experience they were all the same.

Damn it. Why couldn't he remember anything?

After he finished, Mark stepped over to the long granite countertop and peered into the mirror. He looked like crap. His hair was a tangled mess. Half of it hung in his eyes, which were dull and bloodshot, with dark half circles underneath. A scruffy shadow beard covered his jaw, and his mouth was drawn tight.

No wonder she'd bailed. He wouldn't want to wake up next to him, either.

Mark left the bathroom, made his way back over to the bed, and sat down when he noticed the drawer on his nightstand was ajar. Warning bells began ringing in his head as he yanked it open and looked inside, searching the contents. With suspicion creeping in, he ignored the water glass and pills perched on its top right in front of him. He could focus on only one fact:

His necklace was gone.

Instantly he was on his feet and close to full-out panic. *Shit. Shit. Shit.* It had to be here. *Had* to. He couldn't play baseball without it. *Son. Of. A* . . . Where was it?

He dumped the drawer on the floor with a loud thump and stomped out to the living room. His necklace had better be there somewhere. He had a game today!

He searched the leather sofas and chairs, overturned his coffee table. Still nothing.

Next came the kitchen. He tore through every cabinet, scoured the refrigerator. Looked high and low and came up empty. A quick call in to the building's security desk confirmed that no one had turned it in. It was simply gone.

"How the hell did I lose my fucking lucky charm?" He racked his brain. Maybe he and Fonda had got a bit too rambunctious last night, bumped the nightstand, and it caused the drawer to open and the necklace to fall on the floor.

Wait a minute. *Fonda Peters.*

A growl of anger clawed its way up his throat and ripped out on a furious roar. She couldn't have.

His eyes came to rest on the empty glasses. A nasty suspicion began to form in his mind as he stalked over to them. "But you did do it. Didn't you, *Fonda Peters*?"

He was serious about only a few things in his life— baseball being number one. Nobody screwed with his game and got away with it. Especially not a woman who hadn't even given him her real name.

A shiver of dread crept up his spine, but he ignored it and lifted a glass to his nose, sniffing. Nothing.

He reached for the other one and brought it to his nose. Still nothing.

Though his head throbbed like an open wound, his memory of her was still intact. And he didn't like what it was telling him. Not one bit. Fonda Peters was a liar and a thief. He remembered her standing in her bra with that guilty-as-sin smile on her face right before he fell to the bed. She'd drugged him in his own frigging home.

His lips curled in a snarl, his chest heaved. Fonda Peters had gone and stolen his good luck charm like a naughty girl. Now she was going to have a big bad baseball player to pay.

LORELEI WAS OFFICIALLY ticked off. Hanging up the phone with more enthusiasm than it called for, she swore. She'd finally gotten ahold of Dina to confirm their meetup time to unload the goods, and had gotten blown off instead. Apparently Dina had "company" over.

It's not like she hadn't already wasted the day sitting around waiting on the woman. Now it just figured that she'd get stuck hanging on to a stolen item for another day. Why again had she agreed to it?

Oh yeah. The money.

Her niece needed the money.

Slapping her hands on her thighs, she stood from the bed. Nothing she could do about it now. She was just going to have to hang around Denver for another day. Wasn't that lovely?

Anxiety gripped her as she thought about home,

about Michelle. She really missed her. Wanted to hold her and cuddle her and make her laugh. But, it wasn't going to happen tonight. And that seriously sucked.

Tonight she was stuck in a very posh hotel room full of fluffy white towels and complimentary slippers. Room service just a dial away and a mini fridge full of booze. And she, Lorelei Littleton, in a pair of gray sweatpants and a pink tank top without a single thing to do. Who'd rather be at home on the ranch than in the four-star hotel Dina had put her up in.

She supposed she could hit the town, but the idea sent shivers down her spine. Nuh-uh. Mark Cutter might be out there. No way was she going to risk running into him.

She'd be an idiot to venture out tonight. It was room service and cable TV for her. Why not? The room was paid for—compliments of her current cohort in crime. And she was kind of on the lam anyway, so she might as well live it up.

Lorelei crossed the thick carpet and turned on the TV as she walked toward the phone. She called room service and placed an order for a cheeseburger, fries, and iced tea. As she hung up the phone the late news flashed on the big screen.

Her stomach lurched.

There he was, in all his glory, on the evening news recap. Mark Cutter, Denver Rush's star catcher, duking it out over home plate with Luc Lanier from the Arizona Diamondbacks.

An odd tug of horror and fascination propelled her forward until she was on her knees in front of the big screen, eyes glued to the set. They were going at it bare-fisted like two lunatics.

His catcher's helmet flew from his head as the Diamondback clocked him upside his skull, bloodied his mouth. But the crazy man just laughed as he swiped the back of his hand across his split lip.

It took three of Cutter's teammates to jerk him off the other guy. The television made a constant *bleeeep* noise as the network censored the foul language flying around the diamond. All the baseball players had seriously dirty mouths. And the Rush's catcher was having a field day tossing around the F-word.

Lorelei couldn't hear a word the sportscaster was saying—she was engrossed in the cocky, bloodied grin on Mark's face as he was escorted to the Rush's dugout.

She'd stolen that guy's good luck charm.

She was a frigging idiot.

Lorelei rocked back on her bare heels and let out a whoosh of air. She had to get rid of that necklace—fast. Seeing him like that made it very clear just who she was messing with. A person who could smile over a fistfight had to have a few screws loose, right?

Her gaze swept back to the TV. The final score of the Rush vs. Diamondbacks game was painful. A total shut-out with the Diamondbacks winning 5–0.

No wonder Mark had gone out with fists flying. Of course he wouldn't take that well. No doubt he blamed his crappy performance on his missing good luck charm.

Lorelei flinched inwardly and then steeled her mind against the guilt. It wasn't like the jerk was a nice guy.

Good kisser? Definitely. Good with his hands? Oh yeah. Nice guy? Nuh-uh. Not from what she'd heard about him.

From all accounts, Mark Cutter was an all-American asshole. He deserved a little humility.

Still, it did poke her conscience a little to know she was partly to blame for the Rush's pitiful defeat. They were a great team, and only a few games into the regular season. If they blew their chance at the World Series she was somewhat to blame. In a convoluted, roundabout sort of way.

By stealing Mark's cross Lorelei had psyched out their premier catcher—broken his focus, gotten under his skin.

Not many girls could claim that. Sure, plenty got into his pants. And after what she'd seen last night, she didn't blame them. Not one little bit.

But she just bet she was the first to mess with his game. Well, not really *her*—it was his missing charm that had him so unfocused. Oh hell, she'd stolen it from him; she could take the credit if she wanted to.

Lorelei laughed self-consciously. She didn't know if she should or not. Because she knew if he ever found out it was she there'd be the devil to pay.

Her mind flashed to an image of his eyes as they'd been last night. Hot and lethal. Like shards of aluminum.

Unbidden, warmth slid down her torso at the memory of the wild kiss they'd shared. Maybe it wouldn't be so bad if he came for her, after all. Then she might get another chance to kiss him. That might not be so bad.

And apparently pretending to be a tramp last night had warped her mind. One night playing a hussy for

Mark Cutter and she was thinking of all the different positions she knew. Which weren't nearly as many as a real floozy, granted, but she was giving it her best effort.

And that was the problem.

The guy was a cocky, conceited, spoiled sports star. If he found her, kissing her senseless again would be the next thing on his mind—right after he had her arrested. She wouldn't even have the chance to tell him how flexible she was. He'd have her cuffed and hauled off before she could croon, *I do yoga, lover boy.*

And no way was she going to jail. So she'd just have to keep that tidbit of knowledge to herself and not let him find her. But, really, it wasn't possible for him to catch her. He didn't even know her real name. She'd been Fonda Peters.

Even if he did make the connection between her and his missing cross, he had no way of tracking her. She hadn't even used her credit card to pay for her room. His ex-wife had.

She was the person Mark should be going after anyway. Dina was the one who'd approached Lorelei in the first place, offering to pay her one hundred grand to swipe his good luck charm. If anyone was to blame, really, it was she. Well, Mark, actually. He should never have been such an ass to his ex in the first place. Then she wouldn't have been hell-bent on revenge.

Since "company" had waylaid today's plan to meet in the hotel bar, she and Dina had decided to meet tomorrow at Riley's, a quaint Irish pub just off the beaten path. There they'd make the exchange. Cash for cross. The end.

Then Lorelei could hightail it home to Loveland and Michelle.

A knock sounded at the door, surprising Lorelei.

Finally, room service. She was starving. It was a sad fact of her life that she had a heck of an appetite and could pack away more food than even her older brother could. In some very unladylike but highly entertaining contests she'd proven that. And that's why hot dogs now made her turn a putrid shade of green. But she'd showed Logan. *Ha ha*.

And now he boiled Oscar Mayers in the house whenever he was mad at her. The asshole.

Grabbing the remote to click the TV off, Lorelei patted her sloppy ponytail with a hand and made for the door. She should have asked for a double cheeseburger. And a chocolate milk shake. Now *that* sounded good.

Ready to pounce on the delivery boy the minute he wheeled his cart over the threshold, Lorelei grinned in anticipation. Wiggling her booty in excitement, Lorelei gripped the handle, swung the door wide open.

And came nose to chest with a very angry Mark Cutter.

"Hello, Fonda Peters. I believe you have something that belongs to me."

Chapter 5

MARK HELD HIS temper at a simmer and roamed his gaze over her from head to toe. She looked about ready to wet her pants—or faint. Obviously Fonda Peters wasn't too fond of seeing him after all.

Too damn bad.

Mark crossed his strong arms across his chest and leaned a shoulder into the door frame, effectively blocking her from closing the door in his face, and waited for her to make some sort of response. But she just kept blinking her bright green eyes at him with her mouth flopped wide open.

Lorelei Littleton. God, what a name. Old-fashioned and feminine as all get-out. At any other time he might have appreciated the irony of her having a name like Lorelei while she looked and acted more like a Las Vegas stripper.

Except she didn't look much like a stripper now. In

fact, she didn't look much like the curvy vamp who'd worked him into such a lather last night and left him half naked and unconscious on his bed, either.

Except for her breasts—those were just as he remembered. They were still the roundest, fullest, best pair of tits he'd ever seen.

In any case, Lorelei Littleton sure as hell wasn't a name he'd be forgetting anytime soon. 'Cause she owed him. Owed him big.

And more than just his lucky charm, too.

Mark's gazed dropped to her bare feet. Her slender toes were painted deep red, and on the top of her slender left foot perched a small butterfly tattoo in varying shades of lavender, green, and yellow.

A tickle fluttered his pulse at the sexy little mark. He arched a thick brow. Huh. Who'd have thought? Apparently Lorelei had quite a few naughty secrets.

Belatedly, a mildly panicked sound came from her, and Mark raised his gaze. Up over baggy gray sweatpants and a pink tank top thin enough that the dusky shade of her nipples was discernible. And she wasn't wearing a bra, which was so sexy.

He stared hard at her breasts for a moment, until her nipples puckered under the scrutiny, and then slowly slid his gaze up to her face and sloppy ponytail.

Even without makeup she was pretty. Mark felt himself grow semi-hard and scowled. What the hell was he doing growing wood? The woman was the cause of his goddamn split lip. If he hadn't been thinking so much about her when he should have been focused, he wouldn't have played like shit and mixed it up with the Arizona outfielder over home plate. He wouldn't have missed some dumb-ass pitches and taken his eye off the ball. The Rush wouldn't have lost 5-0.

Well, he wouldn't have played like crap and the team wouldn't have lost at least. The other part he probably would have done anyway. Shaking things up on the field was damn fun. Nothing like a good scrum to make a guy's day. But for her sake she'd better have his necklace because he couldn't afford another game like today.

Lorelei brought a hand to her neck and cleared her throat. She tried for a smile and almost pulled it off. Her unpainted lips wobbled only a little.

Mark crossed his ankles and stared at her hard from beneath his Rush baseball cap. She still had that pouty mouth. And it still begged to be put to use. But now it looked softer, more kissable for some reason. His semi grew just looking at it. *Wonderful*. Not.

Mark's brows slashed low over his eyes. It'd been a real shitty day, and getting a hard-on over little Miss Fonda Peters's mouth just capped it. Now he was plain pissed off.

"How did you find me?" Her voice had an edge of panic to it.

Easy. She wasn't the slickest thief around.

Pushing away from the door frame, Mark used his size to intimidate her into moving farther into the hotel room and slammed the door shut behind him, the tension coiling in his body as he advanced. He backed Lorelei until her butt came up against the dresser, stopping her, effectively blocking her in. Now it was time to play his way. *Dirty*.

HOLY CRAP. WHAT was Mark doing here? How could he have possibly found her? And how could he still look so sinfully good with a busted lip, bruised cheekbone, ratty ball cap, and a day's growth of whiskers? If anything, the rough-around-the-edges look made him *more* appealing.

Just what in heaven's name was she doing thinking such thoughts about him? The guy was probably trying to decide which to do first: strangle her or have her arrested. And there she was thinking how sexy his dark blond hair looked curling around the bottom of his baseball cap. Thinking about telling him she did yoga and was real good at the downward facing dog position.

Lorelei took a deep breath, gathered her courage, looked into Mark's brittle eyes, and inwardly flinched. If they got any colder they'd shatter. He was not a happy camper. He was a big, bad, totally irate man.

With her butt pressed firmly against the dark stained dresser and nowhere to go, she had no choice but to face the consequences. But she really, *really* didn't want to. If that made her a coward, so what. She didn't see Mark towering over anyone else with a snarl that promised retribution.

How on earth had he found her so fast? It hadn't even been a full twenty-four hours. Had she left something at his place to tip him off?

With her heart trying to climb up her throat, Lorelei squared her shoulders, which incidentally pushed her breasts up and out toward him. Mark's eyes dropped and she felt his gaze land on her chest, staring hard. They seemed to melt a degree. The snarl twisting his beautiful mouth softened.

Lorelei followed the line of his gaze with her own. She wasn't wearing a bra and her nipples were hard. Suddenly her breath caught in her throat and she found it hard to breathe. With his eyes heating in undisguised interest, the nipples he stared at began to tingle.

For a tense moment neither spoke. Then Mark let out a menacing growl and tore his gaze from her breasts and swore. His voice sounded rough when he said, "Where is it, Lorelei? I want it back, *now*."

"I don't know what you're talking about." And how on earth did he know her real name?

Anger flickered in his clear gray eyes. "Bullshit. You know damn well what I'm talking about. You stole something of mine and I want it back, or else."

Something hot and defiant flared in Lorelei at his threat. "Or what? You'll have me arrested? Make me pay?"

One corner of mouth lifted and his eyes sparked with wicked intent. "Oh, you're already going to pay, sweetheart. In so many ways, your eyes will cross."

She could think of one way that she might like to have her eyes crossed by Mark Cutter. And if he did yoga, too, that could be all kinds of fun.

Right now, though, she couldn't afford to be distracted by naughty thoughts of him. It was time to pick her brain up off the floor and find a way out of this mess.

"How much is it worth to you?" The words popped out of her mouth before she thought better of it. Then her eyes went big and she bit back a smile. Now she was thinking. Her smarts hadn't totally eluded her after all. Thank God. Dina had agreed to one hundred grand for the cross necklace. Would it be worth the same to him to get it back? Would it be worth more?

He scowled and his brows drew together over those clear gray eyes of his. "What did you just say?" His voice had gone dangerously soft.

Okay, so maybe she wasn't that smart after all. "Nothing."

Lorelei watched in fascination as a tic started in Mark's strong jaw and his nostrils flared. His bottom lip was busted and the corner of his mouth bruised, but he still raised it in a chilling smile. Perfect white teeth snarled at her from between his abused lips. She wondered how many times they'd been capped.

She dropped her gaze and took in his clothing while she raced after her scattered thoughts. Last night he'd worn jeans and an expensive sweater. Now her gaze traveled over a ratty gray sweatshirt with the Rush logo on it and a pair of old, ripped jeans encasing his heavily muscled thighs. Then her gaze landed smack on the front of his jeans, and her lungs squeezed tight. Wow.

That was quite an, um, bulge. It was suddenly *very* hot in the hotel room. Or maybe it was just that her face was on fire.

And if he'd only step back she could get some more oxygen to her brain and really put it to use. But apparently Mark didn't know the meaning of personal space. He was so close the heat of his body surrounded her, smothered her. And now he was using it to intimidate her and it was making her claustrophobic.

It was making her think of things she should not be thinking. She needed to put some distance between them. Placing her hands against his solid chest, Lorelei pushed hard. "Get off me, you oaf. Let me breathe."

Amusement flickered across his face and he stepped back, allowed her to move. "Whatever you want, Lorelei. As long as I get what I want."

Inhaling a deep breath, she thanked her lucky stars that she'd left his charm in a plain envelope at the concierge desk. She'd thought it a paranoid precaution, but now she was ever so grateful for her decision. Even if he ransacked her room he wouldn't find it. And no way was she telling him where it was until she got money—from him or Dina. She really didn't care now. Heck, she'd gone this far. She might as well go all the way.

Lorelei crossed her bare arms over her chest, glared at Mark, and considered again. What was it worth to him?

Mark glared right back, his eyes like a gray ice storm beneath the black brim of his hat. Anger fairly vibrated off him. She guessed if she'd played as bad as he had she'd be pretty ticked, too. But she wouldn't blame it on a stupid charm. His lousy performance was his fault entirely.

She broke the tense silence. "I saw the sports recap tonight, Mark. You played like shit."

One corner of his bruised mouth turned up and smirked. Sticking his thumbs in the front pockets of his jeans, he leaned against the wall and replied. "Gee, you think?"

No, she didn't think. Not since she'd met him. And that was a very serious problem.

Lorelei shrugged. "I call it how I see it. You played like crap and took it out on somebody else. What did the Arizona guy do that was so offensive anyway? Make fun of your hair?"

Mark touched his split lip with a long finger, and laughed low in his chest. "He hit a triple on me, sugar. Know what a triple is? I wasn't feeling too friendly about it."

Did she know what a triple was? Jerk. "And here I thought it was because you didn't play well and were being a sore loser. Had to take it out on someone."

Something white-hot and dangerous flashed in his eyes. Apparently he didn't like being called names. Suddenly she wasn't too sure that provoking him was such a good idea, but his arrogance had annoyed her big-time. She'd spoken before she'd thought better of it.

His deep voice was rough with warning. "Now, Lorelei. Calling me names isn't the smartest idea in the world. I tend to take it personally. And I can get real mean, real fast. So, consider this a warning. You're not in the best situation to be provoking me in the first place. Now, I want my cross back, or did you already give it to Dina?"

Oh hell. Lorelei's eyes went huge and she jolted. How could he know that? How could he possibly know his ex was behind this?

Her thoughts must have been written on her face because Mark cocked his head to one side and said, "I may be a jock, Lorelei, but I'm not a moron. Of course I know she's the one who put you up to this. This reeks of her. And because she was the one who paid for your room. Credit cards tell a story, sugar. What I want to know is why. You're going to tell me or spend some time in a jail cell until you decide to talk."

So that's how he'd found her. And to discover her real name all he'd had to do was smile at the desk clerk with his pretty dimples and ask what name the room was registered to and voilà. She was outed. But, how had he known to look to Dina for this? Why did it reek of her? There *had* to be more to the story than she'd been told.

And now here it was. The threat of imprisonment she'd been too confident to consider before. Well, now that it was out in the open she had nothing to lose, did she? She might as well go for broke.

Faking a bravado she didn't feel, Lorelei arched a brow and said, "I asked you how much it's worth to you. If you want it back you're going to have to pay up. Dina offered me a lot of money. You'll have to beat her. Highest bidder gets the prize."

Fury leaped hot and intense in Mark's eyes. Pushing away from the wall with an angry jerk, he crossed to her in a few long-legged strides. "Are you blackmailing me, Lorelei? You'd better hope to God you're not."

Through sheer force of will Lorelei held her ground. *This was all for Michelle*, she thought. "I'm doing what's in my best interest. Either you'll pay up, or your good luck charm goes to your ex-wife." She was forced to tip her head far back when he towered over her, his scowl smoldering hot.

"So it's all about the Benjamins to you, is it? You were at my house last night half naked and ready to do it. If you're only in it for the cash gain, then guess what that makes you?"

Desperate.

Anger balled in the pit of her stomach, bitter and scorching. Lorelei took a deep breath and met his gaze, let her anger spark. "You calling me a whore is laughable, Mark Cutter. Don't think I'm stupid, because I've heard all about you and your women. So don't you dare stand there and throw stones at me. You don't have the right."

He wasn't about to stand there and be lectured by her. His temper yanked off the leash and lashed out, wicked and brutal. "At least I don't fuck for money, Lorelei Littleton. And I don't steal."

Through a haze of red fury he watched her face go pale, saw her jaw clamp hard and her spine stiffen. Saw hurt flash in her eyes before determination settled in. Good. He'd wanted to hurt her. She'd taken something from him and it was more than just his lucky cross.

She'd humiliated him. Last night he'd thought she might be different. Made him think maybe he could have something real for a change. Then she'd gone and drugged him in his own frigging home for money.

That made it personal. Having her ass tossed in jail wasn't going to assuage his ego. No, it was payback time.

"You don't get to stand here and lecture me about moral integrity, Mark. And don't presume to know what my reasons for doing this are. Your ex-wife offered me one hundred thousand dollars, yes. And I'll take it gladly and you can just go to hell." She tossed her ponytail over her shoulder and stared him down defiantly.

He took a menacing step forward until his body was flush against hers and they were nose to nose. His voice dropped low as he said the worst thing he could think of. "You aren't worth a hundred grand."

Something flickered in her green eyes and her nostrils flared. Then she snapped like a rubber band, her body yanking back as she shoved against his chest. "You asshole! My family needs that money! If stealing from you will help my family, then there's nothing I won't do. *Nothing!* I love them and I don't give a damn what you think of me personally. You're nobody. You don't matter."

Now they we're getting somewhere. Some of Mark's anger melted away at her confession. The genuine distress in her eyes soothed the ragged edges in his stomach. Her pain was too real, her anguish almost palpable.

If he was going to get hosed and made a fool, then he supposed at least he was grateful she had reason. Something other than herself and how many pairs of designer shoes she could buy. Which was pretty much what Dina would have done.

Suddenly her words registered in his mind. Mark

yanked off his hat and shoved a hand through his hair. "What about your family, Lorelei? Are they in trouble?"

She stared at him, seething, and he felt a moment of self-consciousness. But only a moment.

"Don't pretend that you give a damn about me. That's an insult to both of us. My reasons for doing this are my own and not any of your business." She crossed her arms and hugged her body, pressing her lips together.

"When you stole from me you made it my business."

For a second he thought she might cave. Her shoulders drooped and her mouth wavered, wobbling at the corners. But then her back stiffened and her face hardened. He almost had to admire her strength and determination. Almost.

It appeared they were at a standoff.

"So now what? Am I supposed to pay you one hundred thousand dollars to get my cross back?" Not a chance in hell.

She didn't even blink when she threw him the ultimatum, "Yes. Or else I give it to your ex-wife. Either way I'm going to collect that money."

So now it was a challenge. Mark always loved a good one.

He suddenly decided that this was the mother lode of all puzzles. This whole thing had layers. His feelings for her, her secrets—the chemistry between them. He could call the cops now, have her thrown in the clink, and get his cross back. That'd be the end and he'd never see her again. Easy solution.

But he'd never been able to leave a puzzle unfinished.

His gut said it was about more than just his necklace now, and he was keeping her until he'd sorted it out. "Not if you're with me, you won't. If I don't let you out of my sight you can't meet up with my ex-wife and make the exchange. Then you'd just be shit out of luck, wouldn't you?"

"No, because you need your cross to play baseball. You'll pay up," she said confidently.

Suddenly Mark laughed. There it was again: the challenge. Mark played baseball for a living, for crying out loud. He lived for competition. And she'd just thrown down the gauntlet. Of course he was going to pick it up. It was impossible for him not to.

Mark slammed his cap back on his head and grinned like the devil. "Pack your bags, Lorelei. You're going home with me."

The look on her face was priceless. Her eyes went round as saucers and her jaw almost hit the floor. "Wh-wh-what? You're kidding, right? Why on earth would I go home with you?"

He laughed and reached out a hand to cup her smooth cheek. This might be damn fun. "Because, sweetheart. I'm not about to let you pawn my cross off to my ex, or let you out of my sight. And I'm sure as hell not going to pay you. So you're moving in with me until either I find it or you give it up."

"What if I refuse?" she asked in a tight voice.

"Then I'll have you arrested and you can spend some

time in jail for stealing and drugging me. " Only as a last resort, but she didn't need to know that. For now the threat was enough.

She continued to stare at him with blank shock. He slid a finger under her chin and gently closed her mouth. Her response was the perfect balm to his bruised ego. She'd just challenged a professional and it was game on, baby.

She'd better be ready to play with the big boys.

Chapter 6

IT WAS FIVE-THIRTY in the morning. Before the sun had even reached the sky. And Lorelei sat awake on the edge of Mark's guest room bed in the dark and wondered how the hell she'd gotten there. It wasn't as if she hadn't protested. Oh no, she'd raised a ruckus, all right. She believed she'd even threatened him with bodily harm. But to no avail. He'd still gotten what he wanted. She had a suspicion that he usually did and it ticked her off that she'd played right into his hands.

She had better things to do than play his warped game. And she sure as hell didn't want to spend so much alone time with the jerk. She might just forget all about her integrity if she saw his naked chest again.

As enjoyable as that might be, she had a life to get back to.

Just because she didn't have an office at a fancy building didn't mean she didn't have a job. She had a life.

She had friends. Most importantly, she had family. Her brother, Logan, was going to start worrying about her if she didn't show back up soon. Mark didn't give a crap about any of that.

Lorelei sighed into the quiet of predawn and stretched her arms above her head, slow to wake up. The outline of downtown Denver was just becoming visible through the open windows in the weak light. The condo was so still she actually cringed at the sound of a yawn that escaped her.

What she wouldn't give for a big, fat, designer triple-shot mocha with whip right at that moment. Full of fat and caffeine and chocolate. Coffee was one of her weaknesses. Another being a sick addiction to rock music from eighties' hair bands. She was not a happy person without her caffeine fix.

If only she could run to a coffee shop and grab a mocha. Oh, but then she'd want a chocolate croissant. No, maybe a chocolate chip muffin. Better yet—both. And a fresh scone to chase it all down with.

Standing up to head to the bathroom, she mentally pictured the room as she evaded a potted palm and a stubbed toe by mere inches. Mark's taste certainly ran toward the contemporary. Not overly so like some decorating magazines she'd seen. Nothing space-age or futuristic. Just clean and simple lines.

Not her favorite style, but then her style didn't matter. Still, she'd have preferred a little more warmth and visual coziness to her prison. Instead, she got a room with Asian-inspired decor, and two black and white photos of nature scenes.

And it was all very neat and tidy.

Lorelei stepped into the bathroom and flicked on the overhead lights. "Shit! Ouch." Pain shot through her eyes at the sudden burst of brightness and she flinched. Her toes dug hard into the green slate floor. Why on earth hadn't someone yet discovered a way for lights to come on gradually? Getting poked in the eye with a thousand pinpricks first thing in the morning ranked right up there with hot dogs on her list of favorites.

Rubbing the heels of her hands into the sockets of her eyes, Lorelei mumbled a curse. She dropped her hands and grimaced at the sight in the mirror. It wasn't pretty.

She looked like hell. She wouldn't be entering the Miss America pageant this morning, that's for sure.

Hair fell in a tangled, snarled mess from her sloppy, lopsided ponytail. Dark shadows dusted the undersides of her eyes, and her usually tawny skin was pale.

Raising her right arm, Lorelei did a quick sniff test and winced. Not good, but not too bad. At least she didn't smell nearly as bad as she looked. Yet. But she could really use a shower before Mark woke up.

Before Mark woke up. Genius! She slapped her hands flat on the cream granite countertops and grinned. She could be out of there and on her way home to Loveland in two minutes. If exhaustion hadn't forced her into sleep moments after he'd planted her in this room, she'd already be home. Frustration gnawed at her over that fact, but quickly subsided. She'd tried her best to stay awake and wait him out. That had failed, but she had another opportunity right now.

Racing from the bathroom, Lorelei stubbed her toe on the foot of the bed and cursed. Hopping around on one foot as pain slithered from her toe up her calf, she gritted her teeth and looked for a lamp. Nothing.

Come on, come on. Limping, she felt around in the predawn darkness for her running shoes. Finding them on the other side of the bed, she dropped to the corner edge and started to slip them on. When she jarred her throbbing middle toe she winced and almost cried out. Biting her bottom lip, she frowned and finished shoving her bare feet into the shoes.

If ever there was a time for her to bail, it was now. While Mark was sound asleep in his big ol' bed. All her problems would be solved. She'd get away from him and his blackmail. She could collect the money from Dina, and she could get back to Loveland and her family. Talk about win-win.

It was about time she finally found her brains.

Her giant overnight bag lay scrunched over on the floor by the door and she snatched it up. She'd just call a cab from the lobby, go collect her car and the necklace from the hotel concierge, and then she'd be on her way.

Thrilled at her thoughts, Lorelei reached into her bag and grabbed a lavender sweatshirt and pulled it on. Then she tossed her purse and bag over her left shoulder and quietly opened the door. Ducking her head into the hallway, she sighed with relief when she saw the living room and the hallway on the other side still dark. Mark was across the living room down that hall in his bedroom asleep.

She felt like doing a Snoopy dance.

Something wild and almost giddy flared hot in her as she began to walk quietly toward the door, her running shoes muffled against the hardwood floors. When she stepped on a board a few feet from the door, she jumped. Its groan echoed in the huge condo.

Oh crap.

She froze. And waited. After a minute she let out a breath of relief and rushed toward the door. It appeared Mark was a sound sleeper.

She reached the door and placed a hand on the knob.

"Leaving so soon, Lorelei?"

Dropping her hand on a screech, Lorelei spun around as the overhead light flicked on. Her heart leaped right out of her chest.

Mark stood at the doorway to the kitchen, shirtless and rumpled from sleep, a pair of plaid flannel lounge pants his only clothing. And he looked good. Really, really good.

If she wasn't so terrified he'd caught her trying to sneak out she might have even been distracted by the sight of all that tanned, scrumptious flesh. She was too scared, though. She didn't even notice the happy trail that shot over his flat abdomen down into his pants. Didn't notice his flat brown nipples and hard chest.

Right. And pigs flew.

Blinking rapidly against the sudden glare of light, Lorelei racked her brain for a plausible excuse. But she couldn't think around all the static in her head. It had whipped out of frequency the moment she'd heard his rough voice.

Now she was back to no brains. And she still wasn't wearing a bra, damn it.

Silence stretched between them. Moments ticked by while he leaned against the doorway staring at Lorelei and she stared at his feet. Big feet. Not surprising since his bulge had been pretty darn big, too.

She'd been caught sneaking out and she was thinking about his crotch again. She deserved to be arrested. For stupidity.

Mark had warned her that if she tried to ditch him he'd call the cops instantly. And he'd been so ticked off she didn't doubt his sincerity for a minute. So she needed to bluff her way out of this. Needed to make him forget what he'd just seen. *Fast.*

It was time for Fonda Peters to make a comeback.

She let her eyes go soft as they traveled over his body, and her lips curved in a warm smile. It wasn't much of a chore. His hard, sculpted body kicked her body temperature up a notch. She just let it show. "Why, hello, Mark. You look utterly delicious this morning. Makes a girl kind of hungry and I haven't had breakfast." Lorelei dropped her bags and sauntered over to him. His muscular arms were crossed over his sculpted chest and he lifted a dark blond brow at her words.

She ignored the fact that she was wearing sweatpants and a baggy sweatshirt. Avoided thinking about how she had looked in the bathroom mirror and pretended instead that she was wearing something very sexy. That she *looked* sexy.

When she reached his side, Lorelei raised her palms to

the flat plane of his stomach and stroked up to his powerful shoulders. Then she slid them down to rest against the waistband of his lounge pants. His stomach quivered beneath her touch, but his face remained impassive. "I was on my way to get some coffee from Starbucks, handsome. Wanna come?"

Humor lit his gray eyes and a smile softened his cut lip. Sleep-rumpled hair added to his sexy, disheveled appearance. "Sweetheart, I always want to come," he said with a slight Southern drawl.

She hadn't noticed that last night. But she did now and it did crazy things to her insides. Mark Cutter was one wickedly hot man.

Lorelei felt a smile tug her lips when she suddenly realized the double meaning. He'd set them up for this. "I'm so glad you like . . . *coffee* . . . as much as I do. It can get kind of lonely for a lady enjoying coffee all by herself. It's nice having a strong, sexy man along once in a while." Her fingers slipped just inside the elastic waistband of his flannels and rubbed softly back and forth. Her pulse leaped at his answering intake of breath and quick jerk.

Big, warm hands smoothed over her hips and squeezed her butt gently. Mark's voice dropped to a husky whisper, "Are you often left to drink your coffee alone, Lorelei?"

If he only knew. It'd been quite a while since she'd shared *coffee* with a man. More than two years in fact. Since before her niece Michelle had been born and her sister-in-law had died, actually.

But Mark didn't need to know that.

Lorelei mentally chided herself. All he needed to

know was that she was interested in an intense game of tonsil hockey. Her family needed her to get back home. And that meant she had to stick out her boobs and rattle his cage. Make him forget about her sneaking out.

And if he didn't forget? What good would she be to Logan and Michelle if she was rotting in prison?

That simply couldn't be an option.

Fighting off the frown she felt forming between her brows, Lorelei tried for a seductive smile and purred, "Honey, it's been far too long since I've had the pleasure of a man over for coffee. Especially one as enthusiastic about it as you."

She watched his gaze drop to her mouth and his nostrils flare. Felt the hot, velvet tip of his erection brush against her fingertips. And it felt nice. Very, very nice.

"That's too bad. Coffee's such an enjoyable pastime. Maybe you oughta forget about sneaking out and running away, and think about grinding beans with me instead," he said, and rotated his hips in circular motion to emphasize his meaning.

Lorelei snorted and then laughed out loud. Who'd have thought Mark had a sense of humor?

He arched a brow, whirled her around until her back was to a wall. "Oh, you think that's funny, do you? Didn't think I was smart enough to get what you were really doing? I see. I'm just a dumb jock who only thinks about his cock, aren't I?"

Still laughing, she sputtered, "You said it. Not me. But that's just pure talent, rhyming like that."

Lorelei looked up to see him smiling, those sexy dimples on display. She noticed when the smile reached his eyes little specks of silver glittered among the pale gray. Sleep-tousled waves of deep blond hair fell across his forehead.

He was simply gorgeous.

"You wanna see talent, Lorelei?" His voice had taken on a rough, raw edge. Without a doubt he had the sexiest voice she'd ever heard. It made her want to call him on the phone just to hear it isolated like that. So male and sexual—it alone got her blood boiling.

Her pulse scattered when the warm hands on her butt streaked up under her top and around her rib cage until they came to rest flat against the undersides of her bare breasts. There they teased, barely cupping, lightly testing the weight.

Lorelei swallowed a gasp. "I don't doubt your *talent* for a minute. But I don't trust it, or you."

He lowered his head until his mouth stopped a fraction above hers. His breath slid hot and promising over her lips. "You don't trust me, sweetheart?" he asked just above a whisper. Then his tongue slipped past his lips to tease the corner of her mouth with slow, erotic strokes.

The hard calluses on Mark's palm gently abused the tender skin of her breasts as he caressed them, sending rivers of need flowing to the pit of her stomach. She couldn't control her response as her knees began to quake and her mouth opened helplessly, eager for his invasion.

But it never came.

Cold air brushed her parted lips as Mark suddenly released her and sneered, "You're damn right you don't trust me. And I sure as hell don't trust you."

Fighting a barrage of unwanted emotions, she swallowed hard and ignored the ache in her breasts created by the cold man standing before her. How could she have so easily lost sight of who, and what, he was?

The only thing they shared was a strong desire to possess a certain necklace. And even that would end as soon as she could find a way to get it to his ex and be rid of it.

Mark Cutter was a means to an end. Nothing more. Okay, right now he was a whole lot more. He was her blackmailer and kidnapper. But he was also the only thing standing between her and a nice long stay at the women's pen.

Not to mention the new star in some very dirty fantasies of hers.

Mark's voice broke into her thoughts. "Hand over your bag and go sit on the couch, thief." The command came hard and unyielding. Without a word of protest, Lorelei handed her duffel over and went to sit on the black leather couch. There was nothing left in the bag for him to find anyway. He'd already taken her cell phone, purse, and keys.

Jerking her head around, she followed his retreat down the hallway with her gaze and asked, "What are you doing?"

He didn't respond as he disappeared into his room. Tapping her thumb impatiently on the buttery leather of the couch, she rolled her eyes and let out a huff of frustrated air. So the guy was going to give her the silent treatment. Real mature.

Lorelei glanced longingly over her shoulder at the door and huffed again. There had to be a way out of this. She just hadn't found it yet. He'd told her she was stuck there for the foreseeable future until he had his necklace, so a way was bound to pop up. The problem was that where he went, she went. It was going to be hard to escape with him glued to her side.

"I used to be smart, damn it. I should be able to figure this out. It's not rocket science, for goodness' sake," she muttered to herself.

"What was that, Hamburgler? What's not rocket science?" he asked behind her.

Startled to find Mark standing behind her dressed in jeans and a green hooded Rush sweatshirt, she did a double take. Frowning at him, she said, "What did you just call me?"

With a rake of his fingers through his thick hair, Mark tossed on a black baseball hat and grinned. Then he winked at her.

Unbelievable. The jerk had the gall to be charming now?

Ignoring her question, he inclined his head toward the door and said on a rough laugh, "You wanted coffee. Come on then."

Coffee? Seriously? Hot damn.

Pushing off the couch, Lorelei glared at him as she walked past. "I certainly don't have a big butt."

"I never said you had a big butt."

"The Hamburgler does."

"So?" he challenged.

"So, don't call me that. I don't have a big butt and I'm not a burger thief." *So there*.

"You're right," he said.

"Thank you." It was good he got that straight.

"You're a jewelry thief," he said with relish.

Asshole.

Lorelei stopped in front of the door and whipped around to face him. "I have good reason for that, Mark. More than you could possibly understand in your narrow, selfish world." Her voice rang with self-righteousness. Not that it mattered. Like he was going to believe her anyway.

Mark ducked his head, the bill of his hat covering his face momentarily. A suspicious-sounding cough caught in his throat.

She hoped he choked on it.

Clearing it finally, he reached around her and flipped some latches on the door. "Yes, ma'am."

She wasn't buying that for a second.

Oh, the slight hint of Southern accent in his tone added to the gentlemanly words, but he was no gentleman. Not by a long shot.

But he was taking her out for coffee. In a way there was something vaguely gentleman-like in that.

Lorelei leveled a hard look on him one last time, straightened her shoulders, and said, "I'm not buying that good ol' boy, Bo Duke charm for a minute, *sweet-*

heart. But as long as we understand each other we'll get along fine."

The corner of Mark's mouth turned up as he twisted the doorknob, sent the door swinging open. Lorelei marched through with her head held high.

"Whatever you say . . . thief."

Double asshole.

Chapter 7

HE REFUSED TO take her to Starbucks. Being a strong believer in supporting local business, he drove right by one and chuckled at the look of longing on Lorelei's face.

She turned her head and glared at him. "I knew you taking me for coffee was too good to be true."

"Nah. Just not hopping on the bandwagon that helps corporate conglomerates crush the little guys." He could tell she wasn't listening, though. She'd already turned her head to stare back out the window.

A small redbrick building came into view and he turned his Rover into the cramped parking lot and nabbed a space. Pocketing the keys in the front pouch of his sweatshirt, Mark hopped out and breathed in the cold, crisp Colorado morning air. Before he could reach the passenger door, Lorelei shoved it open and climbed out.

Her attention was locked on the building front as she fumbled to shut the car door. Reaching over her head he pushed the door closed, then cupped her elbow to lead her toward the coffee house. "You must be one of those people who don't function without caffeine. Such a shame."

She pulled her elbow from his grasp and muttered, "Suck it."

That surprised a laugh out of him and he shook his head, grinning.

Lorelei was prickly as a cactus, Mark thought as he ushered her through the door of Rocky Mountain Coffee Company. The rich, heady scent of ground coffee beans filled his nostrils when he stepped through the door behind her. It smelled great, but he hadn't touched caffeine in seven years and he wasn't going to backslide now.

Now, Lorelei. He could tell she was a real caffeine addict.

Amusement filled him at the almost euphoric look on her face. He watched as her eyes drifted halfway closed and she inhaled deep, her lips curving in a smile of pure satisfaction. His gut tightened at the small purring sound she made low in her throat. It made him think of other ways to make her purr.

And he shouldn't be thinking things like that at all about Lorelei. The woman had his priceless lucky charm in her possession—had acquired it in a rather dubious manner. Hell, he wasn't too sure she didn't do shit like that on a regular basis just for kicks.

Uncomfortable with where his thoughts were headed, Mark turned his head slightly to look more fully at her. She was even more attractive in the harsh light of day than she'd been the other night. And she didn't have a bit of makeup on.

Her hair was a mess, he'd admit that. But for some reason it added to her appeal. Like a mass of liquid chocolate, it tumbled from her ponytail in loose waves, flyaway strands framing her face and neck. He knew it was every bit as luxurious to touch as it looked.

Shoving his hands in his sweatshirt pockets he frowned and continued to study Lorelei as she devoured the menu on the board behind the counter. She had flawless skin. The golden velvet look was real, not some creation of the makeup she'd worn two nights ago. He'd had seen his fair share of women who looked great with makeup and way less than stellar without it.

Fact was, Lorelei Littleton was a natural beauty.

For some reason that kind of irritated him. Mark grabbed hold of her elbow again and tugged her gently toward the counter. At 6:15 in the morning, the café was nearly empty except for an elderly couple at a corner table sipping coffee and sharing the morning newspaper. A young woman wearing nursing scrubs lounged tiredly on the red sofa.

He leaned down and whispered in her ear. "You wanted coffee. Now why don't you stop staring and order yourself something to get your brain working. You're a little slow this morning."

Lorelei turned her stare on him. He was halfway expecting a lecture of feminine affront, but she just smiled and nodded. "I am slow this morning, aren't I? Couldn't be from all the excitement and lack of sleep of the past few days, could it?"

Mark felt himself grin in response. "Nah, couldn't be.

I'm thinking you might be sluggish from all those fries and burgers you've stolen. All that saturated fat, you know."

She rolled her beautiful eyes at him and said with exaggeration, "Whatever."

Chuckling, he slipped his wallet from his back pocket and tossed a twenty down as she stepped up to the counter. "I'll take an orange juice and one of your fresh fruit bowls, along with whatever the lady wants."

Before Lorelei could protest he reached up a hand and squeezed the back of her neck. "Don't worry about it. I've got it covered."

She eyed him warily for a moment, then turned to the barista to give her order. "Thanks."

"No problem."

Grabbing his breakfast and utensils, Mark led the way to a round wooden table in the far corner by the front window and took a seat. His gaze settled on her breakfast pick and his eyebrow shot up in surprise. Apparently Lorelei had quite a sweet tooth.

Munching happily on her double-chocolate muffin, she caught his gaze and muttered, "What?"

He gestured to the assortment on the table before her. "Is that the way you normally eat?"

Washing down a bite of her muffin with a swallow of coffee, she glanced down at her food and shrugged. "Sometimes, yeah. About once a month I get a real craving for all things chocolate. Why?"

Detecting a note of defiance in her voice, Mark raised an eyebrow and gave a shrug of his own. Another challenge. He grinned. "No reason in particular. Just seems like an awful lot of crap there, that's all." He stabbed a cantaloupe ball with his plastic fork and held it out to her. "Here, try this. It's called fruit and it's healthy for you."

Lorelei leaned back in her chair and crossed her arms over her fantastic chest. "You're a health food fanatic, aren't you?" she accused. "What's wrong with what I'm eating? I've got a muffin. It's got flour, which is a grain. It's got chocolate, which is good for you. And I've got a chocolate cherry tart, which has cherries, and they're fruit. So what's the problem?"

He was about to jump right into a lecture about nutrition when he noticed the sparkle in her eyes and realized she was teasing him. Relaxing, he wiggled the small globe of fruit and crooned, "Come on, Hamburgler, you know you want this."

She considered. "I'll make a deal with you. You eat some of my tart and take a swig of my triple-shot mocha and I'll eat your fruit."

Mark picked up his bottle of orange juice and downed half of it before setting it on the table again. He licked the remaining drops off his bottom lip with his tongue and lowered the fork. "Can't. It's game day. No way am I gonna load my body full of that crap before playing Chicago again. I've got to be in top form if I want to play well tonight."

Lorelei took another sip of her coffee and grinned at him over the rim of her cup. Heat slithered into his gut at her saucy smile. "We'll just call it a truce then. Now tell me, did you always want to be a professional baseball player?"

Mark's answer was immediate. "Always. As a kid I wasn't happy unless I had a bat in my hand. It was kind of an obsession for this northern Florida boy and I can't remember ever wanting to do anything else."

The bell above the door rang and they turned and saw a couple with a young boy walk in and head to the counter. Then he brought his attention back to Lorelei. "Why do you ask? I thought you weren't a baseball fan."

"I'm not, really. I've watched a game or two before when my brother had one on, but I don't go out of my way to watch it," she said.

"Do all the big bad men scare you, honey?"

Crumpling her napkin into a ball, she scoffed, "Hardly. I just have better things to do than sit and watch a bunch of men prove their masculinity by trying to bash a ball beyond the outfield."

He raised a brow at her. "Huh. I take it you're not a hockey fan then, either."

Her surprised laugh sounded warm and intoxicating. "Not especially."

A blur of movement caught his eye and Mark turned to see the young boy shuffle over to him, eyes round and full of excitement. Putting down his fork, he turned full in his seat until he was facing the dark-haired boy, and smiled. "Hi there."

The boy stopped so fast his sneakers squeaked against the hardwood floor, and his face flamed scarlet. His young voice came on an excited rush. "You're The Wall, aren't you? Oh man, my friends are gonna be so jealous that I saw you. Can I get your autograph? Please? My friend

Timmy got your autograph last season when you played Atlanta and he's been bragging about it ever since."

Tipping his hat up his forehead with his index finger, Mark chuckled and leaned forward. "You've got the right man, sport. I'm Mark. I'd be happy to sign something for you. What's your name?" Holding out his hand in greeting, he grinned when the boy wiped his palms on the front of his jeans before reaching for a handshake.

"My name's David Muldoon. I'm nine. Oh man. My friends are gonna flip. You're like our favorite baseball player ever. Like, our hero, you know? Here, you can sign this." Reaching into his pocket, the boy pulled out a slightly bent and dog-eared baseball card.

Reaching for the card, Mark felt a jolt of pleasure when he saw it was he. Deeply touched, he asked as he searched for a pen, "You play ball, David?"

A pen appeared in his line of vision. "Sorry, forgot my mom gave that to me. Yeah, me and my friends all play. We belong to a junior league in Lakewood. We're the Eagles."

Mark took the pen and signed the card. Then he handed them both back to the boy. "That so? I bet you're great. What position you play, David?"

The boy's blue eyes lit with pride and his thin chest puffed out as he stood a little taller. "I'm a catcher. Like you. I got your poster in my room to remind me that I can be the best, just like you, if I try real hard. 'Cause I wanna play for the Rush someday, too."

It was moments like this that made him grateful for

his career. Made all the pain and grind worth it. All the stress and sweat. Totally worth it.

Mark motioned the kid closer with the crook of his finger. When the boy stepped close he said in a low voice, "You're already a champ, David, because you try with all your heart. That's what matters most."

Nodding vigorously, the boy nearly vibrated himself across the floor. His voice barely contained his enthusiasm when he thanked Mark and hustled over to his waiting parents. With a last wave and neon-bright smile the boy and his parents left.

Gratitude filled Mark as he turned back in his seat to find Lorelei studying him through narrowed eyes. Uncomfortable under the intense scrutiny and what she'd witnessed, he shrugged. "What?"

"Are you serious? You're going to act all surly and ill-tempered now? Just because I saw you behave like a decent human being?" Her voice was ripe with disapproval.

Unused to being scolded, Mark felt his temper spark. "I can act any way I want. Too damn bad if you have a problem with it." Jerking his shoulder, he began to clean his mess from the table and tried to ignore the pain in the ass across the table from him.

She must have decided to drop it because she changed the subject. "I didn't know you were a lefty."

His mind always two steps from the gutter, he smirked. "Most guys are, sweetheart."

It took her a few seconds, but he saw the instant comprehension hit her. Color tinged her cheeks and she shook her head. "I was referring to you writing with your left hand, Mark Cutter, not from which side you hang your package." She grinned at him. "Besides, I already knew that."

Tension coiled hard in his groin. Slowly, Mark shifted his gaze until it locked on hers. How was it possible that one provocative statement from her got his blood burning? She was an unwanted, unwelcome complication in his life. Hell, he didn't even like her.

So why did he have a crazy urge to skip working out and do his push-ups with her instead?

If he didn't get his head cleared and focus on the game ahead, he'd find himself benched. He hated being benched. It didn't matter if all catchers got pulled from the plate from time to time. For Mark it was an insult and a harsh message that he'd totally screwed up his game.

Mark glanced down at his wristwatch. He had a game today. A very important game that set the tone to the season. And no lucky charm.

There was only one thing to do.

Chapter 8

THE SON OF a bitch had locked her in. Locked her inside his condo with no way out. Lorelei was steaming mad after she'd stepped out of the shower and found that Mark had left. Well, that wasn't what ticked her off. It was discovering the stupid front door had special security locks on it that she couldn't open from the inside—even with a key.

What was she supposed to do now? Crochet a sweater?

Stomping back to the guest room, she threw her towel on the bed and let out a frustrated yell. "Mark Cutter, you pig!"

She yanked her duffel off the floor and tossed it on the bed, rifling through it for some underwear and a bra. "How dare he lock me in like a common criminal." As soon as the words were out her conscience tried to remind her she *was* a criminal, so she ignored it. Told it to shut up. Now was not the time for a guilt trip. He had crossed the line big-time. And after he'd behaved so wonderfully toward that little boy in the coffee shop.

Creep.

Just when she'd started to think there might be more to Mark than a giant ego, he went and pulled a dumb-ass stunt like this. Hadn't he learned by now not to cross a lady?

Lorelei dressed quickly in jeans and a cream V-neck sweater, then finger-combed her hair as she headed down the hall to the living room, her bare feet padding quietly on the smooth cherry floors.

She'd show him. A quick phone call to his ex and Dina'd be there in no time. Surely Dina had more than one spare key to his place. All Lorelei had to do was give her a jingle and Dina'd be on her way in a jiffy with a pocketful of cash.

Only one problem. Mark didn't have a home phone. And he'd taken her cell and her purse.

Looked like he'd cut her off at the knees after all. She couldn't even call her brother to tell him she was fine. And she had no idea how Michelle was holding up.

Tears pricked the backs of her eyes as Lorelei walked over to the plush leather couch and slumped into the cushions. It wasn't even noon yet and her day had already gone down the toilet.

For a few minutes she just sat there in the quiet, fighting tears. Her poor brother. He'd been through hell. Lost so much. She and Michelle were all he had left. Everyone else had died. Their parents and sister, Lucy. His wife. One tragic accident after another.

He already thought he was cursed. It would kill him to lose his daughter, too. Lorelei *had* to get that money, one way or another.

She wished like hell she could snap her fingers and make it appear. Or rewind the clock back a few years to when her credit was good and she could have gotten a loan. But she'd already been down that route before when she'd taken out loans to help Logan pay old medical bills. She was tapped out. No institution would loan her the money needed to cover the costs. And Logan couldn't even ride bulls anymore to win the money. His days with the PBR circuit were history after a bull had hooked him and he'd lost a kidney. He'd nearly died, but she knew he was *this close* to reentering the sport anyway. Although he hadn't said anything, she knew her brother only too well. He'd risk everything he had, including his life, to make sure Michelle was safe. The poor baby had already lost her mom. She needed her daddy, healthy and alive, to raise her.

Getting the money was completely and solely up to Lorelei. That knowledge was a heavy burden to bear. Still, she had to do it—fast. Before Logan went and played Russian roulette on the back of some thundering beast.

Lorelei was desperate to keep what little family she had left.

Dina's offer had been an answer to her prayers. Almost Robin Hood-ish. Rob from the rich and spoiled and give to the needy. She should have known it wouldn't be that easy.

It never was. Didn't she watch the movies, read the

books? There was always a hidden trapdoor. Besides, hadn't her gut warned her?

Lorelei glanced at the clock tucked into Mark's sleek iron-and-glass entertainment center. It was now noon. She'd missed her meeting with Dina. Shit.

Anger surged up inside her. Like hell she'd miss her chance. She wasn't giving up that easily.

Pushing off the couch, she took a good look around Mark's condo for the first time. It was decorated in the same Asian-inspired contemporary motif as the guest bedroom, with a wall of windows overlooking Denver. They cast tons of natural light across the hardwood floor and huge, biscuit-colored rug. Large bamboo planters with lush plants were scattered around the room, the deep green leaves vibrant against the taupe walls. And there was an absurdly large amount of colored rocks in decorative bowls and vases scattered around his place.

What was up with that? Maybe Mark was a Zen Buddhist or something.

The kitchen was more of the same sleek, contemporary look. Stainless steel, glossy black granite counters, glass-topped table. More colored bowls with rocks.

And it was all very, very tidy.

Next she made a beeline for Mark's bedroom. It was time to snoop and see about finding a way out of there. Or see about finding things about the catcher, period.

Lorelei snorted in disbelief when she entered his room and saw the perfectly made bed. Not a single wrinkle to be found on the tan bedspread. Everything was in place. No socks on the floor, no shoes scattered around, no door ajar on the black dresser or matching black bedside tables. The guy was a neat freak. A health-food-fanatical, order-craving neat freak who believed in lucky charms. How odd.

And she wanted to jump square in the middle of that perfectly made bed and mess it up real good.

But first there was one more room to snoop through. Another spare room across from the one she was in. Then she'd give in to the juvenile urge to wreak havoc with the sheets of his bed. She'd loosen the corners, wrinkle the bottom sheet, and maybe shove something lumpy under the covers he wouldn't notice until he climbed in.

It'd drive him nuts. Sucker.

Detouring through the kitchen on her way to the final room, Lorelei opened the fridge and groaned. Vegetables and fruit. Nothing but health food. Where was the good stuff? She had a real bad craving for nachos. Didn't every fridge in America have a block of Velveeta, for goodness' sake?

She leaned inside to take closer look and rummaged through the meat drawer. "Come on, come on. I know there's got to be something in here, some contraband. Even Mr. Health has to have something. Aha!" She grabbed the block of cheddar and slammed the door closed.

A few minutes of cupboard searching and she uncovered some organic corn chips, made a face, and went about fixing lunch. She couldn't help noticing how much more room Mark's kitchen had than her cluttered one back at the ranch. Then again, he didn't live with a rancher and a toddler, either.

Ten minutes later Lorelei had a heaping plate full of nachos topped with gourmet olives, green onion, fresh guacamole, and organic sour cream. Not exactly junk food, but it would do in a pinch. Inhaling the aroma, she popped a corn chip in her mouth and headed out to discover the treasures of the last bedroom.

She left all the dishes on the counter. And she hoped it bugged the hell out him.

Pushing the door open with her hip as she bit into another smothered corn chip, Lorelei stopped short and stared. It was a library. Not another super-clean guest room.

"Holy cow," she muttered around a mouthful of nacho. Trophies, pictures, books, framed posters of Mark in action on the wall. Her eyes grew round as she took in the large room. "Score."

Lorelei pushed the door closed with her behind and made her way around the huge black painted wood desk to the plush leather chair. It, too, was black. Everything in the room matched. In her entire life she'd never been that color-coordinated. Nor had she ever been rich enough to be so, but that was beside the point.

Sinking into the deep-cushioned chair, Lorelei sighed in ecstasy and closed her eyes. If only she could have a chair like this. One with great back support and a thickly padded seat that conformed to her body.

Instead, she had a cheapie from the thrift store that she sat in while she wrote her gardening articles upstairs in her room. It creaked like a rusted door no matter how much she oiled it, and the back was broken. If she leaned back too hard it fell off. She'd landed on her head more than once and had the permanent knot to prove it.

Someday she'd have the money to buy a decent office chair. That thought made her frown.

She hitched her chin and glared at the framed poster on the wall in front of her of Mark snagging a pitch with his glove while crouched behind home plate. He'd ruined everything.

Reignited anger had her reaching for one chip after another while she glared at all his awards and pictures. All his accomplishments.

She polished off the whole huge plate as she compared his pampered life and all its luxuries with the struggling one she and her brother lived. It wasn't that she cared about being rich. Heck, no. That wasn't it.

Lorelei grabbed a small golden trophy off the desk in front of her and turned it around in her hands. It just wasn't fair that one person should have so much while another didn't, that's all.

"That's life, Lorelei. It's not fair. Deal with it." She was, in the best way she knew how.

She stood and walked over to the bookcase. Might as well pass the time while he was out with a good book.

Perusing the shelves, she mulled over her choices. There were a lot of photo essay books, a stack of coffee table books, and tons of magazines spanning from *Ranger Rick* to *Sports Illustrated*. Graphic novels. Even a children's book or two. But very few regular adult novels.

That was strange, but to each his own, she supposed. Everyone had their thing, and obviously he liked pictures.

"Find anything you like, sweetheart?"

Lorelei jumped, a scream lodged in her throat, and whirled around to find Mark standing with wet hair in the hallway. "Would you stop *doing* that? Stop sneaking up on me."

He raised a brow and leaned his large body against the door frame. "I didn't sneak, Lorelei. You were too busy snooping to hear the front door open and slam shut."

He had a point. "Yeah, well, don't do it again. And about the front door. I don't appreciate you locking me in and taking my things."

Mark shrugged a shoulder. "I don't appreciate you taking *my* things."

She huffed and strode across the floor until she was directly in front of him. She held out her hand. "I want my purse and my cell back."

Mark crossed his arms over his chest. "I want my necklace back."

"You don't need it. I do. And I need my stuff, so give it back." Lorelei rotated her outstretched hand and nudged him in his solid chest.

He sighed. "I'm going to make something to eat. Want anything?"

"I've already eaten. I want to go home, Mark."

Pushing away from the wall, he turned and strode down the hall, Lorelei hot on his heels. The frustration of the past few hours, of being locked in, of missing her opportunity with Dina made her voice thin and sharp. "Did you hear me? *I want to go home.*"

He glanced over his shoulder before he disappeared into the kitchen. "Then give me what I want, Lorelei. Hand it to me now and you can leave. Make us both happy."

How could he be so callous?

And what was she doing looking at his butt? He was her warden.

Just then Mark let out a bellow and came rushing out of the kitchen, a fierce frown plastered across his face. Sparks of anger danced in his silvery gaze and a tic worked in his unshaven jaw.

He'd found the dishes.

That'll teach him, Lorelei thought with smug satisfaction.

His voice came low and tight. "There seems to be some dishes on my counter with crap drying on them. Would you happen to know anything about that, Lorelei?"

She grinned like the devil. Dried guacamole was a real bitch to clean. "Yep."

"Plan on doing anything about that?" His voice was carefully neutral.

Oh, this was fun. Lorelei tilted her head to the side and batted her eyelashes. "Does the mess bother you, Mark?"

She held back a laugh as she watched him fight for control. The win was so close she could taste it. Any minute he'd explode. So she thought.

She thought wrong.

Shrugging his broad shoulders beneath his white T-shirt, Mark shook his head. "Nah. Just making sure it was you." He jerked a thumb over his shoulder. "That kinda shit's why I've got a housekeeper."

Her mouth dropped open. How could he recover like that? Go from almost boiling to cool cucumber in a blink? It was maddening.

The cocky grin on his face told Lorelei he knew what she'd been up to. No way was it going down like that. Nuh-uh. Straightening her shoulders, she strode past him and flashed a wild smile.

She wasn't giving up that easily.

Lorelei headed straight for the fridge and threw the door wide open. She needed something messy.

Out of the corner of her eye she saw a pair of very white socks covering large feet come into view. Briefly she let her gaze travel up the faded denim jeans covering muscular legs before she turned her attention back to the contents of the fridge.

"What are you doing in my refrigerator?"

"You said you were hungry. I'm going to make you something to eat. Eew! You have Brussels sprouts in here. You actually eat those things?"

He sounded like a surly teenager when he replied, "They're good for you. You might want to give them a try sometime and lay off the manufactured sugars."

Lorelei scoffed as she reached for a tub of hummus. "I don't think so, buster. Besides, I eat plenty healthy."

This time he snorted. "Since when? And stop wiggling your butt like that, it's distracting."

Emerging from the fridge with her hands full of ammunition, she grinned and closed the door with her hip. "Since always, that's when. It's only during a certain time of the month that my body craves junk food. A guy with as much female experience as you should know that."

Mark leaned his behind against the counter and crossed his arms. His eyes danced with amusement. "Ah, gotcha."

Lorelei opened a drawer and grabbed a butter knife. She dipped it in the hummus and collected a large amount on the blade. Swallowing a laugh, she turned to face him, barely twitched her wrist, and watched as red pepper hummus splattered across the front of his white T-shirt.

"I'M SO SORRY! Gosh, how clumsy of me. Let me get something to wipe that off with."

Mark knew she'd done that on purpose. Her wide-eyed innocent act wasn't fooling him. Not for a second. So she wanted to play dirty, did she?

The brat thought he couldn't handle a little disorder, a little mess. She was about to find out how wrong she was.

He eyed her and drawled, "Now, honey, don't you worry yourself over that mishap." With a finger he wiped the blob off his shirt and flicked it on hers. "Oh darn. Looks like I'm slippery-fingered today, too."

Her gasp of outrage made him laugh. Served her right for snooping around his office.

He saw her go for the hummus tub and snaked a hand

out, snatching it an instant before she did. Mark couldn't resist taunting, "Too slow, Hamburgler. You're not stealing my fries."

She made a face and let out a growl. She lunged for the tub. "Gimme that hummus, Mark."

Amusement rolled through him. God, she was easy to tease. And tempting when she was riled. Color flooded her cheeks and her eyes turned vivid green.

He shook his head and raised his arm, holding the tub high above them. "Come and get it."

"You don't think I will?"

He laughed. "Can you reach it, short stuff?"

She huffed and blew away the hair hanging in her face. He wiggled the tub in challenge.

Lorelei jumped, missing the tub by a good six inches. "Catchers have good reaches, girl. You'd better try harder than that."

She cussed, making him laugh. Then she jumped again. Again and again she tried until Mark was almost doubled over with laughter.

Finally, she stopped and gave him a good glare. "Fine. You win, you big jerk."

He felt a stab of disappointment, but before he could respond she wheeled around and leaped, her legs wrapping firmly around his waist as both her hands grabbed at his arm. Shock and arousal shot through him as she wiggled up his body, using his arm like a fire pole.

The laughter slowly died in his throat when her legs clamped tight around him, pulling her heat snug against him. Her amazing breasts pressed flush against his chest. In an instant he was hard and aching for her.

Turning them, Mark pressed her against the counter. Oblivious to the hunger gnawing at him, she squeezed her legs and thrust up, taking the hummus out of his loose grip.

Her face lit with triumph, Lorelei sat on the counter and lowered her victorious gaze to him. Then she looked at him and her eyes went wide. "Oh my goodness," she whispered.

He couldn't take it anymore. Lust slammed into him and he took her mouth in a hot, carnal kiss. No tender coaxing, no gentle persuasion. He fed her a kiss full of a grown man's raging need. No games. Just tongue, teeth, and raw sex.

She whimpered and it fueled him, ignited him. Made him burn.

He vaguely heard the sound of the tub of hummus as it hit the floor, splattering across the cupboards. Then her hands were on him, yanking at his shirt, pulling at his fly. Her lush mouth was moving wickedly against his, her tongue stroking, demanding.

She bit him and he swore, laughed. His head spun with a sort of delirium. God he wanted her.

Shoving his erection against the V of her thighs, Mark broke the kiss and yanked his shirt over his head. He sucked air like a drowning man as his chest heaved from exertion.

Suddenly he had to see them. In the bright light of day

he had to touch them, taste them. Leaning in, he kissed Lorelei hard before yanking her sweater over her head. Just as quickly he undid her bra, not stopping until her breasts were bare, exposed to his view. Every creamy, beautiful inch.

They were perfect. Full and round with plump, tight, dusky nipples. His cock jumped hard in reaction, straining madly against his fly.

Her voice was a little husky. "I want your mouth on me, Mark. I want to feel your tongue across my nipples."

"Jesus." Something primitive and wicked reared its head at her words. It washed over him, into him, made him grip a handful of her hair and yank until she whimpered and her throat was bare.

Then his mouth was on her, feasting on her breasts. Never. Never before had he wanted a woman like this.

Closing his mouth over her puckered nipple, Mark sucked, using teeth and tongue until Lorelei let out a groan of pleasure and slid her hands into his hair, pulling him even closer. He grinned when he felt her tug his hair and heard her moan his name.

He was so engrossed in the sight, feel, taste of her that he was slow to realize she was trying to get his attention. With a vicious growl he straightened, licked his lips for one more taste of her. And felt immense satisfaction at the dazed, aroused look he saw in her gorgeous eyes.

"What is it?" he asked, his voice sounding rough to his own ears. Desire still pumped a furious pace in his blood as Mark released her hair and slid a finger down her silky throat. He grinned when he found her pulse racing there.

Lorelei closed her eyes and purred, stretched into his caress like a cat. "Mmm, the phone, Mark. Someone's calling."

And that's when he heard it, the sound of his cell phone. He was going to ignore it. Getting Lorelei naked was way more important. Then reality registered.

Instantly the fog lifted, and Mark swore. She'd done it again, damn it. Made him forget his priorities, his job.

He had a game today.

Mark took one last look at her amazing breasts and scowled. How the hell was he supposed to focus on his game after tasting those?

Chapter 9

LORELEI WAS AT her very first professional baseball game. She was seated four rows up and directly behind home plate with a great view of the field. In spite of herself she couldn't help feeling excited as Coors Field filled with enthusiastic Rush fans.

Pregame music blared through the speakers—hard-hitting rock 'n' roll. The smell of vendor hot dogs and cheap beer lingered on the air, mixing with the crisp scent of the freshly mowed ball field. The noise level grew as the crowd shuffled in and began waiting anxiously for the game to begin. Lorelei snuggled deeper into the gold and green Rush jersey Mark had given her to wear. Though it was short-sleeved it was so large on her that the sleeves came down past her elbow.

The Rush were currently on the field for their pregame warm-up. She'd spotted Mark the minute he'd strode onto the field. Of course he was the one with all the catcher's padding and the big glove, but it was more than that. It was the way he moved. So graceful and confident.

A sharp thrill had shot through her when he separated from the team and stalked toward the plate in front of her. After walking around the plate three times and whacking his fist in his glove twice, he'd turned his head toward her and shot her a warning look through his helmet cage. It clearly said, *You disappear, you pay.*

If she was honest with herself, Lorelei wasn't so sure she wanted to skip out just yet. She had a chance to watch Mark "The Wall" Cutter work his magic live and up close. And after what had happened between them in his kitchen she had to admit she was more than a little curious about him.

Besides, she could always bail later.

Yeah, then he'd have her arrested and charged with theft and drugging him. And that was no laughing matter.

Lorelei realized she was glaring at the back of Mark's jersey. She still hadn't figured out how to get the money.

"You missed our meeting today, Lorelei. I'm very disappointed in you."

Lorelei started at the voice coming from behind her and glanced up, tried to turn her head.

"No! Don't turn around. He can't see me talking to you!"

Dina. She couldn't stop the chill that ran down her spine. Lorelei's gaze whipped to Mark as her heart started hammering. He wasn't looking, thank God. The last thing she needed right now was him seeing her with his ex-wife.

Twin surges of panic and excitement darted inside her at what this unexpected meeting meant. The money wasn't lost after all. She kept her eyes locked on Mark and replied, "I won't turn around."

"Good. Now, where is it? Where's that stupid prick's lucky charm?"

Lorelei frowned at that nasty comment. That was a bit harsh, even coming from an embittered ex-wife. "I don't have it on me." It was still with the hotel concierge. "But he knows I took it and is holding me hostage until I give it to him."

Impatience sharpened Dina's tone, raising it almost a full octave. "Well, that's not very smart of you, is it? And that's your little problem to figure out. You do want the money, don't you? God, just look at him out there. He thinks he's something special, doesn't he?" She let out a huff of air and snorted. "He's not going to be so special after I'm through with him."

Unease began to creep along Lorelei's nerves. Dina was sounding downright nasty. Something was off about this whole thing—she could feel it. Glancing out at the field warily until Mark came into view; she took a deep breath and watched him. Her tone was guarded when she replied, "Well, he is a pro ballplayer. That does make him somewhat unique, I would think."

Another snort sounded behind her, full of derision and sarcasm. "Oh, he's *unique* all right. Uniquely stupid. Do you know that he thought I wouldn't catch on to why all of our old friends began snubbing me? That I wouldn't know why I wasn't being invited to all the big social events anymore? I made him look good and he threw it away. Threw me away. And he made me look like a fool. He's going to pay for that. Top dollar, too, because he needs his precious little necklace."

The unease crept up another notch, but she kept her eyes on Mark. If he knew who she was talking to she'd be so done. There'd be no wiggling her way out of this one. "Is that what this is all about, Dina? Payback for losing your membership to the rich people's club? I thought he cheated on you and abused you."

Something very close to venom snaked into Dina's voice, "I *belong* to that club. It's *mine*." It sounded so very different from the wide-eyed, abused ex-wife tone Lorelei had experienced before that she couldn't help swiveling her head around. Before she'd succeeded, a cold, bony hand splayed across her cheek and pushed her back.

"I *told* you not to turn around!"

Well, *excuse* her. Irritation bloomed in her chest. If she didn't need the money so bad she'd tell Dina just where she could stick it after that little stunt. But she did need it, so she remained cool and apologized instead. "I'm sorry."

Apparently mollified, Dina leaned in close and said emphatically, "He did cheat me! I did everything for him and what did I get for it, huh, Lorelei? The bastard took out a restraining order against me. *Me!* I'm the victim—not him. I got publicly shunned and humiliated for that stunt. He ruined my life. Now it's his turn." Suddenly she gasped in outrage and demanded, "Get me the cross, Lorelei. Bring it to me at this address"—she shoved a piece of paper into Lorelei's hand—"and the money is yours. I want to see him humiliated. Shit, I have to go."

The noise level in the stadium rose as fans grew impatient for the game to get under way. Lorelei whipped her head around just in time to see Dina's tall, slender form slip quickly into the crowd and disappear. She tucked the paper quickly into her pocket and frowned. And just what the hell was Lorelei supposed to think about all this, because it was pretty damn apparent that the wool had been pulled over her eyes. A restraining order? What the hell?

Now she understood why Dina needed her.

Before she got a chance to mull it all over, a female voice startled her. "Excuse me, are you Lorelei Littleton?"

Tearing her gaze from where Dina had been, Lorelei turned her head and glanced up. A tall, fit-looking woman about her age stood a few feet down, a tentative smile on her stunningly gorgeous face.

"Yes, I'm Lorelei."

The woman slipped into the empty seat next to her and chuckled. "Oh good." She held out a hand. "I'm Mark's sister, Leslie Cutter. It's nice to meet you, Lorelei."

At a loss for words, Lorelei shook her hand and studied Mark's sister. Took a moment to calm her racing heart. At least she knew Leslie hadn't seen anything— the stadium was way too crowded and people were still standing up milling about.

There was a definite resemblance in the blond hair, the set of the jaw, the shape of the eyes. The color and expression were very different, however. Hers were hazel and Mark's were that pale gray. And his were sulky half the time.

"Y'all are wondering why I'm here, aren't you?" Leslie asked in that softly Southern accent reminiscent of her brother's, only stronger.

Lorelei glanced at Mark just in time to see him salute to his sister. He didn't even look at her. Obviously he hadn't noticed anything, either.

Forcing herself to relax, she answered, "I *was* wondering that, since I didn't even know Mark had any siblings. In fact, I don't know Mark all that well at all."

The beautiful blond tossed her head back and let out a hoot of laughter. "That's just like my brother, all right. Mr. Enigma." Leslie reached for a drink tray she'd set on the floor and handed Lorelei a cup. "Here you go. Mark said you'd probably go for a soda during the game, so I brought you one."

How'd he know that? She *had* been planning on a soda.

Not sure whether to be angry or flattered that Mark had sent his sister to babysit her, Lorelei grabbed the cup and took a sip of the soft drink through the straw. "Thanks, Leslie."

"No problem. So, Mark tells me that y'all have been seeing a lot of each other lately."

Lorelei shifted in her seat and eyed his sister warily. "You could say that." How much did she know?

Leslie took a sip of her drink and pointed the cup and straw toward the field. "It's nice to hear that he's been spending a significant amount of time with the same woman. Since his divorce, there hasn't been anyone who's occupied more than a few weeks of his life at a time."

Lorelei watched as Mark sat on the ground and stretched. The number seventeen slithered over his back as he bent forward to stretch his hamstrings. He was surprisingly flexible. *Hmmm*. Maybe he did do yoga. "Is that so? He hasn't dated anyone exclusively?"

Ripping her gaze from Mark, she turned to look at his sister. Leslie shook her head, her pale blond hair swinging with the movement. "Nope. There's been no one. Until you, that is. When Mark called me and asked me to come meet you, told me that you were very special to him, I was thrilled. He's been playing at being the single bad boy long enough."

She wasn't dumb enough to tell Leslie the truth, but her conscience nipped at her, making her inwardly flinch. Now she was going to have to lie to Mark's sister and for some reason that bothered her. Maybe her conscience was kicking into overdrive, trying to make up for completely deserting her when she'd met Dina.

Glaring again at the hulking catcher, since her lying to his sister was his fault, Lorelei said, "I'm glad to meet you, too, Leslie. You're the first of Mark's family that I've met." That, at least was true. "I thought they were all back in Florida."

"Most of us are. I just moved here a little over a year ago. A change of scenery and all." Leslie's gaze followed a Rush player until he jogged in front of them. Then she put her fingers in her mouth, whistled and yelled, "Whoo! John Crispin, you stud!"

The rugged-looking, unshaven player flashed a smile and raised his mitt, pointing it toward Leslie. Then he twisted on his cleats, sent a spray of dirt flying, and dashed away.

Lorelei held back a smile as Leslie sighed and said, "That's a whole lotta man there, Lorelei. I swear to y'all, his kisses will melt the panties right off a gal."

Lorelei almost choked on her soda. The bubbles went up her nose, making her eyes water and her sinuses sting. Waving a hand in front of her face, she croaked, "Is that so?"

She wondered if Mark could hear them, because just then his head whipped around and he sent her a piercing stare, his eyes as cold as ice behind the metal of his face cage. Tension emanated from him, flowing out in frustrated waves toward her. Or maybe he was just psychic.

"Looks like Mark's in one of his moods tonight." Leslie blew him a kiss. He jerked his chin up, paused, and then turned back around, his movements abrupt. "Unless he gets that under control and focuses, he's going to play like crap."

Lorelei slid farther down in her seat. "Hmm, wonder why he's in such a bad mood?" she muttered vaguely. Like she didn't know exactly why he was in such a foul temper.

Leslie propped a booted foot on the seat in front of her and leaned back, turning her head toward Lorelei. She grinned. "I tell you what, to make things interesting, every time Chicago scores a run, I'll divulge a little secret about him. Something he'd be completely mortified to know I told you. And for every run the Rush scores y'all gotta dish about you."

Lorelei glanced at Mark and back at Leslie. "Seriously?" Leslie nodded. "He doesn't have his lucky charm, you know?"

"Yeah, I know. Won't it be fun?"

A chance to learn some intimate details about him. Lorelei pursed her lips and considered. Then she glanced at Mark again as the game got ready to start and smiled.

She hoped he played like crap.

MARK SWORE AS another ball slipped past his glove and a runner took home. The crowd roared in discontent, announcing another fuck-up of his. Damn that was a stupid mistake. He'd misjudged the ball bounce from left field and his glove had missed it by a mile.

Trying to shake it off, Mark shoved his mask up, yanked off his catcher's glove, and watched as Peter Kowalskin jogged over.

"What's the deal tonight?"

Mark clenched his jaw and glared at a Chicago batter as he warmed up on deck and blew a kiss at him. "Jackass. Why don't you come here and do that again, Gregor, you pussy."

"Hey. He might be a pussy, but you've got to get your head in this game."

Mark shoved his hand back into his glove and

slammed his cage down. "Yeah, I got it. Let's do this."

Kowalskin reached out and smacked the top of his helmet. "Damn straight. Let's do this thing."

Nothing was sweeter for Mark than the time he spent behind home plate. Not even sex. And nothing pissed him off more when things were going bad.

Two up, two down. Top of the fourth. He watched as Kowalskin took the ball back to the pitcher's mound and readied himself for the next batter. Mark assumed the position, muscles alert and ready for action. Adrenaline raged as he watched the batter stride to the plate and stop short of the box. A few swings, a dig of his cleat into the box dirt, and the Cub settled in for the pitch.

Mark signaled to Peter for a slider and narrowed his eyes when the pitcher shook his head, rejecting the pitch. Reassessing, Mark signaled for a curve and raised his glove when the pitch was accepted.

As he shifted his weight on the balls of his feet, his eyes zeroed in on the ball as it was pulled back like a rock in a slingshot waiting for release. He could feel it, almost see the play before it happened, knew a split second before the ball came flying high and fast on his glove side, just inside the strike zone.

He reacted instantly as the batter swung hard, hitting his knees in a butterfly stance. Reaching, he felt the sharp sting of leather hit his glove and heard the resounding thwack.

The umpire behind him yelled out, "Strike!" The batter swore and stepped out of the box.

Mark looked at his glove hand and opened it, the

white leather of the ball bright in the early evening sun. The roar of the crowd echoed in his chest.

He was back, baby.

Mark stood and loosened his shoulders, rolled his head from side to side. Man, that felt good.

As the play began again, he finally tapped into the focus that made him one of the best catchers in the major leagues. As he called pitches and caught every ball, adrenaline tore through him, pumping him more and more.

When a ball whipped into the strike zone followed by a furious swing, Mark shifted forward and caught it.

As the crowd went wild, blood rushed to his head making him feel intensely alive. This was what the game was all about for him. The thrill, the total head-rush. It was him against them—a test of courage, skill, strength, and reflexes.

It was a fast-paced battle of brains and finesse. And Mark loved it like nothing else.

He shut down every attempt at home for the rest of the game, using his toned body and calculating mind to make out after out. Whereas the last game he'd gone to the field in a fit of temper and bad mouth, tonight the attitude from him was minimal. After a few initial bumps, he was totally, completely in his zone.

At the bottom of the ninth the Rush came out on top 4–3, ensuring them one game closer to solid season standings. Intense relief flooded him as he made his way down the line, shaking hands with his teammates.

He'd been able to play a winning game without his good luck charm. Part of him wondered why that was. The other part of him was afraid he already knew. Because there was only one thing different in his life, in his routine that could be attributed to the abrupt change of fortune. Only one thing it could possibly be.

Heading to the locker room still riding high on the Rush's victory, Mark stopped at the edge of the field and glanced into the stadium seats. And there she was. Lorelei. Sitting with his younger sister, Leslie, their heads together, laughing like they were lifelong friends.

Suddenly Lorelei glanced up and their gazes locked. His chest squeezed tight around his lungs, making it hard to breathe. He dropped his gaze and stepped off the field into the dugout, heading to the locker room.

He didn't want to think about her. Didn't want to feel anything for her. She already spent too much frigging time in his head. But there was one nagging suspicion about her he wasn't going to be able to deny much longer. And he didn't like it one little bit.

"Hey, Wall. Good game tonight."

Mark glanced up to see Rush newbie JP Trudeau waiting for him. The kid had taken a beating tonight at shortstop and looked like someone had hit him with a sledgehammer. He had a nasty split lip swelling up on him—courtesy of a collision with a runner at second. His jersey was streaked brown with dirt.

"You look like shit, JP. No girl's gonna want to kiss you tonight with an ugly lip like that."

The young player began to smile and winced. "It's okay. I'll just have her kiss another part of me instead."

Mark's laugh echoed down the long corridor. "Now you're thinking like a real baseball player, rookie."

Together they walked on the painted concrete toward the locker room, the young shortstop towering over Mark. Pushing open the door to the greeting of laughter and celebratory yells, they entered the locker room and crossed the rug with the Rush's logo of Goldpan Sam and his pickax on it. As he passed his teammates they slapped his back and congratulated him on the win.

"Damn good comeback, Wall. You kicked ass out there."

"Another game like that, Cutter, and we move one step closer to that sweet-ass Series."

Mark stopped in front of his locker and dropped to the bench, sweat running down his temples into his damp hair. A bead slid down his throat and soaked into his jersey as he leaned his head back against the metal locker and listened to the guys razz one another.

As the sports reporters made their way into the locker room, he closed his eyes and grinned. He'd pulled it off tonight. He'd played a damn good game without his cross. He'd found his zone. Damn his superstitious hide, but he knew it could mean only one thing: He had a new lucky charm.

It went by the name of Lorelei.

Chapter 10

"You seemed pretty chummy with my sister tonight."

Lorelei tossed her purse on the table and ignored his comment. Her head buzzed from all the juicy tidbits Leslie had shared about what Mark was like growing up.

Even after Mark had started playing like the premier catcher he was, his sister had kept dishing the inside scoop on her famous brother. Lorelei had a little better idea of who he really was, what made him tick.

And now she didn't know what to make of him.

"Hmm," she finally responded dismissively, and changed the subject. "Why don't you have a home phone or a computer, Mark?"

Tossing his bag on the floor, he shrugged out of his navy suit jacket and headed down the hall toward his bedroom. "I hate computers and I have a cell phone. Why? Did you find it hard to get ahold of my ex today?"

Not so much, Lorelei thought. *She got ahold of me.* But she wasn't going to tell him that.

She followed him, the soles of her running shoes squeaking against the floorboards. "I did find it inconvenient, yes. Care to tell me why you don't have those modern household tools?"

She almost swallowed her tongue when he emerged from the walk-in closet with his white dress shirt unbuttoned. The hard plains of his tanned stomach rippled beneath the fabric as he loosened the buttons at his wrist. His fly was open, the waistband of his navy slacks riding seductively low across his hips.

Tousled waves of dark blond hair fell across his brow as he worked the buttons free. Thick lashes hid his eyes from view and a day's growth of whiskers shadowed his jaw.

Mark was raw, sweaty sex undiluted.

Lorelei's equilibrium pitched dangerously off center, throwing her libido into chaos. And it felt damn good. Her last boyfriend, Harry, had tried his best to convince her she was a dead fish with no heat inside her. Now there was this. And this rush of desire was liberating. Proof Harry had just been an incompetent idiot.

The air between them suddenly flashed with tension when Mark looked up and caught her staring at him. He froze, his gaze sharpened, and his body went dangerously still. As if he could smell her arousal, his nostrils flared and he inhaled.

Lorelei felt locked in place, unable to move as he slowly slid his shirt off his muscular shoulders and let it drop to the floor. Swallowing around the knot in her throat, she desperately tried to think of something, anything to take her mind off his amazingly hot body. If she didn't, she'd find herself flat on her back with that spectacular body between her legs. Showing him all her moves and putting her yoga flexibility to good use.

Not that she really had anything against that. It could be the remedy she needed for her two-year dry spell, as long as she kept her head. Maybe that sounded a little shallow, but it wasn't like there was any worry of an emotional entanglement between the two of them. And she seriously doubted that he'd mind being a sex toy.

Right now she had other plans, however.

It took sheer force of will, but Lorelei was able to drag her gaze away from the chiseled muscles of his abs and exhaled on a puff of air. She tugged at the sleeves of his gigantic jersey and took a calming breath.

Time had come for her to negotiate her situation.

"I know why you sent Leslie to me tonight. I don't need a babysitter, you know."

He reached into a drawer and pulled out a faded blue T-shirt. Yanking it over his head, Mark shoved his arms through the sleeves and swore. "I wasn't trying to be coy about it, Lorelei."

"It backfired you know. I learned quite a bit about you from your sister. Things that most people don't know," she said.

That got his attention. "What the hell are you talking about? Like what?"

Pretending indifference, she watched Mark drop his

slacks and toss her a wicked grin. Though it did crazy things to her insides, Lorelei casually leaned back against the wall. "I know that you wore braces for three years."

He shrugged as he pulled on a pair of gray sweats. "So what? That's nothing to write to the *Enquirer* about."

"I know about the time you stole a six-pack of your dad's beer and took the old Buick for a test drive when you were fifteen. And how you drove it into a pond."

Mark let out a laugh and grinned. "Oh yeah, I'd forgotten about that. Dad was real pissed when he pulled the old boat out of three feet of muddy water. Cops never did get wind of that one." He shook his head at the memory and said, "You got any good dirt on me? Come on, hit me with it. Shock me, awe me."

Taking an intense interest in her cuticles, Lorelei studied the nails of her right hand. "You barely graduated high school. I also know you used to stutter when you talked to girls and that you didn't have a real girlfriend until after you were drafted to the MLB."

Moving over to the side of his bed, Mark sat down on the beige comforter and took his watch off. Opening the top drawer of the bedside table, he dropped the Rolex in and closed it with a thunk. His voice was very casual, almost lazy, when he drawled, "Not too bad. But I bet you didn't know I was a virgin till I married my ex-wife, did you?"

He glanced up as if to gauge her response. To hide her shock Lorelei retorted, "Huh, and now you're a complete slut. Go figure."

"Yeah, well, when you find something you do well, you keep at it," he shot back with a grin.

That surprised a snort out of her. "That's true, unless you're the only one who thinks you're good. Maybe all those bimbos were faking it, Mark. Ever consider that?"

"I know when a woman's having an orgasm, sugar." His voice was instantly seductive and warm. "Why don't you come over here and let me prove it to you."

Lorelei tipped her head to the side and looked at Mark. If ever there was a man who could prove definitively whether that was true or not, it was he. No doubt he was the master at giving the big O.

But she wasn't taking the bait. "Some other time, Mark. Like . . . hmm . . . never."

"Chicken."

Too much, too soon, was all she could think. There was so much to consider. She needed some air and some time to consider. What she really needed was her life back.

THE NEXT MORNING brought her a pleasant surprise: her laptop. She'd left it in her car, but it was sitting on the table next to her purse when she stumbled into the kitchen, owl-eyed, only to find Mark fully dressed and making breakfast. And he was utterly gorgeous in low-slung jeans, a navy sweater, and running shoes. His gorgeous mass of hair curled around the collar of his sweater and tumbled over his forehead. Raising a tanned hand, he pushed his fingers into the thick waves and shoved it out of his eyes.

It was too darn early for an attack of animal lust, but

it slapped her smack between the eyes anyway. Scrubbing her hands over her cheeks and biting back a groan, Lorelei narrowed her eyes at him. He grinned right back, the dirty rat. "Are you always so perky in the morning?"

With a flick of his wrist, Mark folded over the omelet he was making in a pan and shook his head. "What can I say? I'm a morning person. Here, I ran out this morning and got you this." He reached for something on the far side of him and turned, handing her a dark red paper cup with a cardboard holder and white plastic lid.

It couldn't be. Was it? With an experimental sniff, the tantalizing aroma of coffee and chocolate hit her nose, cleared her sleep-fogged head, and nearly buckled her knees. *Mocha*.

Instead of taking it from him, she just stood there, staring at the grande cup in his hand. "You got me coffee?"

"That's what it's called, yeah." He shook it gently. "Here, take it. I can tell by your brilliant conversation you need it."

Why did she suddenly feel like crying? Swallowing hard, Lorelei took the cup from him and battled back the urge to bawl. It was just a stupid cup of coffee. A kind act from a confusing man. Nothing more.

It felt like a whole lot more, though.

She noticed Mark was studying her, a question in his clear gray eyes. Blast the man, everything was going to hell, all her careful plans, and it was because of him. She should hate him. She did. She couldn't stand him.

But he brought her coffee. For that she had to like him.

A stunning smile lit his face, revealing those amazing

dimples as he tilted his head to the side. "Are you going to get all girlie on me now and cry?" he teased.

Blinking hard, Lorelei spun around and marched over to the table and plopped down on a chair. A protective hand shot up to rest on the smooth surface of her laptop. "Sorry to disappoint you so early in the day, but no." She took a savoring sip of the rich brew and sat it next to her Dell. "Thanks for this. And thanks for my laptop. I'm assuming that my car is somewhere in the parking garage below now?"

He grunted. She assumed that was a yes. "Did you have a good time snooping?"

He grinned at her over his shoulder and winked. "Uh-huh. Don't get too excited about your computer though. I don't have wi-fi. "

Damn it. She should have known he would've considered that.

Mark scooped up the omelet with a spatula and put it on a plate. He turned and carried the cream-colored plate to the table and sat it in front of her. "Eat up, runt. You need good protein and vitamins in your diet, else you're going to end up stooped over like Quasimodo."

"Wow, I'm impressed. *The Hunchback of Notre-Dame.* You read it?" she asked.

Something flickered in his eyes, a fleeting shadow. Then it was gone and he smiled. "Nope. Watched the movie. We jocks try to avoid reading when at all possible."

Wow, what was that? Lorelei sensed she'd touched a nerve, but why? Though he'd smiled at her, it was strained. "Did I say something wrong?"

He pushed a fork into her hand and ignored her question. "Take a bite. There's things in there called vegetables. You might like them."

She eyed the omelet. "Are there any Brussels sprouts hidden in this?"

He just grinned and motioned her to take a bite. Oh, what the hell. She'd live dangerously. Cutting off a bite with her fork, she asked casually, "Did I upset you with my question? You know I was just asking, right? Some people don't like to read."

A frown pulled at his brow and he moved his gaze to stare over her shoulder. "Just eat your food, Lorelei."

"I want to know what I said wrong."

His gaze snapped back to her, his eyes hard. "I said, drop it."

She had seriously said something wrong somewhere. But Mark stared her down with cold, challenging eyes so she shoved the bite of omelet in her mouth and kept quiet. Her eyebrows shot up at the burst of delicious flavor that greeted her taste buds. Mark Cutter could definitely cook.

"Mmm, this is great. What's in it?"

"Brussels sprouts."

She almost choked. "You're not serious, are you?"

His gaze leveled on her. "Eat." That's all he said. Then he turned and strode out of the kitchen.

"What about you? Aren't you going to eat one?"

His voice sounded irritated. "I already did, Lorelei. Some people get up at a decent hour of the morning, instead of sleeping half the day away."

She glanced at the clock on the stove. It was barely

eight o'clock. What was he talking about? It was still early.

Wait a minute, didn't he have practice? He'd better not even think about locking her in again. No way was she going for that a second time.

Grabbing the plate and fork, Lorelei hurried out of the kitchen and headed down the hall to his bedroom. She found Mark in his closet reaching for a black leather jacket.

Oh no, he wasn't. He wasn't locking her in a second time. "I'm going with you. I refuse to be left here again."

He shrugged. "Fine, but I'm not going anywhere."

She looked at the coat he was holding, pointed at it with her fork. "Sure looks like you are to me."

Mark let out a long-suffering sigh and looked at her. "I was just getting it out for later."

"Well, wherever you're going later I'm coming, too."

Walking over to her, he stopped and said near her ear, "I'm not sure my girlfriend would enjoy me bringing another woman along, you know? I don't think she's into that."

Something hot and hard slammed into the pit of her stomach, almost doubling her over from the force of it. It shouldn't matter. It *didn't* matter.

Taking a deep breath, Lorelei walked over to the dresser and set her plate down. She forced her muscles to relax and said, "Your girlfriend? I wasn't aware that you had one at the moment."

Gazing at her with watchful eyes, Mark replied, "Oh, there's always one or two. I like a little variety in my diet."

Her voice dripped sarcasm. "A redhead on Tuesday, a blond on Friday, twins on Saturday night. Is that it?"

With a shrug of his broad shoulders, he advanced on her. "It's the spice of life, sweetheart."

She felt like kicking him in the shin. And if he came any closer she was going to. "Your life must be well seasoned then, huh? Women waiting for you in every city you play in, cleat chasers ready to flop onto their backs with one word from you."

Body heat radiated off Mark as he stopped directly in front of her. "My, my, Lorelei. That sounds suspiciously like jealousy. I can't be hearing that right, because you wouldn't be jealous, would you? You don't even like me."

The size of him, his closeness was making it hard to breathe. She pushed against his chest in rising frustration. "I *don't* like you, you jerk. Now get away from me. You're too close and I can't breathe."

"Is that so?" he murmured as he brought a hand up and grabbed a strand of her loose hair, rubbing it slowly between his fingers.

Shoving harder as a feeling close to panic tried to grab hold, she demanded, "Save it for your groupies. I said get away from me. I mean it."

Mark stilled and lowered his gaze as a chill crept into his voice. "Or what? You'll sell my good luck charm to Dina?"

She jerked her chin up a notch. "Absolutely." The very next chance she got.

He took a step back. "That will be rather hard, sweetheart, since I've already had a nice chat with my attorney about my ex. He's making it real clear to her right about now that she's damn close to violating the restraining order I have against her and facing mandatory jail time. He's also threatening to put an end to her cushy alimony payments if she goes anywhere near you. Besides, I know what's in her bank account, since I put it there, and she doesn't have the Benjamins. Trust me, you won't be seeing her again."

No! He was lying. He had to be.

One look at his face erased any doubt she might have felt. He'd killed her last chance of being able to save Michelle. Despair gripped her hard in its ugly fist and squeezed. What could possibly be done now?

Lorelei sucked in a deep gulp of air and squared her shoulders. She looked him dead in the eye. "You have no idea what you've just done."

She tried to pass him, but Mark gripped her upper arm and growled, "I did what I needed to do to get my necklace back."

Lorelei slid her gaze from the hand that gripped her arm and leveled it on his, anger burning hot in her blood. "No, you just killed a girl."

His grip tightened and confusion clouded his eyes. "I did what?"

With a furious jerk, she yanked her arm out of his grasp. Without a backward glance she strode to the door. "Get your coat. I'm going home."

Chapter 11

MARK GLANCED AGAIN across the center console to where Lorelei sat silently. Her words echoed hauntingly in his head. *You just killed a girl.*

What the hell had she meant by that?

He had no idea and it ate at him, made him second-guess himself. Had she actually had a good reason for stealing from him? Uncomfortable with the idea that he might have been wrong about the situation, Mark had agreed to drive her to her place. Not that he was leaving her there. He wasn't letting his lucky charm out of his sight . . . again.

He'd agreed to it for the simple reason that he was curious about her. About her life, her home—who she really was.

Early that morning he'd had her Honda Civic brought to his building and had spent half an hour going through it looking for his lucky charm. He hadn't been the least bit surprised the car was littered with empty to-go coffee cups. He'd also found wadded-up receipts, junk mail, and a few candy bars stashed in the glove box.

But nothing good, no lucky cross. A few pens, a small bottle of perfume that smelled terrific, and some CDs. Just enough to whet his curiosity.

He wanted to know more.

Mark knew better than most people that first impressions could be misleading. And he'd be the first to admit he was wrong—if he was, in fact, wrong.

Past experience with the fairer sex had taught him one important thing: There was always a secret motive. His joke of a marriage had taught him that. No woman had come close to touching his heart since he'd handed it over to Dina like an idiot and watched her spit on it. He'd been young and stupid then.

He wasn't stupid anymore. He had his own secrets to keep. Being damn near illiterate from dyslexia wasn't exactly something he went around bragging about.

Lorelei moved in the gray leather seat and turned her head to face him. She'd showered and changed before they'd left and was wearing a sexy black camisole. It dipped low across her chest, and the deep groove of her cleavage was visible.

He knew how that exposed skin felt. How soft and smooth it was. And he knew how it tasted.

Feeling himself grow hard, Mark frowned and cleared his throat. He needed a distraction. "So, we're going to Loveland. Did you grow up there?"

He glanced over at her. She'd done something with

makeup and her eyes were smoky and soft. The expression in them wasn't. Lorelei was still mad at him. "I've never lived anywhere else. In fact, I'm still in the same house I grew up in. Only without my parents."

Mark smiled and flicked on his blinker to switch lanes. He was tired of poking behind Grandpa Jones on the interstate. "Where are they now?"

"Dead."

Shit. That was awkward. "I'm sorry, hon."

She just shrugged and looked out the window. "They died almost ten years ago in a barn fire. I lost my sister, Lucy, too. She died when I was twelve."

Oh God. So much loss. What could he say to that? Were there any words good enough?

There was nothing. So he said instead, though he gave her hand a quick, reassuring squeeze, "That must be nice, being in the same house. Lots of great childhood memories."

"It has its moments." She speared him with a glance. "Your sister's accent is much stronger than yours. Have you worked at losing it?"

So she'd noticed he had an accent. Huh. It didn't even register with him anymore. "Nah, I'm proud of the little town I grew up in. It's just that I got drafted to the major leagues straight out of high school and have been moving all over ever since."

Lorelei turned until she was sideways in the seat facing him, one leg tucked under the other. "How small a town was it?"

"Three thousand people or so."

"Is Leslie your only sibling?"

"Yeah."

"Do you really have a girlfriend?"

Caught off guard, Mark let out a surprised laugh. He knew she'd ask sooner or later. It'd probably been bugging the hell out of her. He liked that she wanted to know. And it irritated him that he liked her wanting to know.

She nudged his shoulder. "So, do you?"

He could tease her, string out the suspense, drive her nuts. He found himself answering instead, "Do you really think I'd try to get down your pants if I had a woman?"

She didn't even hesitate. "Absolutely."

Ouch. Though he supposed he deserved that, it still ticked him off that she believed those things. It just showed how little Lorelei knew him.

"You forget I've heard about your reputation, Mark. I know that fidelity is not your strong suit," she said.

Bullshit. Irritation welled inside him and he shot out, "Did my ex-wife tell you that?" He swore when she nodded. "For your information, sweetheart, I wasn't the one who had problems with monogamy."

"She cheated on you?"

A tic started below his right eye. It always happened when he thought too much about his marriage to Dina.

That's why he didn't think about it.

Until Lorelei Littleton had crashed into his life, he'd managed to avoid thinking about the unfaithful, two-faced money-grubber altogether. Now even the presence of Lorelei was directly related to Dina, and so was his missing cross. It was a hard pill to swallow. He didn't like that those two were connected, didn't like the taint it put on things. The history he shared with his ex held lots of ugly emotions and was full of manipulation and greed. All on her part. He didn't want that brushing up against Lorelei. Though he wasn't sure why, he just knew it didn't sit right and he wanted her untangled from Dina's web soon.

A memory came to him suddenly of a fight they'd had shortly before their divorce. He'd been getting ready to head out for a game and was in the bedroom getting dressed. Just as he'd finished and was grabbing his bag, she'd strutted through the door, fresh from the spa. He could tell where she'd been by the makeup job and new blond hair color.

There'd been no greeting or affection. No kiss or hug hello. Just an accusatory "You didn't put enough money in my account. You did that on purpose, didn't you? I want to go shopping. Nordstrom's is having a sale and I want new boots."

He'd glanced at her across the room, noted that she looked one step away from eating-disorder thin again. It'd been a line she'd struggled not to cross ever since he'd known her. "I just put five grand in there two days ago, D."

She'd turned to him, her hands bunched in fists at her side. "It wasn't enough, okay? God, why do you always scrutinize me? Don't you want me to look good? Be happy?" She'd crossed her arms and glared, her blue eyes frigid. "You always belittle me. You're such an asshole."

It was the same old mantra he'd been hearing for

three years. He was mean. He was unfair. He treated her bad. He didn't love her enough to buy her all the things that made her happy.

Truth was, the only bad thing he'd done was marry her. "If I'm such an asshole, then divorce me." He was tired of being her whipping boy.

She hadn't liked hearing that. In a fit of temper she'd grabbed a vase full of flowers off the dresser next to her and hurled it at him, screaming, "I hate you!"

He'd dodged the vase, and the brush, the picture frame, and the candle. It hadn't been the first time she'd thrown shit at him. Over it, he'd grabbed his bag and strode toward the door, his face set in stone.

As he passed her on the way, she'd clamped a hand around his arm, her acrylic nails digging in like talons. He'd stared straight ahead as she'd hissed, "You stupid jock. One of these days you're going to pay for the way you treat me. I know how to hurt you."

He shook his head to clear the memory and felt his lips press in a tight line. She'd had a way all right.

A small, warm hand slid across his thigh and came to rest on his knee, leaving a tingling trail in its wake. His muscles jerked to attention and his hands gripped hard on the steering wheel of the Rover until the knuckles turned white.

"I didn't know, Mark. I'm sorry. I hope you can understand why I believed her, though. You've got a pretty notorious reputation with the ladies."

His gut felt sour all of a sudden. His reputation had never bothered him much before, but hearing Lorelei talk about him like that pissed him off. "I suppose you believe everything you've heard, too, don't you? Did you ever stop to consider maybe it was all horse shit?"

Mark felt her eyes on him. "You're denying it? That you've had sex in nearly every U.S. state, that you're particularly fond of strippers?"

Oh, that just capped it. Frustration bit into him with vicious teeth. "Damn it, Lorelei. I'm a guy. I've had sex, all right? Lots of it. But I sure as hell don't play baseball just so I can screw women in every major city. And if you believe that load of bull about me having a thing for strip joints and cheap women, then I've given you too much credit."

All was quiet for a moment after his outburst, then she said, "How can you expect me to believe anything else, Mark, when you behaved exactly like your reputation said you would on the night we met?"

That deflated him. She was right. Absolutely, completely, one hundred percent right. And he didn't like what that said about him one bit.

LORELEI STUDIED MARK as they drove up the interstate toward Loveland. She'd never seen him genuinely upset. But she was seeing it now. His brows were pulled together in a deep scowl, his lips pressed into a thin line, and his hands had a death grip on the wheel.

She had a feeling it wasn't too often that he had to account for his actions. Gut checks were few and far between for men like him. Successful, self-absorbed, attractive men in the prime of their life who had just about everything given to them on a silver platter.

Normally she couldn't stand people like that. And for good reason. While they were out in the world living only for themselves, people like her brother, Logan, were swimming in grief, working themselves to death just trying to take care of everyone around them. Trying to find a way to save the life of someone they loved more than themselves.

Heck, he wore her yearly salary on his wrist. No wonder she'd stolen from him.

The turnoff to her house came into view and Lorelei straightened in her seat. "You need to take this exit."

"We're not to town yet."

A wave of irritation washed over her. "I don't live in town, I live over there." She shoved her arm in front of him and pointed out the driver side window. It would do him some good to see how real people lived.

Mark slowed and made the turn off the interstate onto the two-lane road. A smattering of snow covered the ditch on either side from a late season storm. It had melted off the road though, leaving the pavement clear and dry.

Ahead the Rocky Mountains rose, imposing and impossibly beautiful, their snowy peaks sparkling in the sun. Though they'd been driving parallel to them for almost an hour, the dramatic impact of them hadn't been as strong. Not like it was now. Now they were simply magnificent.

The silence stretched between them as they passed small farms and ranches with pastures full of cattle and horses. Lorelei watched a man bundled in a thick flannel jacket toss hay to a line of waiting, mooing cattle from the back of his flatbed truck as it idled along. A young boy sat behind the wheel, his fresh face beaming beneath his cap as he enjoyed the thrill of driving the ranch truck for his dad. Both dad and son waved as they drove by, and her heart squeezed. With a smile she waved back.

They came to a cross in the road and Mark slowed to a stop. "Which way?"

She could see the elms that lined the long driveway just around the bend. "Take a left. You can see the driveway just past the hay field over there."

"I see it." He made the turn and steered the Range Rover to the driveway, slowing, and turned onto the gravel road. "I never would have guessed you grew up in the country."

"That's because you don't know me."

The old white farmhouse came into view as they meandered down the long drive, and joy leaped inside her at the sight. She glanced at Mark to gauge his reaction. How would he respond to the peeling paint on the house and barn? Would he turn up his nose at the rusted brown Dodge truck in the driveway? What about the old tire swing that hung from the towering oak over by the garden? His face didn't reveal a thing.

As soon as he came to a stop behind her brother's extended cab truck, Lorelei flung the door open, grabbed her laptop and duffel, and leaped from the SUV. Just as the front screen door slammed open and her brother stepped out onto the porch. Little Michelle was riding on his hip, her brown ringlets pulled into pigtails, a Dora the Explorer doll clutched to her chest. When she spotted Lorelei she smiled, let out a squeal, and kicked her legs wildly.

Logan tipped up his cowboy hat and scowled at the shiny Range Rover, his gaze traveling slowly over the luxury SUV until they settled on her. He cocked a Wrangler-clad hip and tapped his cowboy boot against the wood boards of the porch. "Where the hell have you been, Lorelei?"

Her heart soared and she felt a grin split her face.

It was good to be home.

Chapter 12

SOMETHING WAS VERY wrong with this picture. Mark blinked and looked again. Why was there a man standing on the porch of Lorelei's house with a baby on his hip?

What was going on here?

He slowly opened the driver side door and stepped out of the SUV. Confusion clouded his mind as he shut the door firmly behind him. He turned to ask Lorelei for an explanation, but she was already jogging up the steps, her arms outstretched toward the little girl. As he watched the scene unfold before him a slow anger flared in his gut, glowing brighter with every passing second. The answer was obvious.

Lorelei was married.

In an instant Mark saw with crystal clarity. The cowboy was her husband and the little girl was hers.

She'd almost slept with him. Jesus.

He'd been wrong about her, so wrong. Lorelei wasn't what he'd thought she was—she was worse.

A tangled, nasty mess of emotions assaulted Mark as he watched her take the girl in her arms and kiss her husband on the cheek. How could she have done what she did with him when she had a family?

An image flashed across his mind of Lorelei topless on his kitchen counters, his mouth feeding on her breasts. Of her moaning his name.

Whatever transgressions he'd made in his life were nothing compared to what she'd done. She'd drugged him and stolen from him, but this was her biggest crime by far.

Mark swiped the back of his hand across suddenly parched lips and swallowed hard. He should leave. Just get in the car and drive away. He should forget about his cross. If she wanted it so bad she'd betray her family, then she could have it. And he'd sure as hell find another lucky charm.

Yeah, he should just go.

He walked to the porch instead. Across the huge lawn he strode, his shoes crunching over the patches of snow until he reached the steps. He paused and looked up.

Something twisted painfully inside him when Lorelei grinned, her smile bright enough to light the night sky. "Mark, I'd like you to meet my family. This is Michelle, the sweetest little girl in the universe. And this cowboy here is Logan, my brother. Michelle's his daughter."

Her brother?

Mark stared unspeaking at Lorelei, his mind reeling from the new information. He was such an ass. His mind tried desperately to backtrack down the path it'd been traveling because like a complete dick he'd instantly jumped to the wrong conclusion.

Belatedly he realized they were all staring at him. He jerked and held out a hand. "Nice to meet you. I'm Mark."

The tall, dark-haired cowboy took his hand in a solid grip and smiled, his dark eyes ripe with question. "Yeah, I know who you are. It's nice to meet you, too. Care to tell me how you tangled with my little sister? I don't reckon you two met at the local Tack 'n' Feed store."

Mark forced a smile in return. "No, we certainly didn't. We actually met at a blues bar a few nights ago, didn't we, Lorelei?"

A flush crept up her neck and flooded her cheeks. She turned quickly and strode for the door. Her voice sounded tight when she finally answered. "Why don't we all go inside where it's warm. Michelle doesn't have a coat on and I don't want her to catch a chill. Logan, why don't you show Mark to the living room while I go make up something to drink?"

Still shaken by the force of his earlier reaction, he gratefully followed Lorelei's brother through the door. The creak of rusty hinges and the sound of wood slapping against wood followed them as the screen door shut behind them. The click of Logan's cowboy boots echoed in the entryway before becoming muffled on the braided oval runner.

Mark glanced around the roomy foyer while Lorelei's brother removed his hat and hung it on a tree rack by the door. It was a big, comfortable house she had. Open and airy. Light filtered through huge windows and cast a warm glow across the scarred oak floorboards.

Beautiful oil paintings decorated the foyer walls, an almost opulent contrast to the faded floral wallpaper. One in particular caught Mark's attention and he stepped over to get a better look. It was a painting of the farmhouse in summer with an older couple rocking together in a swing on the front porch. The man had his arm around the woman's shoulder and she had her head rested on his.

It was happiness and contentment, peace and beauty captured exquisitely in one perfect painting.

"You like that?"

Mark started and straightened. He'd forgotten Lorelei's brother was there. He regarded the painting one more time and turned to follow Logan through the open double doors into a living room. "I do. It's a stunning piece of art."

Logan motioned him to take a seat on a large, deep cushioned brown sofa. The lines softened briefly around his dark brown eyes and a small smile curved his lips. "My wife would have liked to hear that. I always told her she had a gift, but it's good to hear from outsiders, not just those that love you."

"Where is she now?"

"She passed away two years ago."

Not sure what to say, Mark nodded and leaned back into the plush cushions. What *was* there to say?

Lorelei rescued him from having to answer when she

strode in carrying a tray full of glasses and a pitcher of iced tea. The little girl toddled in behind her, the doll dragging on the floor.

"I assumed that iced tea would be acceptable for you to drink, Mark. I didn't add any sugar." She sent him a teasing smile.

The knot in his stomach uncoiled instantly under the warmth of her smile. It felt like being touched by the sun on a warm spring day. He felt himself respond with one of his own.

Twenty minutes ago he'd been absolutely furious with her. What was wrong with him? It wasn't at all like him to be pulled in two completely different directions like that. He was afraid to examine too closely what it all meant.

Logan cleared his throat and gained Mark's attention. With his hat off he looked a lot like his sister. Same straight nose, same stubborn chin. They both had the same strong, striking bone structure. But his eyes were a dark, intense brown and his short-cropped hair was nearly black. And he carried sadness like a heavy cloak, lacking any of the spark so visible in Lorelei. "You think the Rush has a chance at the World Series this year? I caught the game yesterday and the team looks good."

More relieved than he wanted to admit, Mark took the offered glass from Lorelei and nodded his thanks. Baseball talk was good. It was safe. It was his life. "I think we've got a decent shot. If Kowalskin's knee holds up and our new rookie shortstop stays healthy. That kid's a real good player. And he's quick on his feet. He's been a real asset to the team this year."

Out of the corner of his eye he watched the little girl crawl onto Lorelei's lap and felt his lungs constrict behind his rib cage. The child snuggled down and rested her head against Lorelei's chest. When Lorelei kissed the toddler on the head tenderly, he felt it clear down in his toes.

He looked away, breathed deep, and took in the living room. Noticed the warmth and comfort of well-worn furniture and soft colors. Approved of it.

It was Lorelei's home.

When Logan cleared his throat again, Mark knew what was coming. He could see it in the slight frown that marred the sober man's brow. "So, are either of you going to tell me what's going on? Why I'm sitting in my living room with one of the major league's best players?" He nodded toward Mark. "Not that I'm not pleased to have you in my home, you understand. It's just mighty odd that my sister up and disappears for a few days—no word, nothing—only to show back up again with you."

Mark cleared his throat, was about to tell him, when Lorelei piped up. The look she sent him was full of warning. "Nothing's going on, Logan. I swear. I had that meeting in Denver, Friday, remember? Well, I went out for a drink after and met Mark. We hit it off and I've been spending some time in the city with him."

Logan's gaze sharpened. He leveled it on Mark. "Exactly what *kind* of time have you two been having?"

Three things hit Mark at that moment. One: Logan didn't give a shit who he was, he wasn't impressed. Two: He loved his sister very much. And three: He had no idea what Lorelei was up to.

And that made him all right in Mark's book.

So he answered with complete sincerity. "I took her to last night's game and she met my sister. Lorelei is a very special woman. Full of charm, as I'm sure you are well aware. I've enjoyed spending time with her."

He could almost feel the relief wash over Lorelei. For an instant she even closed her eyes. For the grief she'd caused him the past few days she deserved to be exposed. He had a feeling if he told the truth, Logan would demand Lorelei return Mark's necklace. She'd do it, too. His new lucky charm would give back the old one. And that just wouldn't do. He had to let her think that he still wanted the necklace back—which he did. For purely sentimental reasons. As a lucky charm it was worthless now. Somehow its mojo had been transferred to Lorelei when she'd snaked it from him. So now he needed to keep her around if he wanted the Rush to be successful.

He bit his tongue.

LORELEI COULD TELL Mark was on the verge of exposing her. The look in his eye when Logan had demanded to know what was going on told her as much. The chance for the money would disappear entirely. Michelle would be lost.

She'd closed her eyes against the hot rush of tears. Waited for the ball to drop.

But it never did.

She'd gotten so light-headed from relief she almost

passed out when Mark covered for her. Snapping her eyes open, she stared across her living room at him in shock.

Why had he lied for her?

For a suspended moment their gazes locked. The gorgeous gray of his eyes sparked with challenge. What he was up to?

She needed to think. Tearing her gaze from his, Lorelei began to lean forward, only to discover Michelle sound asleep. Her poor niece had dark smudges beneath her eyes. The exhaustion marks were a stark contrast to her pale, alabaster skin. Adjusting her arms until she cradled the sleeping toddler, she pushed out of the recliner and stood.

How could she not do everything in her power to save Michelle? She had to find a way to get the charm to Dina. Even if it meant destroying the strange, tentative, almost-friendship that she and Mark were creating.

Both men were watching her, one with concern in his dark gaze, the other with unreadable emotions shifting behind his silvery one. "I'm going to put her down for a nap."

Without a backward glance, Lorelei swept out of the room and hurried upstairs. Not only was she going to put Michelle down, but when she'd gone to make iced tea earlier she'd slipped upstairs and plugged in her laptop. She'd thought about a backup plan. And that plan was online auctions. All she needed was ten minutes.

Once she reached Michelle's cheerfully painted nursery she placed the toddler in her crib and covered her with a bright patchwork quilt. Out of habit she pressed her hand gently to Michelle's chest, felt her heartbeat. When she was satisfied everything was normal, she kissed the petite girl on the forehead and silently slipped from the room, pulling the door mostly closed behind her.

And jumped when she almost collided with Mark's broad chest.

"What are you doing up here?" she whispered furiously, afraid he'd wake Michelle. And because, yet again, he'd foiled her plans. How was she supposed to log into her laptop now?

"Making sure we still understand each other, Lorelei. You still have something of mine and you're going back with me until I get it."

So that's what he was up to. "How'd you get up here?"

His look was deadpan. "The stairs."

"Does Logan know?" Her brother was usually pretty protective.

"How to use stairs?"

Was he purposefully being dense? "No, that you're up here with me."

He raised a brow in question. "Why wouldn't he?"

Ugh. Never mind. Obviously Mark had passed Logan's inspection or he wouldn't be up there acting obtuse.

She peered around him and glanced down the stairs. "*Shhh.* Keep your voice down. I don't want you to wake Michelle." And she didn't want Logan to overhear.

He actually had the presence of mind to look chagrined. His voice dropped a decibel, but he didn't apologize. "Are we crystal clear on this? You go back with me."

She glared at him. "This whole thing is just so stupid, you know."

"You started it." He jerked his thumb over his shoulder. "Is that your room down the hall?"

She nodded and bit back a nasty remark when he grabbed her by the elbow and tugged her toward her room. Once inside he let her go and gave her room a thorough once-over. Hot prickles of awareness and irritation poked her as Mark stood in her room, his masculine presence out of place and unwelcome. The room suddenly seemed two sizes too small.

"Nice room you got here, Lorelei. Very feminine."

She loved her room, adored it. Every single inch of it. From her white iron headboard and brightly colored quilt, to her vintage cream-painted dressers and braided area rug. She even loved the faded wallpaper with creeping vines and morning glories on it and her scarred writing desk against the far wall. She *didn't* love that damn computer chair, though.

But with Mark standing in the center of her room with his Rolex and designer clothes it felt almost shabby. And she resented him for making her feel that way about a place she'd loved deeply her whole life. Felt anger at herself for thinking that what she had wasn't good enough for Mark Cutter.

Taking a deep, calming breath, Lorelei walked over to the large picture window and looked out at the expanse of snow-flecked lawn below. In the summer, the huge old trees leafed out, casting the lawn in dapples of sun and shade. Flowers would overflow the flowerbeds, bright displays of color. It was the perfect yard for a girl to play, to pretend, to dream. To grow up in.

Lorelei closed her eyes and inhaled, then turned and faced Mark. "I'll go back with you."

"I know you will."

He did know it. It was in his stance, his voice, his smile. So damn self-assured and cocky. Mark always got what he wanted.

Right now that was fine with Lorelei. As long as she got what she wanted, too. She plastered a big, fake smile of her face and asked, "Anything else you want, master?"

His sensual mouth tipped up into a seductive smile and his eyes went lazy. "As a matter of fact," he drawled, "why don't you come over here and give me a kiss. Right here in the middle of your bedroom. Your room, you get to call the shots, sugar."

Lorelei strode slowly over to him, watched his eyes lower, focus on her mouth. She stopped in front of him and licked her lips, lifted up on her toes, and whispered against his mouth. "I'm going downstairs to talk to my brother, but when I come back, I'll give you what you want. Wait right here."

Mark searched her face, his eyes sulky, and said, "You've got five minutes before I come after you."

Lorelei kept the smile on her face and her pace unhurried until she got into the hall. Once there she made her way quickly down the stairs and went in search of Logan. She found him in the kitchen making a sandwich. The sleeves of his ancient denim shirt were rolled up his deeply tanned arms, and his dark hair was smashed down flat in the back from his cowboy hat. Love welled inside her at the sight of him, as it always did.

Her strong, loyal, loving brother. Who hadn't really smiled since his wife passed away, and who was weighed down by grief and hopelessness a little more each day.

Well, that was about to change. "I'm going to get the money, Logan."

His head whipped around and his dark eyes locked on her. "How, Lorelei? By selling yourself to Mr. Baseball up there?" He gestured upstairs with the butter knife in his hand.

Lorelei sighed and shook her head. "You know I'd never do that."

He turned back to his sandwich, added a leaf of lettuce. "You're not pregnant with his kid, are you?"

That one made her snort. "Are you kidding? You have to have sex to get pregnant, and I haven't had any in a very long time."

His voice was almost too low, but she still heard him mutter, "That makes two of us."

Lorelei grabbed a tomato from the hanging fruit basket next to her and handed it to him. "You know the waitress from the café has got the hots for you. And Michelle's therapist is always checking out your butt."

He glanced at her briefly. "I'm not ready." The simple words held a world of meaning. He didn't mean just dating.

"I'm going to promise you something. The next time I come home I'll have the money. We'll be able to do it, I swear. And then everything will be good again. You'll see."

Logan stopped what he was doing and reached for her. "Come here, sis." She went to him and felt his strong arms wrap comfortingly around her. "I love you. You and Michelle are all I've got in this world. I'd do anything for my girls, you know that, right?"

Lorelei nodded against his chest, the worn denim soft against her cheek. "I know that. I love you, too."

His arms tightened around her in a bear hug. "I swear though, Lorelei. You do anything stupid and wind up in trouble, I'll tan your hide like you were caught stealing Mom's prized baking apples to feed the horses. You understand me?"

"I got it, Logan."

Just then his body went still and she knew without turning that Mark was standing in the doorway behind her. Her five minutes must be up.

"It's time to go, Lorelei." His deep, gravelly voice sounded behind her.

Yes, it was. Lorelei reached up on her toes and gave her brother a kiss on the cheek. He gave her a hard warning look and let her go.

It was time to get the show on the road.

Chapter 13

"What is this place?"

Mark reached for Lorelei's elbow and grinned. Yeah, he knew what it looked like. A giant ramshackle old brick warehouse that had definitely seen better days.

It was exactly what he'd wanted when he'd bought it.

His palm cupped her elbow and he tugged her to the huge plank door. Heat from her body soaked into his hand and traveled up his arm in a warm, wandering wave. Already on edge, his pulse leaped at the contact and his blood temperature rose.

It seemed to be a common condition when Lorelei was near. "Are you worried, Lorelei? Afraid of what's inside?"

She leveled a look at him. "It's been my experience that outside appearances are, more often than not, deceiving."

Mark reached for the door and gripped the handle. "Ah. So you don't believe what you see is what you get?"

She scoffed. "Hardly. There's always more to the story,

Mark. Most people don't take enough time to look." Her eyes became cool and guarded. "Most people just don't care."

His mind flashed back to the scene he'd witnessed in the kitchen of her house. There was very definitely more to that story, a hell of a lot more. Emotions he'd never experienced before had slapped him in the face like a scorned woman. Grief, loss, despair. Ugly, desperate emotions so foreign to him he'd almost not been able to put a name to them.

And he hoped to God he never had to experience them again. He liked his life simple and free of complications.

He played baseball. Lived it, breathed it—dreamed it. And he kept his encounters with women brief and shallow. Everyone got out before things got messy and feelings got hurt. Well, most of the time.

He'd learned the value of self-preservation from his first marriage and he'd learned it well. So then what was he doing with Lorelei? She was anything but simple.

"Are you just going to stand there, or are you going to open the door? It's getting chilly out here," she said.

Mark blinked and shook his head. She was right, it was getting cold. Springtime in Colorado was unpredictable and there was a definite bite in the night air tonight.

A car turned onto the street, its bright headlights washed over them. The deep muddled thump of rap music bass reverberated against the pavement and practically shook the car windows. It grew louder as it sped past until it rounded the corner a block down and disappeared from sight.

When all was quiet again, the wide street of Lodo momentarily empty, Mark flung the door open and ushered Lorelei inside. Another blast of music hit them as they stepped onto the landing. A large black man with rolls of muscle stepped in front of them, his huge pecs bulging beneath his T-shirt.

Mark felt her shrink against him and smiled. It felt good to have her plastered to his side. Her curvy body fit snug against him, warm and soft. Settling a protective arm over her shoulder, he raised his other hand and extended it toward the huge man. "Hey, Mario. It's good to see you. How you doing, man?"

The bouncer returned Mark's handshake with a smile. His deep voice rumbled in his chest as he spoke. "Good to see you, brother. It's been a while. Some of the guys are here tonight. Should I tell Leslie you're here?"

Mark gave Lorelei a squeeze. "Nah. I'm sure word will get out soon enough. Sounds like it's the Rhumbi boys on stage tonight. Good. I'm in the mood for some live reggae. We'll head on down and grab a table. Hey, tell Denise I said hi, will you?"

"I will. The guys are at their usual table if you and the lady would like to join them. The band just started their second set of the night."

With a nod, Mark led Lorelei down a flight of stairs to the open main level of the club. He was satisfied to see the place full on a late night. The long bar in the corner was packed and the wraparound balcony was almost full. Even the couches on the left were totally occupied.

Good. His sister was doing a great job with his club.

Lights hung suspended from the two-story ceiling on long poles and illuminated the huge stage. Lively reggae music pumped from the speakers as the band kicked into another song.

The dance floor was crowded as Mark steered Lorelei around the crush to a long table on the far side. Some of his teammates were there, drinks in hand, listening to the live band. The noise level was so loud it took her elbowing him in the side to get his attention.

He smiled down at her and grinned. In the low light she was gorgeous, her pouty lips a mouthwatering shade of pink, her eyes deep as emeralds. His breath hitched in reaction.

"Are you going to tell me now what we're doing here?" she practically yelled.

Mark lowered his head until his mouth was a breath away from her ear. "We're enjoying a night out. Have you got a problem with that?"

He was so close he could smell the warm scent of her skin, feel her hair whisper across his cheek as she shook her head. His stomach pitched and took a long, slow roll.

"I don't have a problem. I'm just surprised, that's all," she replied.

"Even self-centered, womanizing baseball jocks like to kick back once in a while, Lorelei."

A yell from the table caught his attention and he stepped back from her. He looked up to see Peter Kowal-skin waving them over.

"Hey, Cutter! Get your pathetic ass over here and bring the lady. We want to meet her." Peter called out with a grin.

Sliding his hand down until it rested at the small of her back, Mark guided her past a young couple busy shoving their tongues down each others' throats and pulled a chair out for her at the table.

Lorelei sunk into the chair and looked around the table at Mark's teammates. There was Peter Kowalskin and a young kid with a shaved head and nasty split lip. Both of them she recognized from the first night she met Mark. Another was the gruff-looking player Leslie had whistled at. He looked almost more imposing in civilian clothes, his size and brute force even more apparent. The only thing soft about the guy was the brown hair that swept back from his rugged face and curled over his shirt collar.

The fourth guy she couldn't place. Mark took a seat across from her and began making introductions. "Lorelei, I'd like you to meet some of my teammates. The old man there is Peter Kowalskin and next to him looking pretty with his split lip is our new rookie, JP Trudeau. They were with me the night we met."

"That was *you*?" the young player asked, his eyes huge.

She nodded. The rookie opened his mouth again, but Mark cut him off before he could say anything. "She's not kissing anything of yours, rookie, so forget it." He glanced across the table at her, his eyes unreadable in the dim light. "That's John Crispin next to you. He and Leslie have been seeing each other for the past few months. And the delicate flower here next to me is Drake Paulson."

After shaking hands, Lorelei shrugged out of her

coat and leaned back against the seat. Talk immediately turned to—what else?—baseball, so she took that as her cue and tuned out. Her gaze wandered around the huge club and the mass of people.

She couldn't help noticing a lot of eyes kept wandering over to the table of MLBers. A lot of *female* eyes. And they seemed to land an awful lot on the blond-haired catcher with the killer smile and notoriously quick hands.

Lorelei felt a stab of irritation when a man-eater in a six-inch dress and fake breasts the size of melons broke away from a group of similarly attired hoochies and strutted over. She slowed when she reached the table but continued around to the far side, bumping hard into Lorelei as she rounded it.

The bimbo didn't even apologize. She was zeroed in on Mark and apparently couldn't be bothered with common courtesy. Conversation came to a slow halt when she leaned over, her huge silicone breasts almost popping out of her skimpy red dress, and placed her hands on the table. She was so skinny the bones in her chest were visible.

Somebody really needed to feed the poor blond bimbo. She needed some mashed potatoes and gravy or something. Maybe a brownie and some ice cream.

Lorelei felt her eyebrows rise when the woman wiggled her skeleton fingers at the guys and crooned, "Hi there, fellas. I'm Candy."

The guys all mumbled a greeting, except for Mark. His eyes were fixed firmly on Lorelei, his lips pressed in a thin line. Annoyance radiated from him, his body tense.

Why he was annoyed was beyond her. Wasn't this what he waited for? A willing woman and no-strings sex? For crying out loud, she'd propositioned him much the same way a few nights ago in that parking lot. He hadn't been bothered then.

Or was it just that he was irritated that she'd been so right about him?

Suddenly a perverse sense of amusement washed through her. She was going to enjoy seeing how Mark handled this little situation. Grabbing a handful of peanuts from the bowl on the table, she popped a few in her mouth and shot him a smug smile. This was going to be highly entertaining.

At her smile, he scowled, nearly causing her to choke on her peanuts. Laughter bubbled up and almost burst loose and she coughed to cover. Apparently he didn't think the situation was funny.

The great hulking Rush player sitting next to her whipped out a hand and whacked her on the back, the force of it almost toppling her from the chair.

"That's enough. You'll make her swallow her tongue you hit her like that again."

The ballplayer dropped his hand and shrugged as he looked at Mark. "Just trying to help out. She was choking."

"She was fine—"

"Thank you, John," she cut in, and smiled at the gruff-looking player.

The blond wasn't about to be ignored or one-upped by Lorelei's fit of choking and scooted closer to Mark. She cranked up the wattage of her bleached smile and ran a finger along his arm. When he tensed she misinterpreted the action for encouragement and practically purred, "You've got great arms, handsome. Why don't we hit the dance floor so I can feel those strong arms wrapped around me?"

Lorelei had to give her points for that line. But she had a feeling Mark had heard variations of that from women just like her a thousand times. He looked almost bored when he slid his pale gaze up his arm to look the woman in the face.

"It's Candy, isn't it? Right. Well, I appreciate the compliment and the fact that you singled me out, but I'm not much of a dancer." His gaze moved to the bruised man beside him and back. "Now, Drake here is a helluva dancer. Light-footed as a ballerina. Why don't you two give it a whirl and get to know each other?"

Candy stuck her collagen-injected lip out on a practiced pout, but her gaze was assessing. "Are you a baseball player, too?" she asked Drake.

The giant winked at her from his good eye. "That's right, darling."

The blond straightened and pasted a smile on her face. She held out a hand. "It'd be my pleasure to dance with you, Mr. Drake."

The ballplayer downed his drink and pushed away from the table. When he stood he towered over everyone. "Drake's my first name, honey." He slapped Mark on the back. "I'll catch you boys later."

With that they melted into the crowd and Lorelei

looked back at Mark to find him staring hard at her. For a heartbeat their gaze locked, tension flowed between them.

The table was silent until Kowalskin spoke. "You're a real ass, Cutter. Why didn't you send her my way? I haven't seen any action in a while."

That started off a round of good-natured arguing between the players about who really should have gotten to dance with her. The conversation veered straight into the gutter and Lorelei found herself laughing at a highly politically incorrect comment. Until she saw the way Mark was staring at her.

"What?"

He grabbed a passing waitress, his eyes never leaving hers. "Hey, Cindy. Bring me a couple rounds of oyster shooters, will you?"

"Sure thing, Mr. Cutter. The club's been hopping tonight. Everyone seems to really like this reggae band your sister hired. They've become a house favorite. Leslie's really doing a great job managing your club. Business has been really booming since she took over."

Lorelei waited until the waitress left. "This is your club? You own this place and your sister is the manager?"

He folded his arms across his muscular chest and leaned back. "Uh-huh."

"Wow, must be nice to have the money to just buy whatever you want."

His eyes narrowed. "It has its advantages."

A flash of anger caught her off guard and she reacted, lashing out. "I'm sure it does. You get to have whatever your little heart desires, don't you, Mark? Clubs, fancy cars, fast women, designer drugs. Whatever you want is yours for the taking."

He whipped forward in his chair, a warning flashed in his steely eyes. "You pissed about something, Lorelei? Be woman enough to come right out and say it."

Something hot flared between her breasts and she jerked forward across the table until they were inches apart. "You really want me to say it?"

He bared his teeth in a snarl and growled, "*I dare you.*"

The waitress chose that moment to return. Oblivious to the tension, she set the drinks on the table and beamed at Mark before disappearing again.

Reacting before she thought, Lorelei grabbed the nearest shot glass and downed it. Her eyes bulged when she encountered the raw oyster. A shiver ran through her at the slippery feeling and her stomach reacted with a greasy lurch. She almost spit the vile thing out until she saw that Mark was laughing at her. No way would she give him the satisfaction of seeing her gag. Forcing herself, she chewed the disgusting glob and swallowed it down.

She smiled in triumph and smacked her lips. "Mmmm, that was good. Why don't you try one, Mark?"

Still laughing, he grabbed a shot glass and stirred the red cocktail sauce until it was blended with the vodka. "You sure that was good, sweetheart? It looked like you were about to lose your lunch from where I'm sitting."

That was the truth, but she wasn't about to admit it. "Not at all. I positively *love* raw oysters."

He raised the shot glass to his lips and Lorelei felt her skin crawl when she saw the grayish oyster pressed against the side. With a flick of his wrist he swirled the liquid, his eyes locked on her. He must have seen her shiver because he let out a laugh and tilted the glass in salute. Then he tipped his head back and downed the shooter in one fluid motion.

Mark slapped the glass on the table, his eyes filled with amusement, and smacked his lips. "Mmm, that was good."

Smug bastard.

Lorelei wasn't about to be outdone and reached for another glass. Taking a cue from him, she snatched a fork from the table and stirred the liquid until it was thoroughly blended.

"Are you sure you want to do that? I'd sure hate to see you toss your cookies over a little oyster. Maybe you should just set the glass down before you embarrass yourself." His voice shook with suppressed laughter as he issued the backhanded challenge.

Lorelei looked him dead in the eye. "Fuck you, Mark Cutter." Before she could change her mind, she threw her head back and tossed the drink down. Then she slapped the glass on the table. "Bring it on, pansy boy. I can take whatever you dish out."

Laughter erupted down the table and she swirled her head around to see Mark's teammates looking on in avid fascination. JP, the rookie, grinned at Lorelei. "I think I'm in love."

John snorted and cuffed the young guy's shoulder, "You're just horny, boy. Besides, I'm the one really in love."

Kowalskin piped up, his voice full of admiration, "Will you marry me, Lorelei? Forget that pretty boy. Let me show you how a real man treats a lady."

Lorelei laughed in surprised delight. "I'm flattered, Peter. And maybe I'll just take you up on that offer. Can you cook?"

He flashed a grin and ran a hand over the black shadow beard on his square jaw. "Nope, but I can hire you a mighty fine chef."

Mark shoved away from the table and stood up, the humor gone from his eyes. "Forget about it, Pete. She's already taken." He rounded the table and grabbed her elbow. "Come on, Lorelei. We're going dancing."

She let him pull her out of her chair, amused at his reaction to the guys' mild flirting. "I thought you didn't dance."

"I said I didn't feel much like dancing. Now I do."

"Oh well. I beg your pardon." Those oyster shooters had a pretty decent kick to them. Lorelei felt heat spreading out from the pit of her stomach, enjoyed the looseness flowing through her limbs.

As Mark led her through the crowd, the deep beat of the music seeped into her, the groove of the reggae got her blood pumping. The heavy bass pulsed low in her gut and her body started to sway to the rhythm.

Mark's hand slid down her arm, leaving a trail of jangled nerves, until his large, hard palm was flush against hers and his long fingers were tangled with hers. Her head whipped up and her eyes sought his, but he was still pushing his way through the crowd. Didn't he feel it? The hot current of electricity that sparked between their hands and shot up her arm?

Finally Mark stopped and turned. She saw in his eyes the answer. He felt it, too. She wasn't the only one.

She didn't even like him most of the time, but she felt a crazy chemistry with him. And deep down she felt hugely relieved. It meant she was alive. Vibrant. Having experiences and living life—something she'd become desperate for.

For the first time in two years she felt carefree and a little reckless. And it felt *good*.

Someone bumped her from behind and pushed her forward into Mark. Swallowing a yelp, Lorelei tried to push away, but he gripped her hip with his free hand and pulled her closer. When they were flush against each other, he started to move. His hips rolled loosely as he swayed to the side and his hard thighs brushed hers. Taking the lead, he placed his hand on her hip to guide her until they found the rhythm, rocking back and forth.

Heat washed over her, wave upon wave, as they moved together. In time with the throbbing bass they swayed, Mark's finely toned body beckoning her, urging her to sin with every erotic brush against hers. Lorelei felt herself melting, drowning. And she didn't want it to stop.

Giving herself over to the moment, she let the music seduce her, let the man inside. Just this once, for this dance, she fell into the moment.

The music slowed and the tempo changed. Spinning in Mark's arms, she reached for his hands as she backed up against him until she could feel his arousal strain against her butt. She pushed against him in a slow grind, heard his deep groan with a sense of feminine triumph.

Lorelei released his hands and raised her arms to wrap around the back of his neck. Her body shivered deliciously when his hands stroked possessively over her rib cage down to her hips. His fingers dug into her flesh and jerked her back as he thrust forward, ground against her.

She closed her eyes as sensations flooded her. Leaning her head against his shoulder, she gloried in the feel of his heart hammering in his chest. His breath poured hot down her neck as he lowered his head. The ache between her legs grew until she was throbbing in time to the music, her inner thighs slick with her desire.

Damp tendrils of hair curled around her fingers when she shifted to grip his head with one hand, as she turned her face to him and found his mouth. She moaned as his lips covered hers, hard and desperate.

They continued to grind erotically, moving slowly to the music, his mouth devouring hers in a kiss of raw animal need. He placed a hand on her neck and added pressure, gently squeezing in an arousing display of sexual dominance. His tongue thrust into her mouth, stroked aggressively, possessively against hers. And he didn't let up the assault until she whimpered into his mouth in complete surrender.

When it came he ripped his mouth from hers and swore. His voice was rough and primal when he growled,

"I want you, Lorelei. I've never wanted anyone like this. Tell me you feel the same."

She opened her eyes to find him staring hard at her, lust burning hot in his translucent gray eyes. His mouth was slick from their kiss. Lorelei could feel his chest heaving against her back, expanding with great gulps of air.

With gentle pressure to her neck, Mark urged her on. "I know you want me. Your body is so turned on I can feel it. You're practically begging to be fucked. Admit it, tell me you want me and I'll give you the best fuck of your life."

Lorelei stopped dancing and stared at him as the world came crashing in on her. As she looked into his eyes full of passion for her, reality settled heavily on her shoulders. She tried to push away from him, but his grip tightened. A warning sound came low in his throat.

Her body screamed for release and Lorelei had to admit she wanted him every bit as much as he wanted her. It would be so easy to give in to this wild, wanton need inside her to embrace her sensuality with Mark. She ached for it. But suddenly it wasn't as simple as that, and the idea of using him solely for that purpose seemed wrong. Somewhere between oyster shooters and dancing to reggae, something had changed.

She didn't want to be just another name in a long list of fucks in Mark Cutter's life.

Firmly pushing out of his embrace, she braced herself for his outburst and hitched her chin. "I do want you, Mark. More than is probably good for me."

His voice was sharp with sexual frustration and growing anger. "Then what's the problem, Lorelei? What do you want from me?"

"I want you to remember me. My name, my face."

With force, he raked his hands through his hair, the movement jerky. "What do you mean? You're not making any goddamn sense."

"A year from now, Mark, when you've moved through a dozen women and added more to your list of sexual conquests, I deserve to be more than just another faceless screw."

Chapter 14

MARK SWORE AS another ball flew past his glove and sped toward the backstop behind him. On his feet in a flash, he chased it down ruthlessly and spun toward third. A runner had rounded the base and was speeding toward home. Instantly judging the distance to the plate, Mark's feet kicked into motion, determination to tag the runner out his only motivation. That was *his* goddamn plate. Seeing him advance, the runner lowered into a slide, forcing Mark to dive headfirst toward home, the ball stretched out in front of him nestled firmly in his glove.

The impact jarred him, and dirt flew obscuring his vision. He knew he'd tagged the runner, but had he already crossed the plate?

The answer came roaring from the umpire and it pissed Mark off. "*Safe!*"

Like hell he was.

Jumping to his feet to argue the umpire's call as the dust settled, Mark could barely hear the discontent from the crowd around the blood pounding in his ears.

A warning look from the umpire stayed him, though. He'd been tossed from a game on more than a few occasions for arguing calls. Biting back the anger, Mark registered the sound of cheering from the opposing team's fans, their very presence a punch to his already bruised ego.

Thoroughly ticked, he slapped his mitt hard against his thigh and prepared for another batter. The Denver Rush were taking a thrashing. And it was completely his fault. One hundred percent his frigging fault. He wasn't playing worth shit tonight.

He was jinxed. And he deserved it for being idiotic enough to have a woman for a good luck charm. They caused nothing but trouble.

Before play could resume an argument broke out between JP and the runner on second. JP was nose to nose with the guy, spouting obscenities. Adding insult, the shortstop lashed out with his free hand and knocked the runner's helmet from his head. The umps rushed over to break it up, hollering as they waded into the pissing match.

The game got under way again and Mark took his frustration out on any call he disagreed with, criticizing the home plate umpire every chance he got. He knew he was playing a dangerous game, but he suddenly didn't care.

When a runner tried to steal second after a pitch, Mark

caught the ball, leaped forward, and rocketed it off with punishing force. Though the second baseman tagged the runner out, it did nothing to assuage Mark's ego.

The ousted runner jogged toward the dugout and glared at Mark as he came into range. "You're a real ass-hole tonight, Cutter."

"What'd you say, Norton? You whining about something?" Mark rolled his shoulders beneath his pads and shifted on his cleats, ready to take him on.

The player just shook his head and entered the dugout. Smart move on his part, but there was a part of Mark that was pretty bummed about it. He felt like kicking some ass.

Mark tried crossing himself for good luck and shook the feeling off. He hoped to God he'd be able to get his head back in the game.

With the runner out at second, that made two outs in the top of the third. One more and he could take a few minutes, cool down and collect himself on the bench. All he had to do was keep it together. The Rush were down 6–1.

Ten minutes later the bases were loaded and Mark knew his luck had completely deserted him. He'd given up two more runs—easy runs that he should have been able to stop. In a fit of temper he cursed a blue streak. He couldn't remember playing a worse game in his life.

By the time the last game in the series was over Chicago had scored more runs, ending the game in a humiliating 9–2 defeat. The locker room was hushed when Mark walked inside.

They were all taking the loss hard. The Rush had been in the position this game to really put them in the running for the playoffs. They'd blown it.

Now they had a road trip coming up and the Phillies to contend with. Every Rush player despised going to Philly. The fans were notorious and made the games there damn tough. But it was part of the deal and it meant Mark had one day to get his head back in the game. He wondered briefly what it meant that he'd played like ass even though Lorelei had been there. Maybe he'd run out of luck. Or maybe he'd just sucked because he'd sucked. The end.

Drake Paulson dropped down on the bench beside Mark. Shaking himself, he leaned over and began undoing the laces of his cleats.

"You looked like you were struggling out there tonight, Cutter."

Mark started on the other cleat. "You could say that. I played like shit."

The big infielder stretched his leg out and began unwrapping the bandage around his knee. "We all have off games. Don't beat yourself up over it."

With his cleats off, Mark stood and began to undress. "I'm not. I'm just stating facts."

Drake clipped the bandage and tossed it in the open locker behind him. "I should have played better at first. You aren't the only one to blame for tonight."

"Maybe I wasn't the only one, but I was the biggest contributor."

The scarred veteran leaned his huge shoulders against

the metal locker. "When a woman gets under your skin it can really screw with your game. I know." He eyed Mark. "I saw the two of you the other night. You've got it bad, brother."

Denial was swift and strong. "I don't know what you mean. I'm fine."

"How long have we been teammates? Five, six years? This is the first time I've seen you lose focus. It's the first time I've seen you look at a woman the way you did last night."

Mark scowled and yanked his sweat-soaked shirt over his head. "How did I look at Lorelei?"

"Like I used to look at my wife." Drake smiled and shook his head. "Before she left me for my tax accountant."

MARK HAD BEEN awfully withdrawn on the car ride to his condo. In fact, he'd been downright sulky.

Lorelei knew he was upset about tonight, but she had a feeling it was more than that.

She'd spent the game observing him and visiting with Leslie. Turned out his sister went to almost all his games. What she'd observed was that Mark had played like a man haunted by something. And that something wasn't related to baseball. Lorelei was pretty sure she knew what that was.

It was her.

He shoved the door to his condo open and she followed him through. Flicking on lights as he went, Mark shrugged out of his charcoal dress jacket and strode down the hall to his room. Left alone in the foyer, Lorelei sighed. He'd been ignoring her since she'd turned him down last night.

He couldn't have made his feelings any more plain.

She'd been right. To him she was nothing more than a faceless name. It shouldn't bother her. Not when she'd been considering using him the way she had. Mark wasn't anything more to her than a means to an end. He couldn't be.

It shouldn't bother her, but it did.

Why it did, she didn't really want to examine. Lorelei knew what she was, and what she wasn't. She wasn't the type of woman to keep the interest of a man like Mark for very long. It'd last just long enough for one or two nights of steamy sex.

It was her track record. The truth was that most men didn't stay interested beyond the bedroom door. Mostly they hung around long enough to get what they wanted and then they bailed. The last one had been the worst. He hadn't even waited until the sheets had cooled before he'd run out and never called again.

Lorelei sighed again and started down the hall to the guest room. She slipped off her brown leather jacket and hung it on a spare hanger in the closet. Spying her duffel bag on the floor in the corner, she went to it and crouched down.

Mark had already searched the bag for his cross, she knew that. It hadn't been much of a secret, really. And she'd expected it. He could search all he wanted, but he wouldn't find a thing. It was still at the concierge desk at the hotel.

Lorelei straightened and grabbed another bag off the floor. In it were some clean clothes she'd grabbed from her house. When Logan had asked about it, she'd just told him that she was going with Mark on an away game trip. He'd given her the eye, but kept his mouth shut. Not that he needed to say anything, anyway. She already knew how he felt. He'd made that clear back in their kitchen.

Now she pulled out a thin white cotton camisole and a pair of blue jersey lounge pants. They were the only clean pajamas she had. She needed to wash some clothes, but had no idea if Mark had a washing machine or if he sent his laundry out.

Kicking off her shoes, she quickly undressed and slipped the clothes on. Then she pulled the clip holding her hair in a messy bun out and let it fall loose down her back.

Out in the living room she went straight to Mark's entertainment center and perused his CD selection. His tastes ran the gamut from classical to hard rock and she skimmed the spines until coming across one that suited her mood. Slipping it from the rack, she put it in the player. When slow, moody blues came through the surround sound speakers, she turned and sank into the couch and listened. Blues full of sax and guitar always relaxed her.

Mark appeared a few minutes later, dressed only in a pair of flannel lounge pants. Lorelei glanced over the back of the couch and fought to keep her jaw from dropping.

Her mouth watered at the sight of his tanned, sculpted chest and washboard abs. Those deeply cut muscles that V'd down into his low-riding flannels were delicious. So was the dark blond trail of hair that disappeared beneath the plaid fabric.

Why was she hesitating to act on her desire to have sex with him? At the sight of his gorgeous body she was about to experience a total meltdown. And if he never spoke to her again after getting her in the sack? Well, she supposed she could deal with that, if it meant she got to experience a night with him.

He took another step and his abs flexed hard in response to the movement. Oh yeah, she could deal.

He shot her a dark look as he headed into the kitchen. Lorelei guessed he was still ignoring her. Glass clinked as he rummaged in his cupboards. A few minutes later he reemerged with a glass half full of amber liquid and started toward his room.

She sat up straighter and swung an arm over the back. "Why don't you come sit over here, Mark?"

He stopped. "Why would I want to do that, Lorelei?"

Because he looked angry and miserable at the same time, that's why. "You look like you could use a sounding board. I'm a great listener if you want to talk about tonight's game."

"I don't want to talk about it." But he rounded the couch and took a seat. Bringing the glass to his lips, he took a sip and propped his bare feet on the coffee table.

So he didn't want to talk about the game. Fine. She

had a million questions she wanted to ask him. "Did you decorate this place, or did you hire an interior designer?" She'd keep it light until he relaxed. Then she'd ask the good stuff.

Mark took another drink of the amber liquid. The corded tendons of his throat worked and his Adam's apple bobbed. "I hired someone. I can't decorate for shit."

She smiled. "So you don't have an affinity for colored rocks?"

That got a tiny smirk out him. "Nope. But they kinda grow on you after a while." He dropped his head back against the backrest, exposing the long line of this throat. A day's growth of deep bronze hair shadowed the strong line of his jaw and his lean cheeks.

Lorelei tucked her legs underneath her and leaned back against the plush cushions. "Do you ever get tired of the grind of professional baseball? Ever think about retirement?"

He rolled his head along the back of the couch and looked at her. "Every player has to think about retirement somewhere down the line, Lorelei. As much as we'd like, we can't play ball our whole lives."

Curiosity prodded her to ask, "What would you do if you couldn't play baseball anymore?"

"Are you trying to jinx me, sweetheart?"

The day's stress and the alcohol had his voice growing rough. The velvet sandpaper sound of it crept inside her and lodged in her chest. "No, I was just wondering what you would do, that's all. What your other interests are."

"Uh-huh. I'm not going to answer that because you've already jinxed me by stealing my good luck charm. Any chance you're willing to give it back?"

Lorelei shook her head.

"Didn't think so." He sighed. "Am I going to have to have you arrested after all, Lorelei Littleton?"

She leaned forward and took the glass from his hand and swallowed a small amount. It burned a path down to her stomach. "You don't want to have me arrested, Mark. You just want something to blame for your performance tonight."

"Is that so? Maybe I might enjoy seeing your sexy little butt carted off to jail in handcuffs. Ever think about that possibility? You've caused me a lot of grief, sugar." His hand closed over hers and he brought the glass to his lips, took a long pull. His sullen gaze never left hers.

The feel of his large, hard hand on hers sent a spear of heat spiraling up her arm. She dropped her hand and stood. "I'm going to grab the bottle real quick."

"Good idea. I wasn't planning on getting drunk, but now that you mention it. Grab another glass, too."

Lorelei returned with the liquor bottle and another glass. She started to hand it to Mark but he gave a look that spoke volumes and shook his head. "That one's yours. I remember too well what happened the last time you brought me a glass."

Guilt slammed into Lorelei and she nearly dropped the bottle. She recovered quickly, but her hand shook slightly when she poured a drink. He watched until she took a drink and swallowed before he reached for the bottle to replenish his glass.

He had every right not to trust her. She'd done nothing to deserve trust, but it still stung just the same. Before her encounter with him she'd never done anything to deserve distrust and skepticism. And she discovered that it didn't sit well that Mark felt both for her.

If only they'd met under different circumstances he would have seen the real Lorelei. But they'd met under these circumstances and she was just going to have to deal with it.

It would have made the whole thing easier if she could continue believing that Mark was the selfish womanizer she'd first thought him to be. Instead, she was beginning to have a sneaky suspicion there was a whole lot more to Mark Cutter than met the eye.

Turning, she strode over to the panoramic windows and gazed out at the lights of downtown Denver. It was beautiful. It felt almost like being on top of the world with all the shimmering lights sprawling out before her. She hugged her arms to her, the snifter dangling from her fingers, and soaked it in. It was all so different from the world she lived in.

"Little League."

She sharpened her gaze until it focused on his reflection in the window. He was still lounged on the sofa with his feet outstretched and his head tipped back. In one hand he held the glass, the other rested across the flat plane of his belly. His hand shifted and he lazily scratched the skin just above his pelvic bone, and Lorelei felt it in the pit of her stomach like a caress. Heat flooded her and pooled in the same spot on her where his hand touched him.

What was she doing feeling so much chemical attraction for a man who thought so little of her? A man who, with one misstep on her part, would have her arrested without a second thought? It was insane. And stupid.

So why couldn't she stop it?

Movement in the glass caught her attention and she watched as Mark raised his head and looked at her. He was waiting for her response. "What are you talking about?" she said. "You've lost me."

In the reflection she saw him take another drink and lower the glass to rest on his thigh. "You asked what I would do if I couldn't play. I'd coach Little League."

"Really?" That was a shocker. "You'd want to teach kids?"

He pressed his lips together, revealing the deep creases in his cheeks, and frowned. "I'm not a complete ass, Lorelei. I do have a few redeeming qualities. I like kids. To me it's more rewarding to coach them than it is an adult team, all right?"

If she wasn't mistaken, she'd just offended him. And wasn't that strange? She'd insulted a man known by and large to be a completely arrogant jerk. She hadn't known it was possible. An apology was in order. "I'm sorry, Mark. I didn't mean it like that."

"Yeah, you did," he countered. "But that's fine. It doesn't really matter what you think of me. You're only here because I need my lucky charm."

So that's what it boiled down to. The bottom line. Lorelei swirled the half-forgotten drink and took a deep pull of the rich Caribbean rum. Heck, she knew that, but to hear him say it with such annoyed finality was jarring.

The moment at the club last night had been nothing more than a passing urge to him. She could have been any woman last night and he'd have done the same thing. The blond bimbo could have been in his arms and he'd have wanted her, not Lorelei.

She knew that with gut certainty because he was Mark Cutter, and people didn't get a reputation like his for nothing. Women were nothing more than a passing amusement, a moment of distraction.

Last night had been her moment and now it was gone.

Lorelei tossed back the rest of the rum and wiped a forearm across her lips. She turned from the windows and squared her shoulders. Knowing that only made her job easier.

Guilt was a five-letter word that didn't belong in her vocabulary. In fact, it was a good thing that Mark reminded her so bluntly where she stood before she lost sight of what she was doing there in the first place. Before she found herself falling for a cold-hearted baseball player who didn't give a crap about her.

Mark Cutter deserved to be brought down a peg by a woman. And she was just the one to do it.

Chapter 15

LORELEI STILL COULDN'T believe she was in Philadelphia, a city of such rich history. It was home of the Liberty Bell, Independence Hall, and Benjamin Franklin. The former two being places she'd love to see. Still, more importantly to some of the less historically minded, Philly played host to the Eagles, the Flyers, and some of baseball's rowdiest, most enthusiastic fans.

When Lorelei walked into Citizens Bank Park the roar of the crowd was jarring. She couldn't believe the mad crush of fans in red and white jerseys. The atmosphere was nearly manic. Normally baseball fans were the subdued sports enthusiasts—brainy, courteous, quiet unless cheering a play. Apparently somebody forgot to give the Phillies fans the memo.

It was nuts.

No wonder Mark loved playing baseball. It was pure enthusiasm. If these fans were anything to go by, baseball fanatics would be crazy enough to pay an armload for Mark's charm.

Earlier she'd had the brilliant idea to use the hotel's business center to put it up for auction on the net. But before she'd been able to enter all the information she'd caught sight of Leslie searching for her near the bathrooms and she'd had to bail. She'd been so close, too. Maybe his necklace really was charmed, because she was having a heck of a time getting rid of it.

But she wasn't about to give up.

Leslie nudged her side. "Mark got us great seats for the game tonight. We're three rows up from the boards on the first base line. We'll have the best view of all the action. And there's bound to be tons of it tonight."

If the frenzy of the crowd was anything to go by she didn't doubt it.

They made their way down the steps until they found their seats. A balding man with his face painted red and white and sporting a Phillies jersey blocked the aisle. He looked at them and said, "You gonna cheer for our boys? It's gonna be a great game tonight."

Leslie shoved past him, followed by Lorelei. When they were standing before the plastic seats, Leslie turned back to the Phillies fan. "We sure are going to cheer for our boys tonight, aren't we, Lorelei? Our boys are going to kick your boys' butts. The Rush has the better catcher and stronger fielders." She smiled sweetly and plopped down.

"Saying things like that in this stadium could be very dangerous, I'm thinking," Lorelei mumbled as she sat next to her.

Leslie winked and grinned. She turned to the blustering man and said, "Y'all don't mind a little good-natured ribbing, do you?"

The guy shook his head. "Nah, but you got it all wrong. Our fielding is way better and our catcher is ten times better than Cutter is."

Leslie leaned around Lorelei and challenged, "You care to bet on that?"

Here comes trouble, Lorelei thought. Betting on Mark wasn't the wisest choice considering the way he'd played the last game.

"All right. Twenty bucks to whoever's team wins. You're gonna regret betting against the Phillies. They're kicking ass this season. And Cutter's been playing pathetically this go-round. But I'll gladly take your money."

Stretching out her arm, Leslie leaned across Lorelei and shook the balding man's hand. "You're on. And I wouldn't count Cutter out just yet if I were you. He's got a hell of a comeback record."

Lorelei hoped that was the truth as she watched them shake hands on the bet. Music sounded through the stadium speakers loudly as they waited for the game to begin. Lorelei could see JP Trudeau first at bat, Mark on deck behind him.

The guy next to her stood up and yelled, "You suck, Denver Rush! You suck, Cutter!"

Lorelei felt like punching him in his pudgy face. She gave him a good glare instead and stood up.

Placing her fingers in her mouth, Lorelei blew and released an ear-piercing whistle. "Yeah! Go Cutter! You rock! Whoo-hoo!" For added measure she threw her hands up and punched the air. Then she looked down at the man with his red and white face paint and smiled. She had to clamp down on the urge to stick her tongue out, too.

She didn't like anyone bashing her boy like that.

Glancing back at the field she saw Mark looking at her while he swung a weighted bat, his eyes unreadable. For several long heartbeats he stared at her, studying her, before he turned his head.

Lorelei realized she was standing there like an idiot and quickly sat down. It wasn't the smartest idea to stand up in a stadium bursting with infamous Phillies fans while hollering for the enemy for very long. They might start throwing something. Like batteries.

She realized Leslie was staring at her. "What?"

"You really like him don't you?" she said.

More than she should. "I just didn't like that bozo calling Mark names, that's all."

Everyone hushed for the National Anthem and then all of a sudden the stadium went absolutely wild as the music changed. Lorelei watched as the Phillies' starting pitcher warmed up on the mound to the tune of "Good Times, Bad Times" by Led Zeppelin.

And she'd thought the Rush fans were loud.

Leslie leaned close. "It's crazy, isn't it? Milwaukee is the only other city I've been to that rivals Philly for baseball fanatics."

All around her people were standing and yelling for

their team, thousands of voices raised in chaos. "It's mind-blowing," she had to admit. "I never really thought baseball fans were rowdy."

"That's why I never miss an opportunity to come when Mark plays here. It's too much fun to miss."

"So that's why we flew over together? Not because Mark wanted you to babysit me?" It still vaguely annoyed her even though she liked his sister a lot.

Leslie tossed back her blond hair and laughed. "Is that what you think?" She dabbed a pinky finger at the corner of her eye. "You mean Mark hasn't told you?"

"Hasn't told me what?"

"He got us on the same flight because he didn't want you to be lonely. He was worried that you would feel awkward flying into a strange city separately from him. Since I was already planning to come, I agreed."

What a bunch of bull, Lorelei thought. Mark didn't give a damn for her comfort.

"Darlin', my brother is head over heels for you. Can't you see it?"

Like a flash of lightning, shock speared through Lorelei and she jerked in her seat. She shook her head. "No he's not. He barely even likes me. You don't know the whole situation."

Leslie sent her a knowing smile. "You mean about you taking Mark's good luck charm? My brother doesn't lie to me. I've known about that from the get-go. I've simply decided not to ask you about it. I figured you'd talk about it when you were ready."

Lorelei melted against her seat and groaned. "You must think I'm a horrible person."

She felt a hand pat her knee. "I don't think that at all. What I do think is that there's a very strong incentive in your life that's caused you to do it."

"There is."

Leslie looked at her for several seconds, understanding in her hazel eyes. "I know. And y'all trust Mark when you're ready and you'll tell him the truth."

Her jaw clenched. "I'll never trust him. I can't."

"Lorelei, look at me." She looked. "I know you've heard things about Mark. Bad things. I won't lie, some of it's true. My brother's made mistakes, no doubt. But he's a good man. You can trust him."

She shook her head in denial. "I can't."

"I'm asking you to take a chance on him, Lorelei. I was there at the club the other night, you know."

"You were?"

"Yes, and I saw the way y'all were together. I haven't seen him act like that before. Ever."

Lorelei looked out at the field, down at the Rush's catcher. "He was married before."

With a wave of her hand, Leslie dismissed that comment. "That was a mistake. He was very young and she was the first woman to tell him what he wanted to hear at the time. It wasn't love."

"But—"

"Ask him why that cross is so special to him, Lorelei. If you want to get to know the real Mark you've got to take that first step. He's learned from experience not to trust until he's trusted. He's worth the risk."

Well, if that wasn't a cryptic message then she didn't know what was. Trust Mark. Impossible.

Or was it?

"I'm not sure if I can do what you're asking but I'll think about it."

"Hey, you two girls ready to see your team lose?"

Both women spun their heads around at the intrusion.

Lorelei gave him a once-over, leaned close, and said, "I'm going to enjoy watching you eat your words. By the way, nice paint job on your face. But you missed a spot."

The crowd let out another earth-shattering cheer as the Phillies of the National League geared up to take on the Denver Rush. Lorelei forced the doubts and questions from her mind and focused on the game.

Her gaze drifted down the diamond to Mark. He looked positively lethal and focused as he readied at bat. Which brought up a question. "Hey, Leslie? Why is Mark second at bat? I was under the impression that catchers didn't bat at the first of the lineup."

Leslie tossed her a grin. "That's only if they suck at bat, hon. Mark's good. Real good. He's not a slugger or anything, but he's great at base hits and super fast."

Lorelei thought about that for a minute. "And that's what you need at the beginning of a game—to get on base. So, he and JP are good at getting to bases. Makes sense." In more ways than one. Mark definitely was good at getting to bases.

Leslie nodded agreement. "Yep, and they're fast, too. Especially JP. That kid's got fire under his butt. Just watch."

Lorelei shot out of her seat as the umpire came into position and JP stepped into the batter's box, and began shouting and clapping alongside Leslie. The pitcher wound up to the great delight of the roaring crowd. She couldn't help being affected by the energy level in the stadium and felt adrenaline pump into her as the Rush took their first turn at bat.

The Rush came out strong in the first inning, claiming two runs and keeping the Phillies at bay. The heckling and ribbing mellowed a little from the crowd when the second inning got under way. Only about two hundred times did the Phillies fans yell out something rude about a Rush player within her earshot.

When Drake Paulson slammed a homer beyond the center field wall, someone behind Lorelei yelled out, "You're a pansy, Paulson!"

A fight broke out on the far side of the stadium as Phillies and Rush fans clambered in the bleachers for the ball. It quickly turned into a group effort. Before her eyes it seemed every person in those bleachers got into the scramble and began tussling.

Had she ever thought baseball a gentlemen's sport?

She glanced down to see Mark standing calmly at the front of his dugout, a slight smile on his face. He shot a stream of water from a plastic bottle into his mouth and spit it out. Amusement showed on his face as he watched the fans scuffle.

Lorelei studied him from her seat. Damp hair stuck to his temples and clung to the sides of his neck. His tanned cheeks were slightly flushed from exertion and a shadow beard covered his jaw. From a distance his eyes were dark and intense.

Her stomach took a long, slow dive. He was the sexiest man she'd ever seen.

Leslie elbowed her in the ribs. "Y'all want to tell me again that you don't like him?"

Lorelei watched him shrug his shoulders, and roll his head from side to side. Then he retreated to the bench, slipping out of view.

Leslie elbowed her again and she swallowed hard. Her eyes never left the spot he'd been as she slowly shook her head. She didn't answer, couldn't. She couldn't speak at all.

Her heart was in her throat.

ONE OUT WAS left in the bottom of the ninth, Philly at bat. Mark watched Peter wind up the pitch through the metal cage of his helmet. Walskie was pitching his heart out tonight and holding his own. It was impressive he was still going strong in the ninth, his throws still on target and fast. He was definitely earning himself a few days of rest and recovery.

The Rush were up 3–2.

They were hot tonight. They were out to prove themselves and they were pulling out all the stops. Outfielders were making the cleanest relays of the season, the in-field was making double plays left and right, and he was guarding home with ruthless efficiency.

Mark was holding his own.

He had to keep it up for one more out, that's all. One more out and his team moved one step closer to the playoffs. They were busting ass for it. Hell, they suffered bruises and divorces for it.

Now they just had to put the lid on the game.

Like a predator, Mark followed the ball with his gaze, never taking his eye off Peter. At bat was a pinch hitter for the Phillies pitcher—a hard-nosed slugger come to clean up and even the score. Mark knew the player's reputation and calculated the pitch. Signaled it to Kowalskin. He knew the Philly batter was lethal if the ball was low and outside, but weak if it came at him high and inside. In preparation Mark shifted to his left, prepared for the pitch. If Peter threw it right the pinch hitter would swing and find only air.

After an intense moment the ball came and the batter swung hard, missed, and swore. Mark threw the ball back to Peter and signaled the same pitch again. The Philly batter couldn't resist swinging at those high and inside throws.

Again, Peter wound up and released, the ball zooming toward him at an incredible speed. And again the batter swung, only this time catching a piece of the ball with the bat and sending in flying into foul territory.

Two strikes.

On a deep breath, Mark settled into a crouched position again and decided to call the same pitch. If it wasn't broke, now wasn't the time to fix it. Peter nodded agreement and the ball came hard on the inside.

At the last minute the slugger pulled his swing and connected on a bunt. The ball fell dead a few feet in front of home plate. The batter dashed off toward first, hoping to outrun the play.

On his feet instantly, Mark streaked toward the ball, moving with amazing agility and speed. Kowalskin was racing in from the pitcher's mound, and Paulson called to him from first.

In one fluid motion, Mark scooped up the ball, pivoted, and drilled the ball hard toward Paulson's waiting glove. The contact sounded with a thwack as the pinch hitter dove headfirst toward safety at first.

"*Out!*" The first base umpire pumped his arm and yelled.

The crowd went ballistic. Mark shut it out, closed his ears to the noise. Only one thing mattered to him.

The Rush had won.

Back in the locker room the noise level was almost as loud as the arena. Cheers went up as the Rush players congratulated the rookie on his amazing double plays. The kid blushed from all the attention and smiled.

Mark dropped onto the bench and watched with a smile as JP was treated to an old-fashioned noogie by veteran Carl Brexler. Though the kid was tall, the outfielder had a good sixty pounds on him and easily wrestled him into a headlock, rubbed his knuckles over the kid's nearly hairless head.

Kowalskin laughed and announced, "Tonight we celebrate, boys. What do you say to a night of fun and debauchery?"

A round of emphatic "Hell, yeah"s followed.

Mark began unlacing his cleats and grinned at JP. "I think we need to make the rookie our guest of honor."

"You boys know what that means," replied Kowalskin.

The whole team hollered in unison, "It's Miller time!"

JP looked over at Mark, confusion in his eyes. "What's Miller time?"

Mark stood and pulled his jersey over his head. He grinned. "It means, my man, that you're gonna be drinking a whole lotta beer."

"Hey, Cutter."

He looked up. "Hey, Crispy Critter, what's up?"

John Crispin flipped him the bird and laughed. "You want to call Leslie and tell her where to meet us, or should I?"

They all knew there was only one place to go in Philadelphia for a visiting baseball team to enjoy some fun and debauchery. Dirty Harry's Bar and Grill. It came fully equipped with booze, barbecue ribs, big screen TVs, and even a mechanical bull affectionately known as Ballbuster.

"Why don't you give her a call. I'm going to go to my room and change out of my suit before I head out to the bar."

"I was headed back to my room to change, too."

Mark shrugged his shoulders and turned to his locker. "Okay. I'll call. No big deal." He could talk to Lorelei that way.

John's voice sounded behind him. "No, I can do it. I'll give her a call when I get out of the shower."

"Fine." Mark didn't really care.

"Fine."

"All right then." He'd see Lorelei soon enough.

"Fine. Good." A pause. "You gonna call her, then?"

"John?" He was going to bang his head against the locker.

"Yeah?"

"Just shut up and call your girlfriend."

"Fine."

Before he slammed his own head against the locker, Mark stripped and headed for the showers. When he reached the tiles he stopped and grinned. "Hey, John?"

The player looked up. "Yeah, what?"

"Fine."

Chapter 16

A GLASS APPEARED in front of her. Lorelei took it and looked up. Mark stood towering over her, a grin full of rotten intentions on his face.

Suddenly suspicious that her drink contained something gray and slimy, she peered into the glass. "Did you have the bartender slip a raw oyster in my drink?"

He dropped into the chair across from her and laughed. "Now why would you think I'd do a thing like that?"

"Because you would."

Drake Paulson hooked a thumb over at her. "She's got you pegged, Cutter." He looked down at her. "When you going to forget about that loser and marry me, sweet thing?"

Lorelei asked, "What happened with"—she cupped her hands in front of her chest—"Candy?"

Drake's gaze dropped to her hands and back up. "She used me, abused me."

She feigned sympathy. "I'm sorry to hear that, Drake."

"I'm more than just a gorgeous body, you know."

"Yes, you are."

"I'm more than just a thick wallet."

Lorelei bit her cheek to keep from laughing. "Absolutely."

"She did find out the most important fact about me, though."

She was almost afraid to ask. "Oh yeah? What's that?"

"I'm an easy lay."

A burst of laughter erupted and she snorted. Across the table Mark let loose a laugh and shook his head.

Peter Kowalskin swore and retorted, "Like she wasn't."

Apparently the whole table had been listening to their conversation. Several pair of eyes were turned in their direction.

Drake shrugged his massive shoulders and smiled at the guys. "What can I say, it was a match made in heaven."

"You mean a one-night stand, Paulson," another player said from down the table.

He laughed. "That, too."

Still chuckling, Lorelei glanced around the bar and inhaled the mouthwatering scent of barbecue that hung on the air. Three big screens were built into the walls and were tuned to the local late night news. Booths and tables were scattered around the huge open room, two pool tables were to her right, and a round pen with a mechanical bull was set up in the far corner. There was also a small stage for karaoke directly in front of her against the wall.

The bar and grill wasn't crowded, but there were a few groups of people scattered throughout. For the most part the whole Denver Rush baseball team had the place to themselves.

Some of the guys had hopped cabs as soon as they'd hit the hotel lobby and were still wearing their dress suits. Others had gone up to their rooms to change first. Mark was one who'd changed into casual clothes.

Butterflies fluttered deep in her gut when she glanced at him. He was in conversation with another player, his hands laced together behind his neck while he leaned back in his chair. The cuffs of his shirt were rolled up his muscular forearms.

His profile was to her and she studied him. Hair waved over his ear and curled lazily. He'd shaved, and his skin was smooth and very tan against the pale blue chambray shirt he wore. He had such thick lashes. They fanned out and cast a slight shadow below his eyes in the low light.

He laughed at something and the masculine dimples that drove her crazy flashed in his cheeks, teasing her. The top two buttons of his shirt were open and when he moved she caught a glimpse of his sculpted chest. Her lungs tightened. She couldn't take her eyes off him.

He must have felt her gaze because he turned his head. The smile melted and his eyes grew hot. Instantly his body tensed and he stilled.

Why hadn't she noticed the deep bow of his upper lip before? It practically begged to be licked. Or the indentation of his clavicle? Her lips suddenly craved to know the feel of it. Mesmerized, her mouth opened as she stared at the base of his throat, at the smooth skin, and her tongue slipped between her teeth and touched her bottom lip.

Lorelei jolted and she felt her eyes go wide when Mark swore and lurched from his chair. "I'm going to play pool," he growled.

She watched him go as her libido went haywire. Raked her gaze over his broad shoulders, down his back and narrow waist, over his firm butt and heavy thighs. Her mind flashed back to the night they'd first met, to the image of his bare chest and flat stomach. She had to bite back a moan.

Leslie appeared at her side, a glass of red wine in her hand. "Why are you still sitting here? Go after him, Lorelei."

Why *was* she still there? This was her opportunity to experience what it felt like to be truly desired by a man, and to desire him back with equal intensity. Her chance to experience Mark Cutter.

Was she woman enough to handle it?

She glanced up at Leslie and demanded, "Tell me again that he's worth it."

Leslie's smile was sympathetic and her voice was full of encouragement when she murmured, "He's so worth it, Lorelei. So absolutely, totally worth it."

With shaking hands she pushed from the table and stood. She took a step and stopped. The drink Mark had brought her still sat completely full on the table and she snatched it up and downed it in one long gulp, set it back down with a thump.

Leslie gave her arm a reassuring squeeze and nudged her in the back. "Go to him."

She did.

He was alone at the pool tables; the rest of the guys were either still eating ribs and helping the rookie down his third pitcher of beer by chanting, "Go, go, chug, chug, chug," or they were taking turns shouting dirty insults and getting bucked off the mechanical bull.

Mark glanced up from racking the balls, his eyes devoid of emotion. "What do you want, Lorelei?"

You. "Mind if I play?"

"Do you know how?" He rolled the triangle full of colored balls forward and back, settling the yellow one ball on the brown marker.

Lorelei spotted the pool cues and walked over. She grabbed one, held it out in front of her, and checked for straightness. It was too bowed for her taste and she put it back, grabbed another one, found it satisfactory. "I can hold my own."

"What's the ante?"

"What?"

Mark smirked and carefully removed the wooden triangle. "What's the bet? You can't play pool without one, or are you afraid I'll kick your cute little butt?"

He thought her butt was cute. That was good to know. "I'm not afraid of you, Mark Cutter."

Rounding the pool table, he stopped behind her and said against her ear, "You should be. If you knew even half the things I want to do to you, you'd be very afraid."

Oh, this was getting good.

Her stomach flopped and took a nosedive. "Nothing you say could scare me."

Hot breath feathered across her cheek. "Wanna bet? You forget who I am, Lorelei."

A delicious shiver raced down her spine. "Remind me, bad boy."

Heat pooled between her legs when he moved behind her and she felt a hand smooth over her butt, stroke down the center seam of her jeans. It stopped just before the junction of her thighs and curled, pressed strong fingers into the cleft between her cheeks.

"Ever been kissed there, sweetheart?"

She shook her head.

"Want to be?" His voice was low, rough with arousal.

He was trying to shock her, scare her with his vast experience. It wasn't working. "Are you offering, Mark?"

The hand on her butt jerked slightly and she thrilled at his quick intake of breath. Two could play this game.

Teeth nipped the curve of her ear, sending a jolt of electricity down her neck. "Anytime, anyplace. I'll kiss you, lick you wherever you want. Just tell me where you want it and I'll make you scream."

The air was too thick, too hot. It was like syrup in her lungs. Arousal like she'd never felt before washed over her on a tidal wave and settled between her thighs.

It was terrifying. It was exhilarating, this game of naughty taunting. It made her bold.

She turned her head slightly so that only he could hear her scandalous words. She couldn't believe she was about to say it, but he'd dared her, challenged her. Called her bluff. On a lot of different levels. Because she knew in her heart now that she wasn't just another conquest of his. She was more—so much more.

And that changed everything.

She swallowed hard and whispered, "Do you want to kiss my pussy, Mark? Lick it until I come?"

His whole body convulsed and his hand squeezed her, hard. He swore violently. "Fuck, yes."

Charged silence stretched between them. Neither moved for several long seconds, then he slowly unclenched his hand and slid it back over her butt and let it drop away. She heard him suck in a deep breath as he stepped back and put some space between them. Cool air swept over her, a startling contrast to the wicked heat of his body.

They both looked up when they heard someone call his name. A group of the guys were heading in their direction, beers in their hands, completely oblivious to what was going on in the darkened corner where Lorelei and Mark stood.

She felt more than heard him move. He was suddenly beside her, his butt resting on the edge of the pool table. His voice was low and urgent. "This isn't over, Lorelei."

"Hey guys, mind if we get in on the game?"

Mark's teammates crowded around the table and headed for the pool cues on the wall. Drake Paulson picked up the stick Lorelei had dropped on the table, raked his gaze over her and Mark. He laughed at them as he handed her back her pool cue. He, at least, knew *exactly* what he'd interrupted.

Lorelei took the offered pool cue and fought to get control of her emotions. There was no escaping the brood of slightly drunk baseball players crowding in on her, so she had no choice but to get a handle on her hormones for the time being and resign herself to a few rounds of pool.

Apparently Mark also realized the futility of trying to slip away because he let out a frustrated sigh and said, "Which one of you pansies wants to take me on first?"

A ballplayer she didn't recognize stepped forward. "I'll take you on, Cutter. How about loser buys the next round of drinks?"

Mark looked down at her before he stood and walked around to the head of the pool table. "You're on, Brexler, but I break."

For the next twenty minutes she watched Mark play and eventually felt her equilibrium return. When Mark won the first round of pool, Brexler shrugged and happily ordered a round of beers. Before she knew it, a pint had been shoved in her hand and she found herself laughing at something Peter Kowalskin said.

Another player stepped forward and issued the same challenge—a round of beers on the loser—only *he* got to break this time. "You had unfair advantage, Wall. We'll see who wins this time."

Lorelei brought the pint glass to her lips and was about to take a drink when JP Trudeau stumbled over to the table. Over the rim of her glass she saw that he'd downed one too many pitchers of beer. He was totally smashed.

He raised his nearly empty pitcher and said around a belch, "Iz Miller time."

It must have been some inside joke because all the guys—including Mark—laughed, raised their beers, and shouted, "It's Miller time!" Then they took a drink.

Baseball players.

"Somebody needs to pour that boy into a cab. I think he's about to pass out," she said to no one in particular.

Another player she didn't know came forward. "I'll take him back to the hotel. It's about time I call it a night anyway. The wife will be calling my room before much longer to make sure I'm there."

Everyone said their good-byes to the inebriated shortstop and then attention turned immediately back to the pool game. The guy who'd challenged Mark was just about to break when Kowalskin spoke. "Not so fast there, Jim. I think our boy here needs something tougher than a round of beers from the loser. Let's make it interesting."

MARK SET THE butt of his cue on the floor and grinned. "Oh yeah, old man? You wanna take me on instead?"

Peter crossed to the table. "If Jim here's willing to give up his turn I will."

He turned his head to see what the second-string third baseman's response was. Jim smiled and handed Pete his cue. "He's all yours, Walskie."

Mark eyed ballplayer. "You want to make this interesting?"

Pete looked over at Lorelei and winked, irritating Mark. "Uh-huh. New bet. Loser has to stand up on that stage over there and sing a karaoke song for the great enjoyment of the team."

He considered. "What's the winner get?"

Pete laughed and clapped him hard on the back. "To pick the song."

Mark heard Lorelei gasp and snort with laughter. He straightened. "You're on, Pete."

"You'd better tune up your vocal cords, boy, 'cause you're gonna be singing like a canary in a minute."

For the next half hour Mark and Peter battled it out, the crowd of onlookers cheering like it was a baseball game instead of pool. When Mark tried to bank the seven ball and it missed the corner pocket by a mile, a collective gasp came from the players. Even Lorelei was getting into the sport of things, and she gasped right along with them.

"Your turn, Walskie."

As Peter lined up his shot, Mark quickly surveyed the table. The seven ball was his last one before sinking the nine ball. If Pete didn't dislodge it from its spot by the middle pocket he shouldn't have a problem getting it next time. And Pete still had two balls to get in the pockets.

His shot set up, the pitcher pulled his stick back and let it go. The cue ball smacked hard into the striped ball, sending it straight into the pocket. "Are you ready to sing, Cutter?"

Mark stared at the table with a sinking feeling. "A bet's a bet."

With efficient strokes, Peter cleared the table and sent the nine ball home to rest in the corner pocket. Looked like he was going to be singing.

Shit.

A shout went up from the guys as they congratulated their pitcher. Then the heckling started.

"Whatcha gonna sing, Tweety Bird?"

"Oooh, The Wall gets to perform for us."

"Does he have to dance, too?"

The group gathered around him and started pushing him toward the small stage by the bar. A liberal amount of alcohol made the shoves a little more enthusiastic than needed and Mark tripped on the step as they hauled him up on stage.

They'd made enough noise that the whole bar was now looking at him, watching with avid curiosity. The only way Mark was going to get out of this was by force.

He tried to decide whom he wanted to deck first.

Peter appeared on the stage beside him and took the microphone out of the stand. He flicked the on switch and tapped his fingers on the mouthpiece. A resounding thump, thump, thump came through the speakers.

Mark glared at the pitcher. "You know I'm gonna kick your ass for this, don't you?"

The dark-haired player laughed. "Yep. But it's so worth it. Come on, Wall, show us what you're made of."

"I need a drink." He tried to step down from the stage.

Kowalskin shot out an arm and stopped him. "No time, Cutter. The song's loaded and your fans are waiting eagerly." He looked around the bar. "Isn't that right, everyone?"

Even the bartender shouted and applauded.

Mark surveyed the bar and saw all the faces watching him. Leslie let out a whistle from the back table and yelled, "You go, boy! Show us your stuff!" He vowed he'd get even with her for that.

Hoots and hollers came from his teammates and he realized there was no escape. He was stuck.

Mark slid his gaze over the crowd until it landed on Lorelei. She'd moved off to the side and was leaning against the wall, a fist pressed against her mouth in an attempt to hide her smile. It wasn't working—he still saw her laughing at him.

He'd show her.

He reached for the microphone and yanked it out of Peter's grasp. "You'd better not have given me a chick song."

The pitcher pointed to the monitor where the name of the song was displayed. "I did. The eighties at its best, man."

"You're a dick, Kowalskin," he said after he read the title.

"So they tell me." Peter raised his arms in the air and announced to the bar, "The one, the only Mark Cutter will now present us with a song." The bar erupted in applause and whistles.

Hopping from the stage, Peter melted into the crowd of onlookers and hollered, "Give 'em hell, tiger!"

LORELEI SHUDDERED WITH suppressed laughter. Mark looked so damn uncomfortable all alone up there on stage. He just kept staring at the monitor in front of him and scowling. When the music started she understood why.

Instantly she recognized the song and burst into a fit of laughter. Everyone else in the bar recognized it, too, the hoots and hollers escalating to a frenzy. Mark was going to sing one of the most famous chick songs of the eighties.

"Hungry Eyes."

The theme song from eighties blockbuster *Dirty Dancing* starring Patrick Swayze. One of the best romantic movies of the decade. She could remember the song playing on the kitchen stereo when she was a kid. Swinging her hips to the tune had made washing the dinner dishes go by in a flash.

Dear God, how bad was he going to butcher it?

She watched Mark shrug his shoulders as he did during a game and roll his head from side to side. Then he raised the microphone and said into it, "All right, here goes."

Lorelei waited with trepidation for the first notes, tensed for Mark to tank big-time. She closed her eyes and flinched when his mouth opened. She couldn't help it—he'd finally made her afraid.

A rich baritone with a raw, sexual edge greeted her ears and her eyes popped open and zeroed in on the stage. Mark was watching her and grinned when her gaze met his.

He could sing. Holy crap could he sing.

Her mouth dropped open in shock and she pushed away from the wall. His voice started soft and easy as the song began, seducing her through the speakers.

Shouts of encouragement came from a group over in the corner as he neared the chorus and his voice grew stronger, more emotional—rougher. It filled with real desire as he started singing about having hungry eyes.

The banked passion from earlier flared hot again as she watched Mark brace his feet apart and roll his hips suggestively, getting into the moment. A round of whistles followed, but she barely registered them.

All she could hear was Mark.

Her stomach took a long, liquid roll when his eyes locked on hers and he began singing directly to her. Need, desire, carnal lust—everything he felt was in his gaze, written across his face as the words of the song became his personal message to her, his plea. No man had ever wanted her that much before. Something shifted inside her, cracked. Without a fight she opened herself, let him in.

When the interlude came and saxophone wailed through the speakers, Mark placed the microphone in its holder. Then he raised a hand toward her, his palm to the ceiling, and crooked a finger at her. Beckoned her to him.

She went.

His hand wrapped around hers and he pulled her onstage into his arms. The bar went wild. Yells, whistles, catcalls.

She didn't even hear.

Mark surrounded her, a strong arm wrapped around

her waist, the other dove into her hair and fisted. Then his mouth was on her and he was kissing her. Hot, wet, demanding.

He tore his mouth from her and lowered his head until his lips caressed her ear. "It's time, Lorelei." His voice shook with his need.

She nodded. "Yes, it's time."

They were gone before the song was over.

Chapter 17

HIS HANDS WERE everywhere the second the door closed behind them. He had to touch her. If he didn't he'd go crazy. Hell, he already felt crazy. For Lorelei.

They stumbled together in the dark hotel room. He roomed alone and hadn't pulled the drapes open earlier. Mark tore his lips from her. "I can't see. Shit, I can't see a goddamn thing." He tried to find the light switch on the wall.

He felt her hands race over him, searching until she found his hand. She placed it on her breast. "Feel your way, bad boy." His hand squeezed in reflex.

"Jesus." The air rushed from his lungs.

Her other hand stroked up his stomach and she tore at his shirt. Buttons popped open and her mouth was on his throat in an openmouthed kiss. Her tongue licked his skin, burning a path down his chest.

It nearly buckled his knees.

With his free hand he gripped her hip, walked her toward where he remembered the bed to be. She tripped and they went down hard. Reacting instantly Mark grabbed her arms and turned until he hit the floor first and she landed on top of him. The wind was knocked out of him and he grunted. Lorelei sprawled across his chest and he heard her whoosh of air.

Then she was laughing.

He found his voice. "What's so funny?"

"It looks like I've fallen for you, Mark."

A rush of heat pooled in his gut, twisted it in a tight knot. God, he wished it were true. He suddenly wanted Lorelei to be falling for him in the worst way. The thought of it set his heart racing.

They had their issues. No doubt about it. And they had secrets from each other. Didn't know every detail about each other, or even birthdays and all that trivial bull.

But he'd be damned if he didn't want Lorelei to fall for him. He wanted it bad. Because like a fool he was falling for her. In a way that he never had before. For anyone. She pulled emotions from him that stole his breath away and made him think of picket fences and buying a puppy.

She slid over him until she was straddling him on the floor in the dark. He could barely make out her silhouette in the near blackness. But he could feel her. How he could feel her. Her heat, the weight of her, the hands that seared a path down his bare chest. And it turned his cock to stone.

"I've wanted to do this, wanted to run my hands over your hard body, Mark." Her voice was husky with arousal.

It washed over him and settled in the pit of his stomach.

He tried to reach for her. "I want to touch you, Lorelei. Kiss every inch of your gorgeous body. I've been going crazy with wanting."

He growled when she stopped his hands. She pushed them to the floor with a laugh. "Uh-uh. I get to do this my way, Mark. Now lie there like a good boy and keep your hands to yourself until I tell you otherwise."

If he didn't get inside her soon he was going to go insane. Or come right there in his jeans. "I can't wait. I want in you." Her fingers skimmed low over his stomach and he hissed, "*Now*, Lorelei."

She reached his fly and pressed her palm over his hard-on. She sounded amused when she teased, "My, my, aren't we in a hurry?" Her hand squeezed him through the denim. "I thought professional athletes were trained to go the distance."

He rocked against her. A groan tore from his throat as she stroked him with a sure hand. "Later. I'll go the distance later. Right now I need to be inside you. God, Lorelei, if you don't stop that I won't even make it that far."

His breathing grew ragged. He was tuned into her every movement in the darkness. Lightning skittered along his nerves, his senses heightened to an almost painful alert. When she undid his fly and took him in her hands it was almost too much. He arched helplessly into her and ground out, "Hell, yeah."

"You like that?" She ran her palm up his shaft and gripped him. Her thumb slid over the head and rubbed a bead of moisture into the sensitive flesh and he nearly lost it. She moved over him; he heard rustling, could tell she was taking her clothes off. Unable to hold back anymore his hands reached for her, slid over her hot, bare skin.

He had never felt like this before—like a wild animal. Something primitive tore through him as his hands cupped her full breasts and she moaned. He flicked the pad of his thumb over her nipples. A sharp tug pulled low in his stomach and his groin ached so bad it throbbed. He didn't want it end, knew it would.

"Mark, kiss me," Lorelei demanded in a low whisper.

He flexed his stomach muscles and sat up, ran his hands over her to fist in her silky hair. A growl rumbled in his chest when his mouth found hers in the dark and he fed her a hot, hungry kiss. She moaned. He yanked her head back and trailed openmouthed kisses down her throat. She arched against him as his mouth covered her breast and he sucked her nipple.

He held her like that as he tongued her hard peak and cupped her other breast with a hand. They were perfect, full and ripe and darkly sweet. He wanted to devour her.

It didn't matter that she'd stolen from him, that he still didn't know why. All that mattered was her ragged breathing and the nails that bit into his shoulders telling him she was turned on. That she was ready for him. But there was something he had to do first.

LORELEI FELT MARK's toned body flex, the hard muscles bunch, and then she was on her back. He was looming over her in the darkness, his erection rubbing against her crotch. She bit her lip when he shoved roughly against her. It might have hurt if she wasn't so turned on. Instead, it sent tremors shooting off inside her like fireworks.

"Now you're in for it, sweetheart. You're going to pay for teasing me," Mark growled against her neck.

God, she hoped so.

Power still swam in her brain like a heady concoction. She'd made him hard, mad for her. Her. Lorelei Littleton. It made her drunk from the knowledge.

She'd needed to know how much she affected him. Though she'd been teasing earlier it had been the truth. It didn't matter that it was the stupidest thing she could do, that it ruined everything, all her plans. She couldn't help it.

She was falling for the catcher with the fast hands.

A gasp escaped her when Mark's hand undid her zipper, dove inside. Through her cotton panties he cupped her.

"You're wet, Lorelei. Your panties are soaked with your juice. I can smell it on you, your desire for me. But I want to hear you say it. Tell me how you feel," he demanded.

In the darkness, lying on the floor, she felt his fingers rub her through her panties and she groaned. He slipped a finger around the cotton and found her. Touched her where she wanted him the most.

"Say it, Lorelei. Tell me you're wet for me." His mouth found a spot below her ear and he kissed her there. His tongue slid over the curve of her ear and he nipped her with his teeth. She moaned and arched into his fingers.

"I'm wet, Mark," she whispered. Her stomach turned to liquid. She felt like she was about to burst into flames.

He trailed a searing path of wet kisses down her chest. His tongue flicked over the hard peaks of her nipples before he continued on his path. "No," he said against the flat of her stomach, "tell me I make you wet. That I make your pussy ache. Say the words, Lorelei. It turns me on to hear those dirty words come from your pretty mouth."

He was making demands, trying to shock her. Instead, her arousal only grew hotter. She thrilled at the dirty talk, her body responded to the call of it. Responded to him.

She went wild. "You make my pussy ache, Mark. I want you inside me now. Only you have what I need." It was true.

His gravelly laugh echoed in her gut. He pulled his hand from her pants and yanked them off. Her panties followed. He disappeared for a second. She heard him strip and the sound of foil tearing as he covered himself. Then he was back and his hard hands were running up the length of her bare thighs. His hot breath whispering across her skin. He traced a finger over her wet curls. "That's right, baby. Only I have what you need. But not yet, Lorelei. You tormented me, now it's my turn. Ask me again. Ask me again what you did at the bar."

Lorelei reached for him, touched him everywhere she could reach. Arms, shoulders, the back of his head. He blew on her crotch and her body ignited like a flash fire.

She knew what he wanted to hear. "Do you want to kiss my pussy, Mark?"

His answer was swift and hard. "Fuck, yes."

Then his mouth was on her in a hot, wet, openmouthed kiss. A sound of primitive aroused male tore from his throat. He found her clit with his tongue, rubbed over it in circular motions, sucked. Lorelei thought she was going to die from the feel of it.

When her inner muscles starting to clench and she neared orgasm, Mark shifted. His toned athlete's body covered her and the plump head of his erection pressed between her slick folds.

This was what she wanted, craved. She needed to go over the edge. Hunger clawed deep in her belly and she arched her hips. With a ragged groan he sank into her. His thick shaft stretched her, filled her, and she gasped.

"Oh God, Lorelei. You're so tight around me." He thrust deep and her inner muscles clamped around him, started to quiver.

He kissed her and she could taste herself on his mouth. His tongue thrust inside, over hers as he started to move in slow, long strokes.

She didn't want slow. Raising her legs, Lorelei wrapped them around his muscular back. His hard body strained from exertion as she took him deeper still until she felt him against her womb.

Nothing else existed. Only the man above her and the thick erection stroking into her.

"I want more." She bit his corded neck and he swore.

"You want more?" He panted, his breath harsh.

"Yes!" She raked her nails down his back. He responded with a growling sound deep in his throat.

And he gave her more, his body pounded into her

harder, faster. He gave her more until every nerve in her body sparked like an electrical current and need became a white-hot ball in the pit of her stomach. Until all she could do was feel, cling to Mark.

Their breathing grew more ragged. Over and over he thrust into her until suddenly she gasped. Crying out in the darkness, her body burst and an orgasm tore through her. It flooded through her, over her as her inner muscles convulsed against his shaft. Her body sucked him in, pulsed around him until he pushed deep and went still. A groan tore from his throat and his body went rigid as he climaxed.

They lay there afterward not moving, their breathing rapid, their hearts pounding. Neither spoke for a long while.

Later his hand stroked over her hair and he shifted. "That was utterly, completely amazing."

It was more than amazing for Lorelei. It was the best sex of her life. Incredible, earth-shattering, mind-blowing sex.

They'd damn near set the room on fire. And she couldn't have felt better about that if she tried.

Mark rolled off her onto his back. His arm reached around her and he pulled her against his side. "I suppose one of us should turn on the light," he murmured.

His fingers trailed a lazy path up and down her arm. Her palm flattened against his damp chest and she rested her head on his muscular shoulder. "No. The dark's nice." She couldn't get up if she wanted to—her thighs were still trembling.

His chest rumbled when he chuckled. "Yeah, you're right. The dark's nice."

He shifted slightly under her and she felt one of his hands run over her hip down to her knee. Gripping gently he lifted her leg and settled it over his. She nudged his testicles and felt the crisp hair covering his heavy thighs tickle the sensitive skin of her leg. He kept his hand on her knee.

"When's your birthday?" His voice was the rough, deep sound of satisfied male.

Idly her fingers began to explore his chest. "May twelfth. When's yours?"

"November fifteenth. How old are you?"

So he was a Scorpio. Didn't that just figure? She vaguely remembered reading his birth date on his bio page, but she'd forgotten about that little fact. "I'm twenty-eight. Why do you ask?"

Firm lips pressed against her forehead and he sighed. "Just curious is all. I figure I need to know these things. Women tend to get upset when you don't know."

The warm, contented afterglow that had settled over Lorelei abruptly disappeared. She was sure that he hadn't meant to, but that comment had just reminded her who Mark Cutter was. He'd probably had to remember a lot of birth dates in his lifetime.

She tried to sit up, but he tightened his arm around her like a vise. A heavy leg tangled with hers and clamped down. She couldn't move.

"Where do you think you're going?"

For air. But she didn't think he wanted to hear that so

she said instead as she settled back down, "Nowhere, just getting more comfortable."

His grip loosened and he relaxed again. His hard leg rubbed over hers in a slow rhythm. "You want to get on the bed?"

Her body and mind melted. Not particularly. It felt incredible in his arms. Even the doubts couldn't overshadow that. She had a fleeting thought about why that might be, but it dissolved into nothing when his fingertips skimmed her bare back. His touch felt decadent against her skin.

There would be time later to think on things. "No, I'm fine," she said.

They were quiet for a moment, their even breathing the only sound in the room. Mark began stroking her arm with his fingers again. It felt so good she closed her eyes and sighed. Let her hand glide over the dips and planes of his corrugated stomach. He had such an awesome body.

"Lorelei?" he said quietly.

"Hmm?" Her fingers reached springy pubic hair.

"What do you do for a living?" He sucked in air and his stomach muscles quivered beneath her hand.

It mildly surprised her that he was asking. That he was interested in her beyond a bout of sweaty sex. She decided to take that as a good sign. "I write articles for gardening magazines."

"You mean like stuff on how to grow tomatoes and keep bugs from eating your flowers?"

She gave a low laugh. "Something like that. It's a little more exciting than that to me, but that's the idea."

Mark was silent for a moment, and then asked, "Do you like it? I mean is that what you've always wanted to do?"

She supposed he would look at in that way. Baseball wasn't just his job, it was his life. He'd probably been born knowing he was bound for the major leagues.

"Gardening is one of my passions, writing is another. So for me it was only a natural step to combine the two."

"So you like it?"

"Yes I do. I get to work from home, call my own hours, spend lots of quality time with my family. But the pay could definitely be better."

"Is that why you stole my necklace? Because your job doesn't pay well?" He asked it casually, but Lorelei could hear the edge he tried to hide in his voice.

She removed her hand from his body and placed it on her hip. "I can't tell you why. It's too personal."

His body tensed and steel entered his voice. "I think we just got pretty damn personal, Lorelei. I deserve an answer and I want to know why you did it."

He was right. He did deserve an explanation. But she couldn't give it. If she did it meant laying her family open to an outsider's view, giving them opportunity to judge. And once they started, they never stopped.

For as long as she could remember she'd had it drilled in to her that family business stayed in the family. It didn't get shared for other people's scrutiny. After her sister's death her parents became almost fanatical about it in their grief. Even now, after they were gone, being closed-lipped was a habit she couldn't break. Even if it upset Mark not to get an answer.

If she told him one thing, it would lead to another. Then another. Pretty soon her family's entire closet of skeletons would be on display for his perusal. He would eventually find out the truth about her mother. Though her mom had always had problems, after Lucy's death she had gone off the deep end and hurt a lot of people. Lorelei was sure that's why her parents had become so paranoid about privacy. Because Barb Littleton's crazy behavior had created more buzz than a swarm of bees. There were still things that happened that she and Logan never talked about, shared traumas that had shaped and molded them both. More things still that her father had kept from them.

It was her mother who had started the barn fire. On purpose. Though it had never been openly acknowledged by their parents, Logan was sure that she'd been schizophrenic and had lit the hay on fire during a delusional episode. Her father had tried to save her, but they didn't make it out on time.

What would Mark think of her if he knew all that?

She wasn't willing to be that exposed and vulnerable— that open to rejection. She didn't have that kind of trust in her. She could, however, turn the conversation back to him, and ask him about his necklace. Put the spotlight back on him and see if he was willing to open up.

"Why is that cross so important to you, Mark?" She really wanted to know.

"Why's it so damn important to *you*?" he shot back. With a curse he moved and rolled Lorelei on her back. Pinned her arms above her head. His hard thighs straddled her and his hands gripped her wrists. The hair on his calves rubbed against her legs and his feet wrapped over her shins, held them to the floor. Instantly heat flashed in her stomach and her blood warmed. All her senses were alert in the dark and it excited her to feel his large, hard body over her but not be able to see him clearly. It sent a shock of feminine wariness zinging through her.

"I'll make a deal with you, Mark. When you tell me your secrets, I'll tell you why the necklace means so much."

"They're none of your business. They're mine." His silhouette lowered toward her on his warning. His breath washed over her neck and she felt the weight of his erection on her stomach. Annoyance mingled with arousal inside her. Arousal won when his mouth found her jaw and he began kissing a moist, slow trail to her mouth. She strained against the hands still holding hers and released a soft moan. In one fluid motion he stretched his large body and settled over her. Hot flesh came up against her and her nipples grew tight. It was full body contact, bare skin to bare skin.

His mouth reached hers and he licked the corner of her lips until she opened it for him. Then he whispered, "Do you know what a triple is, Lorelei?"

She was melting again. "Yes."

"Good, because I plan on hitting one tonight."

Chapter 18

MARK HIT TRIPLES for three straight days off the field.
By the time they were back in Denver, Lorelei was pretty
darn sure she'd made up for her celibate streak of the past
two years in spades. Boy, he'd been right about one thing:
When he found something he did well he kept at it.

The door opened and he walked in to his condo just
as she was finishing up lunch. Two plates loaded with
grilled chicken salad sat on the black granite counters.
It had been a struggle to cook the chicken breasts since
all he had was a hunkering stainless steel contraption out
on the balcony. After ten minutes of muttering and then
five more of flat-out swearing she'd figured out how it
worked. Then she'd felt like an idiot. Turned out all she'd
had to do was push a stupid button.

She'd stood there frowning, thinking to herself that
she was glad no one was out there to witness her blond
moment when she'd caught wind of a snickering above

her. Her gaze had whipped up to see a young teenage girl hanging over the balcony above her; she'd obviously enjoyed eavesdropping.

Lorelei had turned to walk back inside when she'd realized that just about every teenage girl had a cell phone. So she'd strolled to the edge of the balcony, smiled up at the young girl, and introduced herself. She'd figured with the cell phone she could call Dina and be out of the locked apartment in no time.

After a few minutes spent convincing the girl to loan out her precious cellular, and then a few more spent finagling the phone down with a roll of blue yarn, Lorelei had grabbed it. Then she'd wasted no time dialing the number she'd memorized. She could still remember the conversation clearly.

Dina had answered on the fourth ring. "This better be good."

"Hi, Dina."

"Well, well. Look who's decided to grow some balls after all. Since you're calling me I assume you have the goods?"

Lorelei glanced through the glass doors at the living room. "Not exactly. I have it," she rushed on before Dina could interrupt, "but I need your help."

A drawn-out sigh came through the phone. "Really. What is it that I'm supposed to help you with?"

Talking to the woman was like listening to nails on a chalkboard—they both grated. "I'm still stuck in Mark's condo, but he's gone. I need you to come let me out and then I'll take you to get the necklace." It didn't sit easy with her, but she still needed the money. So much had happened between her and Mark since the beginning, and she was trying like hell to keep a divisive line between business and personal. But she couldn't help wishing there was another way.

Dina cut into her thoughts. "Silly girl. I can't help you. Have you forgotten that the prick has a restraining order against me? I'll be arrested if I step within a thousand feet of his place."

"But—"

"No buts. I'm paying you an ass ton of money, so figure this out yourself. I have better things to worry about than the two of you playing hanky-panky."

Frustration made her tone sharp and she snapped. "I'm beginning to think you don't actually want his charm after all."

Dina snorted and replied coldly, "I'm beginning to think you don't want the money after all."

Exhaling, Lorelei grasped at her composure. "I'm sorry."

"You might be sorry, but you better not make me sorry I hired you." There was a shuffle in the background. "I'm late for an appointment. Get off your ass and do something, Lorelei. Or stop wasting my time."

On that note the line went dead.

And that had been that. A perfect opportunity completely wasted.

Lorelei had stared at the phone with a sinking feeling and then gave it back to the girl. Maybe she was cursed. Because it seemed like every opportunity that cropped up just got smashed to bits, and that there was simply no way for this to work.

Or maybe was there a way and she just didn't want to see it because of what it would mean for her and Mark.

"What smells so good?" The deep timbre of Mark's voice drifted in from the foyer, pulling her back to the present. He appeared in the doorway and she saw his mouth drop. "You made me lunch?"

Lorelei glanced down at the plates and back to his shocked expression, her heart suddenly a little bubble of happiness. "Yep. I thought I'd prove to you I can make more than just brownies and junk food." She handed him a plate. "Here, eat this one. There's things in there called vegetables. You might just like them."

He laughed at the words she threw back at him and took the plate in a strong hand. The other ran intimately over her butt and squeezed. His mouth lowered to her neck and he nuzzled the sensitive skin. "I'd rather eat you." He gave her a playful nip and straightened. "But a guy's got to get his protein and roughage first."

She watched him swing a denim-covered leg over the back of a chair and sit down, laughter rumbling deep in his chest. He was doing crazy things to her emotions. And if she didn't watch it, her heart would start overruling her head. Veering into that sticky territory with a man like Mark was a surefire way to get her heart stomped on. Men like him didn't make love—they had sex. They didn't fall in love—they made women fall in love with them. And when they were bored or things got too real they bailed. Plain and simple.

Good thing she wasn't in any real danger. Sure she had feelings for him, but she had a handle on it. Absolutely. She could control her emotions and keep it all on the superficial level he was comfortable with.

She could and she would. Because she didn't want to know what it felt like to be left crying in Mark Cutter's dust.

"Hey, Lorelei. Why don't you come over here and sit by me. This is great, by the way. Any chance you could grab me a bottle of water from the fridge on your way?"

She grabbed her plate and reached inside the fridge for two bottles of the Rocky Mountain's purest. Nudging the door closed with a bare foot, she made her way over the cold tile and sat down across from Mark. His gaze traveled down her, over her snug white T-shirt and jeans, to stare intently at her feet. She wiggled her toes, and his mouth tipped at the corner in a small, crooked smile.

"I've been fantasizing about that little tattoo you got there, Lorelei." A hum of appreciation rumbled in his throat.

Her eyebrows shot up. "You have?"

Clear gray eyes filled with bad intentions lifted to hers. "Uh-huh. And it's sexy as hell."

Her gut tightened. She took a drink of water, let the liquid cool her insides. "That so? Is it dirty?"

The fork stopped halfway to his mouth. "As a mud pie, baby."

She let her eyes slide over him. "Is it kinky?"

The fork clattered to the table. "Why don't you define your idea of kinky for me?" His voice had taken on a decided edge. She felt a running shoe slide intimately up the inside of her calf and saw the look on his face. Her stomach quivered.

"Eat your lunch, Mark. I went to a lot of trouble to make that." Before she forgot all about it and jumped him like a nymphomaniac. Never before had it been quite like this. She was beginning to wonder if she should be worried.

She shivered when the shoe reached the junction between her thighs and pushed into her. His eyes were hot when he said, "Why don't you be my lunch? I'll eat as much of you as you want, sweetheart."

"Say pretty please with whipped cream on top."

Something hard flashed in his gaze and his brows lowered over his eyes. "I never say that word, Lorelei. *Ever.*"

Defiance sparked behind her ribs, lodged in her chest. "And why is that? Because you're a spoiled badass sports star and you think you're above politeness?"

He leaned back in his chair and crossed his powerful arms across his chest. "No. Because I don't beg and I'll never be brought to my knees like a pussy over a woman."

Pain slashed her, swift and vicious. "Is that a challenge?"

His smile was cold and his eyes hot when he said, "It's a fact."

For several tense seconds they stared across the table at each other. Battling back the wave of pain and anger that tried to wash over her, she took a deep breath and notched up her chin. No way in hell would she give him the satisfaction of knowing what he'd just said hurt her.

"Lucky for me I don't give a shit." It was the truth. Had to be. She turned back to her lunch and speared a piece of chicken and lettuce with her fork. There was nothing going on between them other than sex and his cross anyway. It shouldn't hurt her to hear him say how he felt.

But it did.

Damn it! Shoving away from the table, Lorelei strode to the counter and forced deep breaths. It wasn't supposed to go down like this. Mark was supposed to be nothing more to her than a means to an end, an enjoyable diversion from the monotony and oppressiveness that was her life.

When she'd first agreed to Dina's plan she'd had a secret. Not the theft, not the exchange of money. No, her secret was more personal than that. She'd wanted to feel something—anything—different from the smothering weight of emotions she'd lived with since the day her sister-in-law had died. A chance to feel alive, carefree, unhindered. To focus on something else for a moment in time other than Michelle's life-threatening heart defect, the mountain of medical bills, the way her brother was being eaten from the inside out.

It was a chance to be selfish and do something completely insane. To be a wild woman—free and spontaneous.

Strong hands gripped her hips and yanked her back against a rock-hard body. Breath rushed down her neck and his voice rumbled against her ear. "You don't give a shit about us, Lorelei? About what's going on here?"

She kept very still while her heart leaped behind her sternum. "That's right."

Mark's hands slid to the front of her jeans and he spread his palms just above her pubic bone. The heat seared her. "Oh, there's something going on, all right. You're just too cowardly to say it."

He was everywhere, his heat surrounding her. Anger and desire rolled off him and washed over her. She could feel his heart beating fast in his chest. Could feel the hard length of him pressing against her butt, the immense strength he kept on a tight leash. It vibrated through him.

She wasn't a coward. Not by a long shot. Lorelei was a realist. "The only thing between us, Mark, is sex."

He tensed. His hands slid up her body and cupped her breasts. "Not ordinary sex, Lorelei. The best of my life."

Arousal shot straight down to her crotch when he pinched her nipples between his fingers. "That's quite a compliment to me, considering how much you've been laid."

His teeth bit into her neck and Mark pushed her forward until the counter cut into her stomach and she was sandwiched between two granite surfaces. "Now that wasn't nice. You've gone and hurt my feelings."

He didn't have feelings. Bitterness swept through her at the unfairness of it all. Control was slowly slipping through her fingers and she lashed out, tried to grab it. Tried to gain the upper hand. "Sex isn't the only thing between us. There's something else."

He said with a growl, "Damn straight there's more. You've crawled inside my head. And I can't seem to get you out."

His words sent her heart racing and emotions bubbling up inside her so fast she nearly choked on them. She shook her head against the onslaught and swallowed hard. That wasn't what she'd meant.

"That's not it." She was fairly sure he was lying anyway.

He bent his head to her ear and said just above a whisper, "What is it, baby? What else do you feel between us?" His hand crept under the hem of her T-shirt.

"Your good luck charm."

The hand froze and he swore. "Why did you just have to say that? Goddamn it, Lorelei."

"Because it's the truth."

His deep intake of breath pushed his broad chest into her back. He dropped his hands. She thought he was going to step back, but he just spun her around to face him.

When she got a good look at his face something close to panic barreled hard into her solar plexus. He was furious. One hundred percent pure, pissed-off male.

"It's still just about the bottom line for you, isn't it? You really *don't* give a shit about this, about what's happening here."

This was her chance to lash out, define her boundary, and she took it. "That's right. It's all about the money. Nothing more."

Quicker than she could blink he picked her up and tossed her over his shoulder. She didn't have time to do more than gasp before he'd walked to the spare room and dumped her down on the bed. The bed creaked and she bounced once before she righted herself. He was already turned from her, crouched down in front of her bag and yanking clothes out.

"Don't do that. Let go of my bag."

His eyes spit anger at her when he looked up. "I can do whatever I want. You stole from me. Then you went and screwed me till my brain scrambled, got under my skin, and all you want from me is the money my cross will bring you?"

"I need the money. It has nothing to do with you. It's just the money. If I knew how to get it somewhere else I would, believe me." Scrambling off the bed she walked to him. He fairly vibrated with anger, but she wasn't scared. It was the first time he'd let slip how she made him feel.

"Tell me why you need the money so bad. What's so horrible in your life that you need money to fix?" His voice was low and hard.

"Do *you* need all the money you have? You make millions a year. What's so bad in your life that you need all that?" she flung at him.

He stood slowly and straightened to his full height. Then he braced his feet spread apart and clenched his hands into fists at his sides. "My life is damn near perfect. I'm trying to figure you out, so don't change the subject again. I want to know what's going on."

"Have you ever lost someone? Someone you loved?" She crossed her arms across her chest and stared him down.

Mark raked a hand through his hair in frustration and sighed. Some of the anger seemed to drain out of him. "Is this about your brother's wife?" he demanded.

She found no reason to lie. "In a way, yes."

He slowly advanced on her. "Is Logan in trouble?

Where are your relatives, can't they help? Tell me, Lorelei, I want to know." It was less a demand that time.

Taking a step in retreat she backed into the bed, almost fell down. She couldn't tell him. No matter how many times he demanded. "There are no other relatives."

Compassion softened his gaze. For some reason, seeing that made bitterness swell inside her. She didn't want his sympathy.

"I'm sorry. I didn't know. But you didn't answer my other question. Is your brother in trouble?"

Again, she didn't have to lie. "In a way, yes."

Warning flashed across Mark's face as he stopped in front of her. "Stop that. Tell me why Logan's in trouble."

She stared out the big window at a beautiful, cloudless sky. It was so blue it almost hurt her eyes to look at it. "Would you let me sell your necklace if I told you?"

He sighed and she turned back to him. "You know I can't do that. It means something to me."

"Who gave it to you?" She really wanted to know.

Mark sighed again and briefly closed his eyes. Then he opened them again and relented. "A girl. The first girl to ever kiss me."

"How old were you?" She asked because she remembered his sister saying he didn't have a girlfriend until after high school. Maybe it had belonged to his ex-wife.

"Seventeen. I keep it because she saw *me*. Saw beyond the imperfections, the defects."

What was he talking about? What defects? He was perfect. "Are you talking about how you used to stutter when you talked to girls?" That wasn't a defect. That was kind of cute, actually. If she'd been a girl he'd talked to with a blush and a stutter she'd have been a goner. His name would have been written all over her notebooks with little hearts.

Mark reached for her again, let his hands settle on her hips. "It's more than that. She saw value in me, told me I was special. She kissed me and gave me her necklace— told me it was for luck. I haven't stuttered around a woman since then. And I kept it close until you swiped it from me."

Now they were getting somewhere. And they'd effectively changed the subject from her family. Lorelei ran her hands up the soft merino wool of his sweater and sidled up against him. "What other problems did you have, Mark?"

He shook his head. "I'm not telling. You have to go first."

Never. "You've been playing well without your cross. Maybe you don't need it anymore."

His hands closed over hers and clamped them against his chest. A spark lit his eyes and turned them silver. "Maybe. But, I want it back, Lorelei. That hasn't changed. I won't let you take the money and run."

"Would you have me arrested if I do?"

Brows slashed low over his eyes and he glared at her. For a moment Mark was silent as a tic worked his jaw. Uncertainty flashed across his face and he sighed. "I don't know anymore. Hell, I might. I might let 'em cuff you and haul you down to the station just for kicks. Because I'd be really pissed if you did that to me after all this."

But he might not. That much was clear to her. He might not forgive her, their affair would most definitely be over, but there was a chance he'd let her walk. That was good to know.

He squeezed her hands, got her attention. His voice was ripe with warning. "Don't even think about it, Lorelei. I said I don't know. That doesn't mean you should go and find out. I'm unpredictable. Remember that."

She would. Definitely. She'd remember that today was the day she saw a crack in Mark Cutter's armor.

He stepped back and pushed up the sleeve of his sweater. He checked the time on his watch and raked another gaze over her that said they'd have a day of reckoning if she betrayed him. "I'm going to say it one last time. I want my lucky charm. If you run you'll regret it."

"You're threatening me?" She couldn't believe it. Well, yeah, she could. But still.

"Damn straight, sweetheart."

"All right. I'll give it back. You want it back, I'll give it back, but you've got to do something first." Lorelei held back a grin. The cocky jerk deserved what he had coming. She walked to the door and looked back at him.

And saw he'd been checking out her butt. His gaze wandered over her body, a grin cupped his mouth, and she could see his eyes were filled with male appreciation. "Yeah, what's that?"

"You have to get on your knees and say please."

LORELEI HAD THOUGHT her comment would get to him, but he'd surprised her. Instead of responding he'd just smiled, grabbed her hand, and tugged her from the room. Now she was standing with him in the parking garage, an incredulous look on her pretty face.

"You own a Ferrari? You have *got* to be kidding me."

Mark laughed and pushed the unlock button on his key ring. "She's beautiful, isn't she?"

He glanced at Lorelei over the gunmetal gray hardtop. She had her jaw open just staring at his baby. Then she asked, "Do you know what these things cost?"

God, she was a delight. "I've got an idea, yeah. Since I bought it."

She looked like she wanted to deck him. He grinned.

"You going to get in, or am I going to leave you here?"

Scowling at him, she opened the door to the sleek car

and got in, muttering, "People like you make me sick, you know that?"

He slid in beside her and ran a hand over the glass-smooth gearshift. "Yeah, we should all be shot. Buckle up, sugar, 'cause it's going to get wild."

"Up yours, Cutter."

"I love it when you sweet-talk me." He started the car, hit the gas pedal until the powerful engine roared, and smiled across the interior at her. "Call me an ass again. That one gives me serious wood."

Even though she tried to hide it, he saw a smile tug at her lips. She shook her head and looked out the passenger window as he made his way through the parking garage. He launched the sports car up the ramp and they merged into downtown Denver traffic.

When they came to a red light and stopped, she said, "You know what these are called?"

Yeah, Ferraris. The light turned green and Mark barely touched the gas—the car leaped. "No, what are these called?"

"Penis extensions."

He said around a laugh, "Honey, you've seen my penis. We both know there's no problem in that department."

She just gave a sexy little hmmm in her throat.

"You think there is?"

Finally she glanced at him, down at his dick, and back up at him. Laughter lit her green eyes and turned them to liquid moss. "I'm not answering that. It'll get me in trouble."

He knew she was goading him, but he fell for it

anyway. As he sped the car up the interstate on-ramp he said, "Is ten inches too small for you?"

"Ten inches? Huh. Felt more like five," she said, and laughed.

Saucy wench.

"Now, Lorelei, we both know that's not true. But if you want I can pull it out right now and we can measure it."

Her mouth dropped slightly and kind of floundered, making him laugh. Then she blushed. His breath lodged behind his rib cage and his hands gripped the steering wheel. Why did an innocent blush have such a strong effect on him?

"You've actually measured your penis before?" she said when she recovered, her voice full of curiosity. He slid his gaze from the road and his stomach tightened when he saw her gaze was firmly locked on his crotch. His dick jerked to attention and pulled his fly tight across his lap. Her eyes grew round.

"I was lying, Lorelei."

She licked her lips and a spear of lust shot to his groin. "You were? About what?"

"It's actually ten and a half inches." Now he really was lying. It was eight. And, yeah, he'd actually measured his pecker before. What guy hadn't?

"Lord have mercy." Her faced flamed.

Something settled around his heart, squeezed. He ignored it. "Why are you getting embarrassed now?"

"It's just hearing you say it, that's all. It's like me telling you my bra size." She paused, shook her head. "Wait, no, it's *way* worse."

Mark tapped the gas and whipped around a blue Ford Explorer. Conversations with Lorelei were never dull, that's for sure. She wasn't shy about things. He loved that about her. "What is your bra size? I've been wondering that actually, 'cause you've got great tits. They fill my hands up real nice."

Her laughter snuck inside him and warmed his chest. "Gee, that's a real sweet compliment, Mark."

"Anything for you, baby." He grinned. "So what size are you? D cup?"

She pursed her lips as she considered him. God, that mouth of hers drove him crazy. If he had to pick a favorite feature on her it would definitely be her lips. And in the past few days they'd been all over him.

"Thirty-four D," she said finally.

Hot damn. "Nice. Very, very nice."

Before he combusted or drove his shiny car off the road he changed the subject. But they'd definitely be fogging up the windows later. "Ever taken the interstate to Vail?" She shook her head. "There's this real pretty drive along a windy road up there that'll take us to Lookout Mountain."

"What's Lookout Mountain? A teenage make-out spot?"

They'd just passed Golden and were steadily speeding up into the base of the Rockies. Pine trees and aspens with their new spring leaves began to close in around them.

"It's actually not really a pull-out spot, but a windy road that rings the side of the Rockies. It's got a helluva view of Denver. I thought you might like to see it." He grinned and downshifted as they started to climb. "It's also a great make-out spot."

For the next hour conversation meandered casually from one trivial subject to another. Since their little entanglement earlier that day, Lorelei had been determined to keep the talk casual. Mark knew that he'd touched on something back in the bedroom. He'd seen it on her face. She was hiding something big. That wasn't a surprise. What was—what had bothered him more than he cared to admit—was that whatever it was hurt her deeply. The pain in her eyes had nearly undone him.

He didn't want to care. Didn't want to feel like someone had cheap-shot him in the gut with a line drive. Things weren't supposed be complicated for him. No messy feelings, no attack of conscience. Nothing but fun and games until it was time to move on. That was the way it had always been. Hell, he hadn't dictated it. He'd only followed the lead from the women in his life. Now he made no apologies for how he'd chosen to live. And, yeah, he knew what that said about him and he didn't care. He was trying very hard not to care.

After he'd found out about Dina's infidelity he'd vowed not to be a fool again. Not only that, but he'd made a promise to himself that he'd never tell another woman his secret. The way Dina had treated him after she'd found about his illiteracy had proven to him it was a mistake to admit to such a weakness.

Only one woman had ever known the truth about him—other than his mother, Leslie, and Dina. Molly

Sawyer. Sweet, innocent pastor's daughter and the first girl he'd ever loved. He used to sit behind her in church and spend the hour inhaling the rose scent of her shampoo. Then he'd go home and spend his nights fantasizing about her. He'd been a real Sunday regular there for a few years.

It never seemed to bother her that he'd get tongue-tied, stumble over his words. That he wore braces and had an acne problem. Or that his hands were too big for his frame and he tripped over his size thirteen feet regularly.

All she'd cared about was what was inside him. When he'd told her about his dyslexia she'd smiled so sweet his heart had nearly exploded. She'd told him with such youthful conviction that God didn't mess up when he made people. He'd made Mark perfect, just the way he was. She'd told him that he was special in the best way possible.

Then she'd taken off her little cross necklace and put it in his palm, curled her fingers around his. Told him to keep it for every time he felt unworthy and to remember what she'd said. And she'd kissed him. Soft and innocent on his trembling lips, and his world had burst with young love for her.

And that's why he kept the cross for good luck. Every time he felt overwhelmed, worthless, frustrated beyond endurance, he reached for it and it reminded him. Even after Dina had slept around on him, called him stupid, and broke his heart, he remembered.

It had kept him going.

And now there was Lorelei Littleton, come to take his

necklace from him. He wanted to be able to categorize her with all the rest—with Dina, the dozens of meaningless women of his past. It was where she belonged. No one special, no one to think about a year or two down the road.

But he couldn't do it. Beyond his control, his better judgment, his past experience, he was beginning to cast her in the same pure light as an innocent preacher's daughter with a heart of gold.

It scared the living shit out him.

The sun had sunk behind the mountains by the time he reached the winding curve of road that opened over Denver. He slowed the Ferrari and pulled over on the shoulder, the passenger side facing the city lights. He heard Lorelei's intake of breath as he put the car into neutral, shut of the engine, and pulled the e-brake. He left the interior lights on so the dash lights glowed over them before he turned to her and looked out the window.

The city stretched below them like an ocean of lights. Everywhere he looked he saw them glittering. To his left he could see Boulder and Longmont, their lights bleeding into the outskirts of Denver. Straight ahead he could see the long straight run of Colfax Avenue.

He liked the view from his condo. It was up close and involved. But this—this kicked ass. Almost otherworldly from the perch halfway upside the mountains. He liked to drive up there in his car, hug the Ferrari to the winding curves as he sped along. When he found an unoccupied spot he'd pull off and sit. Sometimes he'd pop in a CD, but most of the time he liked the quiet.

He'd wanted to share it with Lorelei.

"Mark, this is beautiful. Absolutely breathtaking."

His eyes skimmed over her and he felt his chest tighten. "Yes, beautiful. Breathtaking." he agreed, and didn't mean the city lights.

She turned to him. "Do you come up here often?"

He heard the question she was really asking. "I like to drive up here by myself time to time. I don't bring women up here, if that's what you're asking."

Her voice was soft, "You brought me."

Yeah, he had. He wondered briefly what that said about him, what it meant, then decided he really didn't want to know. His head was already too full of unwanted thoughts.

Reaching his arm out, he gathered a thick strand of her silky hair and rubbed it between his fingers. "I thought you'd enjoy it."

Her breath hitched and she whispered, "I am enjoying it."

He smiled at her and leaned close. "And I thought we could neck in the car like teenagers."

Her smile warmed his soul. "It's been a long time since I've had a make-out session in a car."

Tension curled in his gut when she licked those lush lips of hers. He made a strangling sound low in his throat. "God, you're so hot, Lorelei. Do you have any idea what your mouth does to me? I think about it a dozen times a day sliding warm and wet over my cock and it makes me burn for you."

She sucked in air and it shoved her amazing breasts

out toward him. Her voice sounded kind of breathy when she said, "I haven't done that yet, Mark."

An ache started in his balls and wove up his shaft. He shifted to relieve some pressure. It didn't work. Sliding his hand to the back of her neck, he pulled her close and whispered against her mouth, "I know. But a guy can dream."

She held him off by placing a hand to his lips. He slid his tongue out and licked the seam of her fingers. She moaned and her hand shook. Good. He was so hot and hard for her that he wanted her wet for him. "Tell me what you want."

"I want to kiss you."

His tongue slid between her index and middle finger and stroked the junction in lazy swirls. "Just move your hand, sweetheart, and you can kiss me however you want." He let his teeth nip the fleshy side of her index finger and she jumped. He grinned.

"Not there. I don't want to kiss your mouth." Her free hand slid up his thigh and settled over his hard-on, squeezed. "I want to kiss you here."

Mark froze as every nerve in his body screamed. He sucked in a breath. Before he could say anything Lorelei's hands were undoing his fly and shoving his briefs down until they caught beneath his testicles. Then her hands closed around him and he swore. Flexed against her hot little hands.

"Did you do this in the car as a teenager?" she asked as she lowered over him and her breath branded him.

He could barely speak. Couldn't think at all when her

wet tongue touched the base of his erection. She made a purring sound in her throat and her tongue slid up the length of him. *Sweet Jesus.*

His knee rammed the steering wheel when she gripped him in a hand and licked her tongue over the head in a long, lazy stroke. He thought he was going to come right then and there. "Lorelei," he growled, and grabbed a handful of her hair, arched into her mouth.

And when she finally closed that hot, wet mouth over him he almost did come. Desire tore through him and a groan ripped from his throat. With his heart pounding in his chest he stared down at her, and her mouth slid over him, gently suctioned him. When a lock of her hair fell across her face Mark brushed it away and held it at the back of her neck.

It was better than his fantasies—way better. He let out a growl and watched her, whispered, "I want you, Lorelei. I want to be inside your tight body."

Her movements stilled and she looked up at him, sat up. And it felt like he'd been gut-shot. The wind rushed from his chest. She was so incredibly sexy. Her green eyes glowed in the dim light, her lush mouth was slick and swollen, her hair a dark, tangling mass, her skin flushed with arousal. His lungs squeezed painfully. He'd never seen anything more beautiful in his life.

Mark pulled gently on her hair. "Come here."

She shuffled and he pulled her across the center console. Lorelei's butt landed against his hard-on and her hands dove into his hair. She licked her wet lips, desire in her eyes. Hunger clawed at him but something else was there, too. Something deeper. He kept his eyes open and locked on hers when he lowered his mouth. Instead of attacking her lips, he touched his tenderly to hers. When her eyes went wide and a little wary he smiled against her. "What's the matter, sweetheart?"

Hot breath puffed against his skin and she shook her head, lowered her mouth to his again. Mark watched her eyes drift closed and felt something inside him shift. He cupped the sides of her face in his hands and nibbled at her full lips, felt them tremble. Instead of devouring her, he let his lips trail over her face. Kissed her eyelids and heard her soft gasp. Pressed his lips against the warm skin of her temple and breathed in the scent of her.

He didn't know what was happening, was terrified to know. But when he felt her body shudder against his he felt it somewhere deep in his soul, in that place that hadn't been touched by anyone in years. And when he traced his lips over her jaw and saw a tear shimmer on her eyelashes, slide down her cheek, it almost unmanned him. He kissed the teardrop away and felt the rush of her breath against his left cheek.

"Oh Lorelei," he breathed. "What are you doing to me?"

She shook her head as a sound almost like a sob caught in her throat. Her plump lips pressed together and her chin quivered. On a ragged whisper she asked, "What are you doing to *me*?"

Her eyelids fluttered open and her beautiful eyes focused on him. Emotions swirled in the glimmering depths. "This was supposed to be easy. I don't know you."

He brought his mouth back to hers, his hands still cradling her head. Fire burned in his blood. "You know me, Lorelei. Better than anyone else has in a long time." Suddenly he couldn't remember why he'd ever wanted easy.

When she shook her head again he frowned and his throat squeezed. His voice was raw. "Say you know me, Lorelei. Tell me you know who I am on the inside. Not who the world sees, but who I really am." It was suddenly very important for him to hear her say it.

Something was happening between them and he wasn't sure if he was ready for it, or if he really even wanted it. But he knew that if all she still saw him as was the professional catcher with the bad rep he might just go crazy. God knew he'd made mistakes, but he was more than his reputation, he knew that. He needed Lorelei to know it, too.

Her small, soft hands covered his and his heart stopped. "You're not who I first thought you were."

It started beating again, a hammer in his chest. Touching his mouth to hers he felt the current of electricity that flowed from her—took it into him and welcomed it. Sinking into the kiss, his hands slid over her body and pulled her close.

He wasn't going anywhere.

Chapter 20

LATER THAT NIGHT Lorelei slipped back into Mark's condo and walked silently down the hall, his necklace cradled in her hand. She was thankful the hotel concierge had kept her envelope. She'd been a little worried that things left there had a shelf life. If so, she'd gotten there in time and that's all that mattered.

As she tiptoed down the hall the small metal cross warmed against her palm. When she stepped through the doorway to his room he was there, sound asleep in the middle of his bed just the way she'd left him. Moonlight streamed through the massive windows and sent shadows dancing over his prone body. Even in sleep it was hard and unforgiving, years of honing every muscle evident in the power of his shoulders, the strength of his thighs. In every way he was her fantasy come to life.

Stepping softly across the wood floors, Lorelei kept her eyes on him. If he made a move she'd lose it. Lose courage and the strength to do what she knew was right.

The game was over.

When he shifted in his sleep and turned his face to her, she was sure he'd woken. Her lungs seized up and fear skittered down her spine. But he didn't say anything and soon he was softly snoring again. The air she'd been holding rushed out of her on a whoosh.

Before she could change her mind, she very gently set his necklace on the bedside table where he'd see it in the morning. Then, unable to resist, she stared down at him one last time. Memorized the way he looked relaxed in sleep. His hair tumbled across his brow and his sensual lips were slightly parted. Deep, even breathing raised and lowered his broad chest in a slow rhythm.

The last time she'd stood over him like this he was a stranger to her. This time he was so much more, and it hurt to walk away worse than she'd anticipated. Much worse. But it was better that she did it now while she could. That she be the one to call it quits, put an end to the affair. She had to do it before he did.

The car ride had changed everything—every single game piece on the board. In one fell swoop it had sent them flying. It had stopped being a game and become oh-so-very real. So much was at stake.

Hearts were on the line.

She'd never felt more vulnerable. It was only a matter of time before hers was flattened. And Mark wouldn't even know he'd devastated her. She didn't blame him for it—it just happened with men like him. But she had to get out before it all came crashing down.

Relationships without trust always crumbled. No matter how true the emotions. She was realist enough to acknowledge that fact. But she was still too cowardly to risk the rejection. A little tiny part of her soul hated herself for that. Wished she were braver.

She wasn't.

Shaking herself, Lorelei turned to go. Mouthing a silent oath she spun back around and pulled her hair back with a hand. One last time to feel him against her lips, then she'd leave. She'd go back to her life and get over him. Forget about the ballplayer with the fast hands.

But right now she needed to kiss him. In the dark and quiet while he was deep asleep and he couldn't see that it hurt her to do it. She leaned out of the shadows and bent over Mark. The sleep-warmed scent of him filled her nostrils along with the lingering scent of their earlier sex. She refused to call it lovemaking. It might have been different from all the other times—more tender, less hurried, more intimate. But it wasn't love. They hadn't made love.

But it had felt awful close to it.

Her lips touched him and she felt the jolt all the way to her toes. It made her lips tingle and her abdomen turn to jelly. And not just with need.

She pulled her lips away.

A lock of wavy hair fell over his eye when he shifted and she reached up, brushed it back. She heard a low masculine groan and whipped her eyes to his. They were still closed, but his mouth had curled in a slight smile and he stretched like a panther awakening from a nap.

His voice was raspy. "Mmmm, what are you doing, baby? Come back to bed."

Panic slammed hard into her. He wasn't supposed to wake up! She had to get out of there—fast. If she didn't go now she'd miss her chance and then everything would go straight to hell. She didn't want to be there when that happened.

"I'll be right back," she whispered. "I'm going to get some water."

His hand reached up and found her breast, squeezed it.

Sleep made his voice heavy as it dragged him back under. "Hurry back, 'kay?" His hand dropped from her breast, left it achy with need.

Raking her gaze over him, Lorelei whispered, "Okay." Then she slipped to the door and stepped over the threshold. She grabbed the door, pulled it closed behind her. "Good-bye, Mark."

It took no time at all to grab her bags and leave after that. He'd never bothered with the extra locks. All she'd had to do to leave earlier to get his cross was flip the deadbolt and turn the regular lock. This time she didn't even have to do that. She just opened the door and was in the elevator less than a minute later.

Though she felt tears sting the backs of her eyes she refused to give in to them. Lorelei Littleton was made of sterner stuff than that. At least that's what she told herself to keep from bawling like a baby. Crying wasn't allowed. She'd known that from the beginning. Hell, she'd made the rule. So why was she being such a wimp?

Because for a suspended moment in time Mark had held her heart in the palm of his hand and made her cry. Made her feel such intense emotion it had terrified her.

She thought over that on the drive up I-25 to Loveland. When she pulled into her driveway at two in the morning she'd come to a lot of conclusions. None of which she liked the answer to.

Now she had to face her brother and tell him she'd failed. Explain to him that she'd had the money in her hands and she'd let it slip right through her fingers.

A sob ripped from her chest and Lorelei lowered her head until her forehead rested on the steering wheel. Giving in to the hot tide of despair and self-disgust, she let the tears come. The floodgates opened and like rain they fell in a steady rhythm down her cheeks, dropped to her lap. Inside the house fifty feet from her lay a little girl with a deformed heart of pure gold who was going to die.

But it was more than that. So much more. Feelings so complex and strong that she had trouble identifying them ripped at her chest. Grief for Michelle was there, yes, yet something long buried and deeply personal thrummed a wounded rhythm in her, too.

She'd had it—the passion, the adventure, the *life*. Everything her secret heart had longed for while it had been shoved to the back of her emotional closet and more urgent issues had taken precedence. It had huddled there, untended and ignored for years. Yet it had persisted. And just when it had finally been brought gently from the dark and set to bask in the warm, nurturing sun, she'd had to shove it back in again.

She ached. In a way that bordered on desperate and inconsolable. To have tasted her dream and had it in the palm of her hand, only to see it slip through her fingers like sifting sand, nearly undid her. The thought of going back to the life she'd had before Mark was crushing. Worse yet was the thought of the life that waited ahead for her now that there was no hope for Michelle.

Lorelei threw her head back and cried out, "What is wrong with me?" Why couldn't she do it? Why hadn't she been able to sell his necklace? Why all the half-assed attempts and self-sabotage? The answer was right there in front of her, naked with uncensored truth. She hadn't done it because Mark had once been a lonely, awkward boy who'd been given a gift by a girl. And Lorelei couldn't take that away from him.

She sat up and thumped the heel of her hand hard against the steering wheel. "Damn it, Lorelei! Damn you." Self-loathing washed through her and she welcomed it. Deserved it for the fate she'd resigned her niece to.

On top of it all she'd broken a promise. When she'd left she'd promised Logan the next time she came back she'd have the money. It was one more transgression on her list of things she'd screwed her family on. One more lie.

Logan and Michelle were all she had in the whole world. She couldn't bear it that she would lose one of them. She'd lost so many people she loved and didn't know if she'd survive losing another one.

Sitting up, Lorelei wiped her hands over her face and sucked in air. Logan might very well hate her afterward, but he deserved to know.

She stepped from the car and quietly closed the door, then walked to the house. All the windows were dark except Michelle's. A faint light glowed there from the teddy bear nightlight. But she doubted Logan was asleep.

When Lorelei stepped through the front door she knew her suspicion was right. She heard fabric rustle and saw the shape of her brother move through the darkness toward her. He never slept anymore and she knew it was from all the demons that chased him, cornered him in his sleep. He'd loved Susan more than she'd ever seen anyone love anybody and it was eating him up inside. Instead of getting better, slowly moving through the grief, he seemed to be sinking further into it.

She knew he felt like it was all his fault. Which was so wrong. He couldn't have known about Susan's weak heart, Susan hadn't even known. Not until it was too late. Even when they'd discovered the problem with Susan while Michelle was still in the womb they hadn't been able to abort her. It was their baby and they'd wanted her to live.

Lorelei cleared her throat and let the truth fall. "I couldn't do it. I had the chance and I screwed it up. I'm so, *so* sorry." Her voice cracked.

His arms came around her and he pulled her close. "*Shhh.* You didn't screw up anything, Leelee. I'm the one who should be apologizing, not you. I realized after you left the other day all the burden I've put on your shoulders and I'm sorry for it. It's not right for you to have to miss out on a good life, a happy one."

"Stop it. You're not a burden, damn it. You're my

family. I would do anything for you. And I tried. I really did, but in the end I just couldn't steal from him."

Logan kissed the top of her head and rocked her gently. His voice was tired and weary and full of love. "You're a good girl, Leelee. Of course you couldn't steal from him, no matter how much you might have wanted to. I would have been disappointed in you if you had."

She sighed into his arms, comforted by his embrace and the use of her childhood nickname. "But what about Michelle's surgery?"

He was quiet for a moment. "You let me worry about that. I know you love her, but she's my daughter. I've been thinking on something lately that might just work."

Instantly alert, she raised her head and demanded, "What? You're not thinking about riding bulls again, are you?" He kept silent and she knew she'd guessed right. She'd suspected as much. "Logan Michael, you can't afford to go back to rodeoing and have another bull tear into you like Sampson did."

His sigh was strong enough to part her hair. "Lorelei."

"Logan."

"I just don't see another way. If I can make it to Vegas and win, the pot would be more than enough to pay for Michelle's surgery and the rest of Susan's medical bills. I know it'll be cutting it close, time-wise." He tightened his arms around her. "I've been giving this a lot of thought and even if I don't make Vegas I think I can still scrape together enough for her surgery at least."

Lorelei felt a new worry settle on her shoulders. "But—"

"No more talk, Lorelei. I've made up my mind. We've got some time yet before we need to out-and-out panic over Michelle. I'm going to enter some local contests and get ready to take on Cheyenne in July. I've been out of the pro circuit since Susan died and I reckon it's well past time for me to get back in the saddle."

"You mean the back of a one-ton Brahman bull." Just one more thing for her to freak out about. Lovely.

Logan patted her back and stepped away. "Hey, you used to love watching me ride."

That was before he'd almost been mauled to death by a cowboy killer with razor-sharp horns. "Promise me you'll be careful. I don't want to raise Michelle alone."

"I promise, string bean." He ruffled her hair like only an older brother could get away with. "Now get up to bed, you've interrupted my reading."

As soon as she hit the upstairs landing, she headed straight for her niece's room. As she slipped inside quietly, her heart swelled with tenderness at the sight that greeted her. Flushed from sleep, Michelle sat in the middle of her crib cuddling a teddy bear, her dark hair a tangled mess. When she spotted Lorelei her mouth bowed in a sleepy smile.

Tears came to her eyes as she went to her niece. "It's late, sweetheart. What are you doing up?"

Big brown eyes looked up at her, innocent and sweet, and broke her heart. Reaching into the crib, Lorelei bundled the little girl in her bright quilt and cradled her in her arms. Leaning her head down, Lorelei inhaled the scent of her shampoo.

Michelle snuggled under the blanket and said, "Rockie." Then she pointed to the rocking chair in the corner.

"Do you want me to rock you, love?" Lorelei was already headed in that direction and sat on the blue cushioned chair.

She felt Michelle's head rub against her chest in agreement and started rocking gently back and forth. Her niece snuggled even closer and whispered, "Love, love."

Lorelei's heart squeezed painfully as a tear slid down her cheek and her arms tightened. She kissed her baby girl with trembling lips and whispered back, "That's right, baby. Love, love." So very much love.

MARK SLOUCHED AGAINST the bus seat and scowled as it traveled through San Jose traffic on its way to the Giants stadium. A hot ball of confused anger churned in his stomach. He still couldn't believe it.

Lorelei had left him.

When he'd woke this morning and found his necklace on the bedside table he'd known instantly. But like a fool he'd searched the condo, hoping that she'd turn up in one of the rooms. Hoping that she'd decided to give his necklace back and take a chance at an honest relationship with him.

He should have known better.

Just as she had the first night they'd met, Lorelei had bailed while he was asleep. Only this time she'd put something back, not taken something that didn't belong to her.

It didn't matter. He didn't care. Hell, his life was back exactly how he liked it. If he wanted to bang some anonymous woman after the game tonight he could. He had no strings holding him down, no girlfriend to answer to, nobody to care about his actions. And especially, no one trying to be his conscience, telling him he was more than he was. He didn't need any of that crap. He didn't need Lorelei Littleton and her complications.

In fact it was a good thing she'd left. Now he could get her out of his head and get back to being Mark Cutter. Get back to fast times and faster women. Be just like he was before she'd come crashing into his life with big breasts and bigger problems. Yeah, he could do that.

"Hey, Wall. You ready to rumble tonight?"

Mark turned to Drake and forced a smile. "You know it. First game in a new series—I'm all over that, brother. What about you?"

The first baseman scratched his huge chest and grinned. "I enjoyed some well-deserved R and R with a lusty redhead last night I'm all set."

Mark smirked. "How's a guy as ugly as you get so much action?"

"I'm charming," the veteran said seriously, then laughed. "And I'm loaded."

Mark's brow arched. "Ah. Gotcha."

Someone reached over the seat and slapped his shoulder. He turned to see Kowalskin grinning down at him. "So how's things going with you and the love of my life? She dump your sorry ass yet?"

Like last week's garbage, but he wasn't about to admit it. "It's going."

"So she gonna be at the game tonight?" Peter smacked his head when he didn't answer quickly enough.

Mark whipped around in his seat and snaked a hand out to clock him, but the pitcher moved pretty quick and he missed. "She's at home, and if you do that again I'm going to thump you. You forget I still owe you for the karaoke, old man. Why do you want to know so much about Lorelei?" It was beginning to piss him off.

The ballplayer grinned and said, "Because I've got a serious case of puppy love for your girlfriend." He ducked out of the way just in time and Mark's fist glanced off his shoulder. The jerk laughed. "Man, you've got it so bad."

He did not. "I do not, peckerhead."

"You're whipped, admit it. That gorgeous brunette has you by the balls."

He gave Peter the finger and turned around. "I ain't whipped." No way. He couldn't be. Lorelei didn't have him by the balls.

She wasn't even around anymore to grab them.

He brooded about that for the next hour, until the team hit the stadium and readied for the game. Then he blocked out everything and went to work.

The game flew by in a tunnel of concentration. Though he had his necklace back, he still played like hell. The team managed to pull off the win, however. 4–3, with the final run scored in the top of the tenth.

After the sports reporters had left and he'd showered,

Mark stepped out of the locker room with his duffel slung over the shoulder of his navy suit jacket. A couple of the guys were lingering in the corridor. Brexler motioned to him and he jerked his chin. "What's up?"

The fielder waggled his thumb at the other guys. "Some of us were just getting ready to head out for something to eat. Want to tag along?"

Maybe. It might be a good diversion—get his mind off Lorelei. "Yeah? Where you headed?"

JP spoke up. "To see boobs."

Paulson added, "The Frisky Kitten."

Huh. Topless women, booze, and nachos. Sounded like a dream come true. A real treat.

It sucked that he wasn't interested.

The guys were all staring at him waiting for his answer. "I think I'm just going to head back to the hotel and grab something from room service."

Drake eyed him and let out a knowing laugh that made Mark feel like punching him. "Catch you later then."

He turned, began walking and heard one of them making the sound of a whip cracking. Bastards. He rolled his shoulders and stopped. "Screw it. All right, I'm in."

He should've taken the hotel and room service.

All those gyrating bodies with naked breasts and it turned out he only wanted to see a certain pair of 34Ds topless. It'd taken him less than ten minutes after arriving to discover that lovely little fact. And he'd left, two hours and too many beers later, less than thrilled with what that said about him.

Chapter 21

FOR FOUR DAYS Lorelei kept up pretenses. Smiled and put on a happy face. Played with Michelle and dabbled at a few articles, helped Logan around the ranch. She even started to till the vegetable garden, prepping it for the seedlings she had started on the back porch. On the outside she looked like she was just fine.

Inside she was miserable.

Her brother was returning to riding bulls, she was afraid Michelle was coming down with a cold—which was never good and always terrifying, and she missed Mark. She'd gnaw off her left foot before she'd ever admit to it though.

It was for the best that she'd ended things. She knew that. He had a demanding baseball career, she had gardening articles. It didn't take looking beyond their jobs to see how very different they were.

Even if he showed up and asked her to take him back

she'd say no. It would never work between them. Men like Mark married flashy, exciting women. And women like her settled down with dependable, steady types.

She kept telling herself that as she pushed open the screen door and stepped outside. With Logan and Michelle gone for the day at the doctor for a regular checkup and physical therapy, she'd taken the opportunity to air out the house and clean. While she'd been away Logan had let the laundry pile up, and she'd spent the past few hours washing and folding.

She reached the clothesline and set down the basket full of wet clothes. With a snap of fabric she draped one of her brother's denim shirts over the line and shook her booty to Aerosmith's "Dude Looks Like a Lady" as it spilled through the open windows of the house.

Since it was laundry day and seventy degrees of Colorado perfection she had on a baggy sweater and her wash day shorts. They were hot pink cotton short-shorts that barely covered her behind and gave her legs a good tan.

She had to admit it felt good to be home. For a moment Lorelei closed her eyes and raised her face to the sun, let the warm rays wash over her. She stood there enjoying the slight breeze, the happy sound of birds chirping nearby, and the simple joy of hanging laundry on a warm spring day.

The phone rang, startling her. Lorelei hung another shirt before she reached for where it lay on the grass next to the wicker laundry basket. She bent down, her behind wiggling in time to the music, and snatched it up.

She hit the talk button on the cordless and draped a white T-shirt on the line. "Hello?"

"Lorelei?"

She almost dropped the phone. "Mark?"

"I've got an issue with you, sweetheart."

Her heart slammed into her chest. Why was he calling her? She dropped a pair of her wet panties. When she bent to retrieve them she heard him groan into the phone and she asked, "Are you all right? You sound like you're hurt."

"I'm fine." He didn't sound fine.

She ignored that because something else occurred to her. "How'd you get my phone number?"

His deep voice growled into the phone, "Don't change the subject, Lorelei."

Her stomach turned to liquid. She distinctly remembered wishing she could talk to him over the phone to hear his voice isolated like that. Now she was and his voice was like sex. Raw, rough, hard. Just like he was.

And what was she doing thinking about him like that anyway? It was over between them.

She grabbed another shirt, hung it, and tried for blasé. "What do you want, Mark?"

"You, sweetheart. I've missed you."

Well, that plan was shot to hell. She couldn't pull off blasé if her life depended on it. Not with his rugged, masculine voice saying things like that to her.

"Do you often pull your hair up on your head with a scarf like Daisy Duke? Did I ever tell you she was my first crush? It does wild things to me that you do your hair like her."

She frowned at his odd questions. "Sometimes I pull it up with one, yeah. Why are you calling, Mark? You got your lucky charm back."

His low chuckle sent shivers down her spine. "I've been thinking about you, fantasizing about you in a skimpy pair of hot pink shorts. Makes me want to take a bite out of you. Would you want that, Lorelei? Do you want me to eat you?" His voice had dropped to a hot whisper by the time he'd finished.

Of course she did. That was part of the problem. Being eaten by Mark Cutter was as addictive as a drug and she was an addict. She needed AA. *Hello, I'm Lorelei Littleton and I'm addicted to Mark Cutter's spectacular mouth.*

But he didn't need to know that. "Not particularly."

His laugh came through the phone and she felt her lips twitch in response. He had the best sense of humor.

"Be that way, then. But I'm wise to you, honey. So, question: What do you think about squirrels?"

Squirrels? What in the world? "In what context?"

"Cute or menace."

Lorelei contemplated and snapped another shirt, shaking out the wrinkles. "Cute, I suppose. Why do you ask?"

"Look around."

She spun and looked down, a gasp stuck in her throat. Sure enough, there was a fat, brown squirrel rifling through the wet laundry. She took a step forward and it leaped from her basket, dragging a pair of her wet underwear with it. The rodent raced, tail twitching, toward the nearest tree. Lorelei dropped the phone and dashed after it. What the hell was wrong with that animal? Somebody needed to tell it that squirrels collected nuts, not Fruit Of The Looms.

The faint sound of laughter stopped her dead in her tracks and twirled her right back around, her panties instantly forgotten. It was Mark's laugh. And it didn't sound like it was coming from the phone. It sounded far too close. Wait a minute . . .

Where was he?

Her gaze raked over the backyard, hungry for the sight of him. Nothing. Only the big old white house behind her, tulips and daffodils spread at its feet. Nothing but Steven Tyler, the great expanse of lawn carpeted with spring grass, and the tire swing swaying gently in the breeze.

Disappointment speared through her. Mark had just made a lucky guess, that's all. It's for the best, she told herself as she bent to retrieve the phone, held it in her hands, and stared at it. Should she even talk to him anymore? Torment herself with what she couldn't have? Draw out the misery? She hung up the phone.

Mark was a game she couldn't play anymore. Had stopped playing that night when everything had changed between them. It was her choice.

So why did she feel like crying?

Lorelei scrubbed her hands over her face, pressed fingers against the bridge of her nose, and closed her eyes against the hot sting of tears. Hadn't she vowed not to get in so deep with him that he could hurt her? That she wouldn't hang around long enough to see him leave? Well, she'd been the one to do the leaving. That was true. But her plan had backfired—her heart had gotten involved after all.

"Don't you know it's rude to hang up when someone's talking to you?"

Her body tensed, every single nerve went pinging through her. Opening her eyes, she dropped her hands and slowly turned around. Felt her world tip dangerously beneath her feet.

There he was, standing in her backyard in a pair of jeans, a black baseball cap, and a faded gray T-shirt that said "Baseball Players Give Good Wood," looking better than any man had a right to. And her heart plummeted right down to her pink painted toes. "What are you doing here, Mark?"

His running shoes made a muffled sound on the grass as he advanced on her. He hadn't shaved in a day or two and had the stubble to prove it. Dark blond hair curled around the bottom of his cap and smudges darkened the undersides of his eyes. They were hot, but his scowl was hotter.

He was mad, bad, and so damn good it hurt her heart to look at him.

Lorelei tore her gaze from him and swallowed hard. Focusing on a new foal and its mother in the pasture to her right, she said, "Go away, Mark. There's nothing here for you."

He didn't stop until he'd invaded her personal space

and his body heat washed over her. His voice had a hard edge. "You owe me an explanation, Lorelei."

Her jaw clenched and her eyes narrowed. It wasn't fair, just wasn't fair at all. She'd given him his stupid necklace back. There was no reason for him to be there, messing with her emotions. "I don't owe you anything. That stopped the minute you got your necklace back."

The brim of his hat shadowed the top half of his face when he lowered his head to her and demanded to know, "Are you telling me I'm nothing to you? That what we've shared means nothing?"

It meant everything. "That's right. It was a good time while it lasted, but I got bored so I left. No offense."

He made a warning sound low in his throat. She still refused to look at him—couldn't. "You got bored?"

She swallowed around the lump in her throat, nodded. "That's right."

"Prove it," he demanded after he cursed.

Why was he doing this to her? Wasn't he glad to have his life back? No strings, no complications. Wasn't that what he wanted? "I don't have to prove anything to you."

His hands shot out and gripped her hips, pulled her close. "Why?" he taunted. "Afraid you'll show your bluff? That I'll know you're a liar? News flash, I already know that. You've done nothing but lie to me—now it's time for the truth."

Emotions crashed over her in brutal waves, too much for her to take. She pushed hard against his chest. Taken by surprise by the attack, Mark rocked back far enough for her to yank out of his grip. The second his hands released her she was running to the house. She heard him let out a string of curses, then take off after her. "Damn it, Lorelei," he called after her, "come back here, you little coward. I'm not through with you."

Her pulse leaped at the threat and she barreled up the steps to the back porch, swung the door open, and had it ripped out of her hands and slammed shut. Mark spun her around and pinned her to the door as his large body came up hard against her. Air rushed from his chest and washed hot over her face. When she struggled he just gripped her hands and flattened them over her head.

"Let me go." She was breathless. His body was so close and it was making her crazy. He was making her crazy. Too many emotions racked her. It was just too much, period.

"No. I'm never letting you go again." Hard gray eyes stared her down. "Get used to it."

Lorelei stopped struggling. What was he saying? "It's over. We both know it. Maybe you just don't want to admit it because you're a sore loser."

Full, sensual lips scorched her skin when he kissed the side of her neck. "It's not over between us, sweetheart. Not even close. Now kiss me and prove to me how bored I make you because you don't feel bored now. You feel hot and soft and so damn good." His open mouth trailed over her jaw, making her knees weak.

His voice was caught between a demand and a plea when he whispered roughly against her mouth, "Kiss me."

She kissed him. Against her better judgment. Despite

the voice in her head screaming at her not to. She did. On the back steps of her house because she couldn't stop it. And because she wanted to more than she wanted anything.

A groan rumbled deep in his chest when her mouth opened under his. He released her hands and shoved a heavy thigh between her legs, pushed it against her crotch. The brim of his baseball cap hit her in the head and she ripped it off, flung it away. Then her hands were in his hair, pulling at him. They were streaking over his shoulders, her nails digging into the hard muscles. They were tearing at the waistband of his faded jeans.

She couldn't get enough of him.

When her hands dove under his shirt and encountered the hard, corrugated plane of his stomach he tore his mouth from her and growled, "To the bedroom. *Now*."

Because she couldn't help herself she clamped her legs around his lean waist and gave him wet, drugging kisses. She felt him fumble for the doorknob and push the door open. As he stumbled through the door into her house, the screen door slapping behind them, she ran her tongue over his throat. Tasted his skin.

"Jesus." His hands gripped the backs of her thighs below her butt, hard.

She laughed against his neck when he stubbed his toe against the wood stairs and almost toppled them to the floor. He released a very creative oath and flung a hand against the wall, saving them. When she sucked the skin below his jaw he tripped again. "Am I distracting you?" She bit his ear.

"Hell, yes," he ground out. "Don't stop."

She didn't, and when they crashed through the door to her room and hit the bed she was so turned on she almost came. Almost climaxed right then, when he fell on top of her and thrust his erection hard against her. Tremors started and her muscles clenched. She gasped, "Hurry."

Sunlight streamed through the open windows and fell across his face when he leaned back. He was so beautiful to her that her heart floundered in her chest. His normally clear eyes were totally glazed with passion. His lips were slick from her kisses. "Tell me what you want," he panted.

His hands raced over her stomach as he pushed her sweater over her head and threw it on the floor. Her white cotton bra went next, and when her breasts were free he groaned.

"I want you naked," she demanded, impatient for the sight of him.

In less than a minute he stripped until he was wearing nothing but skin and a condom. Her gaze ran hungrily over his body until it settled on his heavy erection jutting out from the patch of dark blond pubic hair. Her stomach shuddered in response to the sight of him, made her ache for what he had. She licked her lips and his hard-on jerked in reaction. He smiled and moved to her.

He stopped at the foot of the bed by her feet and Lorelei watched him reach out, felt the callused palms and strong fingers wrap around her ankles. Honed muscles flexed as he yanked, pulled her down the bed. "Your turn, sweetheart," he said with a wicked grin.

Then his hands stroked up the insides of her thighs, and nothing had ever felt better in her life. Lorelei knew it didn't change anything. There was no way for the two of them to work. They lived in different worlds.

But when his hand was palming her through her shorts and his fingers were slipping behind the cotton fabric to touch her where she throbbed for him, she didn't care. All she knew when his thumb found her clitoris and rubbed was that she'd explode if he didn't take her soon.

He shifted her, and then her shorts and panties were flying through the air. They landed on her computer desk, her flower-printed panties draping from the corner of her open laptop.

His harsh voice made her wet and achy for him. "I've spent the past week hard for you. Nothing's worked to cool the fever you've started in my blood. I'd think of your mouth, the way it had felt so slick and hot around me that night in my car, and my cock would turn to stone. When I'd try to take care of it I'd see your hot little pussy and my hand wasn't enough. I wanted your hands on me stroking me off, not mine." He dropped to the floor between her knees. "I needed you."

"Oh God," she breathed. Her hands fisted into the quilt.

Mark laughed and slid his hands under her behind, spread her thighs, and pulled her to his mouth. "He's not going to save you now." His wet tongue stroked boldly, aggressively over her. "You're mine."

A strong finger slid inside her as his mouth covered her fully and it made her cry out. "Mark!"

Another finger joined the first. His tongue rolled over her clit and he sucked. Used tongue and lips and suction on her with single-minded intent. Her muscles started to quiver on the edge of orgasm. Wanting more, wanting to go over the brink, she raised her knees and placed her feet on his shoulders, arched into his mouth.

A growl ripped from him, vibrated against her before he pulled back. His voice was rough, raw with arousal. "Look at me," he demanded.

She opened her eyes and stared down her body. Sexual desire rolled off him and slammed against her. His body was rock-hard beneath her knees. "Don't ever leave me again. Do you hear me? I don't think I could take it." Mark straightened slowly, pulled her bottom off the bed until she was positioned over him, the thick head of his penis pushing against her. "Say it. Tell me you'll never leave me again."

His hard hands gripped her butt and she tried to slide onto his erection, but he held her off. He rubbed the hot length of him against her opening until it was slick with her moisture and she was panting with need. "I need to hear the words," he said just above a ragged whisper. "Tell me you'll stay." This time it wasn't a demand. It was a plea.

But she couldn't say it. So Lorelei did what she knew they both wanted instead. She gripped the end of the bed and shoved off the edge, buried him all the way inside her in one long thrust. The hot circumference of him filled her up and she quivered around him, moved against him.

He gasped. "Damn you. Why can't you just say it?"

Because she was still so scared. So she shifted her hips and rotated them, ground flush against him. Rubbed against the base of him. Mark swore violently and pulled out, rocked into her. Thrust in deep again on a primal moan.

They forgot all about talking.

Chapter 22

"Come back to Denver with me."

Lorelei pulled her shorts over her hips and sighed. "What just happened doesn't change anything."

His voice was hard behind her. "It changes everything. Go throw some clothes in a bag. I'll buy whatever else you need to stay in town with me for the next few days."

And that right there was part of the problem, Lorelei thought. Mark could just about buy whatever the hell he wanted to just like that. No thought involved or financial struggle. Anything at all. He wanted it and it was his.

She and Logan had trouble some months buying groceries.

Not that she begrudged him the money, really. Some people just had it, some didn't. She knew that, was fine with it. Except when there was a situation like Michelle's. Then it got to her. Made the unfairness of it burn in her chest.

Glancing over her shoulder, she saw Mark pulling his

shirt over his head. A flash of gold metal caught her attention before gray cotton covered it. Bitterness and guilt mixed hot in her abdomen.

His good luck charm. Funny how she hadn't noticed it ten minutes ago when he'd been naked.

But she wasn't the least bit surprised he was wearing it. No doubt he'd kissed it like a long-lost girlfriend and put it on the second he'd spotted it. He'd probably permanently fused the clasp so it could never come off again.

Seeing it around his neck served a purpose, though. It reminded her that there was no solid, honest foundation for them to build a relationship on. When she'd pushed him that day he'd told her it had been a girl's—but whose, she still didn't know. Something else was missing, too. She just couldn't put her finger on it.

"I'm going downstairs to finish hanging the laundry. The front door's unlocked. You can leave that way." Lorelei didn't look back when she walked out.

She had just hung a pair of Michelle's little pink Wranglers when the creaking of the screen door signaled Mark's presence behind her. A small stain on the hem of the tiny jeans suddenly caught her interest. *Wonder how that got there.*

Out of the corner of her eye she saw him lean his tall frame against the trunk of an old maple. He rubbed back and forth against the bark as he scratched at an itch, then he crossed one foot over the other and hooked his thumbs in the front pockets of his jeans. The black ball cap was back on and pulled low over his eyes.

He looked casual, totally relaxed.

She knew better.

"Care to tell me what's going on in that head of yours, Lorelei?" Wow, he even sounded casual. Mark was a dang good actor.

Lifting the pant leg for a closer inspection, she scraped her thumbnail across the teeny mark. "Nope."

His sigh could have parted the tree branches. "All right. We'll play a round of twenty questions then. Are you mad because I didn't call or come by before today?"

I'll be damned, that looks like a grape jelly stain. She'd have to remind Logan not to feed Michelle peanut butter and jelly sandwiches. Too much sugar. "Nope."

"Are you upset because I didn't let you lead back there in your room just now?" He jerked his head in the direction of the house.

She snorted. "Get over yourself."

"I promise, next time you can tie me to the bed and have your way with me. How's that sound? You can do whatever you want. Except whips and chains—I'm not into pain." He was quiet for a moment. Then he said, "Well, except maybe some spanking. That might be all right if you ask me real nice."

A smile tugged at her mouth and she bit her cheek to stop it. Tried for a frown instead. "There's not going to be a next time, Mark."

"So spanking's out?"

She choked back a laugh. Smart-ass. "Go home and leave me alone. I've got work to do and Logan should be bringing Michelle back from therapy soon. Go harass someone else."

Lorelei didn't realize what she'd let slip until he asked quietly, "Why does Michelle need therapy?"

Shit. All humor left her and she grabbed up another damp pair of toddler jeans, hung them on the line, pinned them. "Never mind."

His voice was soft with his next question. "Is she who you were talking about that day in my room? Is Michelle sick?"

She spun to face him and threw the clothing in her hands at him as hot grief overcame her. "I said drop it!" Tears burned the back of her throat and stung her eyes. What right did he have to ask that like he really cared? Damn him. She just couldn't deal with this right now, not when so many emotions were at the surface. Raw vulnerability ripped through her and she pushed back violently, an instinctual response to the overwhelming emotion.

He pushed away from the tree and strode across the grass, avoiding the wet wads of clothes. "That's it, isn't it? What this whole thing has been about. Something's wrong with Michelle." His eyes filled with instant understanding and sympathy.

Feeling scared and cornered, she lashed out, all rationality lost in the face of such emotional bombardment. "You don't get to ask me questions about my life and my family like you give a shit. I want you to leave. *Now*." It was too much. He was tromping all over her personal boundaries and if he didn't leave soon she was going to lose it. She wasn't ready to let him in.

He was relentless. "Is she going to die, Lorelei?"

It was all suddenly way too much. Michelle, Logan, Mark. She lost it.

Tears sprang up and spilled down her cheeks. When he tried to reach for her she slapped out blindly against his hands. Something close to hatred flooded her. His life was so perfect. *He* was so fucking perfect. "I said *leave*! Go back to Denver and leave me and my family the hell alone."

His hands grabbed hers and he pulled her roughly into his arms as she fought him. He grunted when she elbowed him and said against her hair, "No. I've already told you that. Damn it, Lorelei, calm down and talk to me."

That was rich. "Talk to you? Why should I when you don't say a single thing to me?" She gave up on struggling when she realized the futility. His strong arms held her effortlessly. Her gaze lifted to his and she glared at him instead.

He stared down at her with confusion in his eyes. "What are you talking about? You know how I feel about you."

Did she? She knew he wanted her, found her desirable. Even that he found her funny. But, no, she didn't know how he really felt.

But that wasn't what she was talking about now. "What about you, Mark? Your secrets?"

A hard glint came into his eyes. "This isn't about me. This is about you finally telling me the truth about why you stole from me. It's because Michelle needs help or she's going to die, isn't it? And you and Logan don't have the money to get her the help. That's why you needed the money my necklace would bring so bad, isn't it?" He gave her a gentle shake. "*Isn't it?*"

She snapped like a wishbone. "Yes! She's going to die because I couldn't do it! I couldn't sell your cross. I couldn't do it because of how I feel about you. And I hate myself for it!"

Mark sucked in a breath. "Don't say that, honey. You don't mean it."

She wasn't so sure.

Blood roared in her ears and a hard ball was lodged deep in the pit of her stomach. She shoved out of his arms, leveled her gaze on him, and sent him away. "I *do* mean it when I say I want you to leave."

He let her go and she walked to the house. She refused to look back when she opened the screen door and stepped inside. She didn't stop until she was in her room. And she didn't give in to the feelings tearing at her until she heard a door slam and the sound of wheels crunching gravel as his car pulled away and sped down the drive.

Then she gave in and let the flood take her.

MARK PUNCHED THE gas pedal and the Ferrari responded. It rocketed down the gravel road. A turn came up and he took the corner at sixty, sent the car into a slide to make the Duke boys proud and grinned over the quick rush.

It was about frigging time he'd finally got some answers. Man, had he got them. Lorelei had folded like a deck of cards. He supposed he should feel guilty for what he'd just done, and a big part of him did. He felt bad for pushing at her, bullying her for answers until she'd snapped. But it had been necessary. It was way past time for her to come clean, and he'd realized that for her to do it she'd need some serious prompting.

See, he was learning how she worked, what made Lorelei Littleton tick. He'd reached a point of near desperation that night the guys had invited him out to the strip club. Ten times he'd picked up the phone to call her. Ten times he'd dialed Lorelei's number and hung up before it rang. And that was when he'd had to admit the truth, admit the guys were right.

He was totally whipped.

He wasn't ready to call it love, but it was way more than he'd felt for a woman in a long, long time. It was more. Stronger. Deeper.

So he'd sat there after hanging up the phone for the last time wondering when he'd become such a sissy. And that's when it had hit him. Just because Lorelei had a hold on him didn't mean he had to be a pansy about it. Instead of staring at the stupid phone like an idiot he could be figuring out how to get what he wanted. He'd always been more of a doer, so he got off his ass and did something.

He'd stayed up that night watching girlie movies and downing Lorelei's favorite drink. Triple-shot mochas with whip. Those he'd drunk because he was pathetic and had wanted some sort of connection to her while he'd been twelve hundred miles away. And probably because deep down he was a real sick, twisted masochist who liked to be punished.

Man, he'd paid for it the next day. But it'd been worth it. Well, not the mochas—hell, no. That'd just been plain stupid on his part. There was a reason he stayed away from caffeine. Now he remembered. Boy, did he remember.

But all those movies had been worth it because they'd showed him the same thing. When pushed too far the women got pissy and blew up. Then the poor, abused guy was able to get down to the real important stuff.

It had seemed like it might work for him, so he'd planned, strategized. And he'd managed not to call her for four whole days.

Late at night had been the toughest. He'd gotten used to her being with him so quick it was a little scary. And when she hadn't been there it'd been tough. He'd had a few sleepless nights. Well, all right. All of them had been sleepless. But he'd got what he wanted today so it'd been worth it.

Now he knew what she'd been hiding from him. And he was still jarred by the truth, but he'd wanted to know. Had needed to know deep in his gut that Lorelei was someone he could trust enough to tell about his dyslexia and know she wouldn't someday use it to belittle him. To make him feel worthless like his ex-wife had.

Now that he knew *why* she'd stolen from him, he felt much better. He'd needed the truth. And it turned out it was something he could help with.

Now he had some plans to put into action.

Chapter 23

HE GAVE HER a tomato plant.

She cried when she saw it. Bawled just like a baby.

Lorelei found it on the front porch wrapped up in red ribbon just like a Christmas present. A plain white card was tucked among the tender young leaves. It said:

For your writing inspiration. Think of me.
   Mark

How could she not think of him? He occupied her head every minute of every day. Days had passed since she'd blown up at him. Long, agonizing, awful days.

Sitting down on the top step of the porch and stretching out her bare legs, Lorelei picked up the plant and set it in her lap. Stared at it as she blinked back tears and felt sorry for herself. She missed him so much it was just pathetic.

Then she got mad. "Ugh. You were the one that ended it." She pulled the card from the fuzzy green branches and looked at Mark's message. His handwriting was terrible.

Logan rounded the barn, turning her attention. Lorelei watched him stride over to his pickup and toss a pair of spurs, some braided rope with a bell, and his black and red chaps into the backseat.

So he's going to do it, she thought. A part of her had known he would eventually. There really wasn't another option. And to be honest she couldn't blame him. He'd always been an amazing bull rider and stood a decent chance of making some real money if he stayed healthy.

That's what scared her. Logan was only thirty-two and had more battle scars than most men obtained in a lifetime. He'd been hooked, stomped, mauled, and kicked. And the idea of him climbing on the back of a living tornado again made her insides shrivel.

"Hey, Lorelei. Can you bring me my riding glove? It's sitting in the rocker over by you." Logan glanced at her from beneath the brim of his black cowboy hat. "Thanks."

With a sigh she pushed off the porch and set the tomato plant on the railing. Sliding the card into the front pocket of her running shorts, she grabbed the tan kidskin glove and walked over to him. "So you're really going to do this."

His jaw tightened and he slid the glove between his leather belt and Wranglers. "We've talked about this."

"No, we didn't talk. You informed me of your decision. There's a difference." Anger rose up and she clamped it down. She reminded herself he was only doing what he had to.

He sighed and looked down at her. "I'm sorry for that, sis. But we both know this is something I have to do." He reached into the backseat and grabbed a black protective vest. "I'll be fine. I knew you'd worry so I got one of these. I reckon a bull's horns will have a mighty hard time getting into me with this on."

Not if it really wanted to. But it was pointless to argue. "I'm not going to waste my time fighting with you over this, Logan. You're even more stubborn than I am. All I'm going to ask is that you be careful. And that when you sit down on the back of whatever beast you're riding today you remember you have a daughter and sister who love you very much."

He looked down and studied her profile. "I will, I promise. Have you been crying?"

Lorelei hugged her arms to her and nodded. "Yeah."

He grabbed her jaw, turned her face to him. "Shit. I'm sorry if I've made you cry."

"It wasn't you." She pushed his hand from her chin. "It was another jerk."

Logan searched her face, brows drawn together over his dark eyes. He asked softly, "Does he mean that much to you?"

She shrugged. There was no use talking about it, anyway. It was over. "He doesn't mean anything to me. We enjoyed each other for a while, that's all. We don't even know each other."

Her gaze slid over Logan when he turned and jogged to the porch. Once there he grabbed the tomato plant and walked back over, placed it in her hands. He read the question in her eyes. "I saw the note when you were on your run. Seems to me a guy who'd drive over an hour to bring a woman a plant is more than just *enjoying* things for a while. Too much work for a fling." He looked purposefully at the plant. "He brought you a tomato plant, Lorelei. How'd he know that would get to you more than roses ever could? It means he's either been paying very close attention, or he's a damn good guesser. Nobody's that good."

The delicate little leaves beckoned her and Lorelei traced a finger over a branch. She caved. "All right. I care about him, Logan. A lot. But it's over."

He raised a black brow at her. "Yeah? Doesn't look like it to me." He gestured to the plant in her hand.

Maybe Mark was still interested, maybe not. It didn't matter, not if they didn't trust each other. "He's got a secret. Something that he doesn't want me to know."

Logan considered. "Have you asked him about it?"

She shot him a look full of exasperation. "Of course I have."

He gave her a small lopsided smile. "Yeah, I'm sure you have. Forgot a moment who I was talking to."

Enough. She was done talking about Mark Cutter. He spent far too much time in her head as it was; she didn't need to fill her days with conversations about him, too. "I'm heading inside. Michelle should be getting up soon and I want to take a shower before I get breakfast ready for her. Did you want me to make you something, too, before you go?"

"Nope. I scrambled some eggs and cooked some bacon earlier." He started to turn, paused, turned back. "Hey, Lorelei?"

She looked up from her plant. "What?"

"I went out to feed the horses about six this morning and saw your plant then. I just realized your ballplayer must have got up damn early to get that here, is all."

Yeah, she'd thought about that, too.

The phone was ringing when she stepped in through the front door. Doing a quick search she found it under a mountain of newspapers. She grabbed it. "Hello?"

"Good morning, sweetheart. Did you get my present?"

Since he couldn't see her she gave in to the urge and smiled into the plant she still cradled in a hand. "Maybe."

Goodness, his voice was sexy. His deep chuckle had lust snaking through her. "You wearing any skimpy shorts today? I've been fantasizing about those little pink ones of yours. Want me to share the details?"

Absolutely. "Not really."

Lorelei belatedly realized what he'd asked and looked down at her black running shorts. Her head snapped up and she darted to the front window, looked out. "You're not hiding somewhere outside again, are you?"

"No, why?" He sounded sincere.

Maybe he really was psychic. "Never mind."

His voice took on a tense note and he said just above a whisper. "You're wearing Daisy Dukes again, aren't you?

Lorelei grinned. She wasn't, but it'd be fun to mess with his head. "Uh-huh. Black silky ones."

He groaned into the phone and the ragged sound had her biting her lip to keep from laughing. He was too easy.

"Are you wearing panties?" Heat flooded his voice.

Yep. Granny panties. Ugly cotton ones she wore when she went for her runs. "No." She made her voice sound a little breathless. "Just smooth bare skin."

She heard a clunk and a curse and realized he'd dropped his phone. Laughter bubbled up and she put the phone between her breasts and covered her mouth with a hand as it let loose.

Lorelei gulped in air and forced the giggles under control. She put the phone back to her ear just in time.

"Are you saying what I think you're saying?" Mark asked, his voice all hoarse.

The connection crackled with static and she moved to the dining room for a better signal. "Uh-huh."

He sucked in air. "Whew." He didn't say anything else for a moment. Then he growled, "That's so hot."

Suddenly she didn't have to fake a breathless voice. Her lungs squeezed and her nipples grew tight with instant arousal. She opened her mouth to say something about it when she heard another voice in the background and said instead, "Who did I just hear?"

His voice was strained when he answered, "Peter Kowalskin."

Warning bells went off in her head. "Where are you?" She had a feeling she knew the answer.

"On the plane getting ready for takeoff."

Oh God. "You've been talking to me like this when there've been other people around?"

"Nobody can hear me and most everyone's asleep anyway," his deep voice responded.

Her face caught fire. "I'm hanging up now."

"Wait," he rushed. "Don't go. Come to my place for dinner Tuesday night. I'll make something."

She wanted to. She *really* wanted to. But she wasn't sure if she should. "Mark—"

"I want to talk to you, Lorelei. About things."

Mark wanted to talk about *things*. That could only mean a few *things*.

How could she refuse?

She sighed and hoped she was making the right decision. "All right."

MARK HEARD THE knock. Heat coiled in his abdomen.

He reached for the wineglasses and called over his shoulder, "It's open."

The door shut softly and the sound of boots clicking on hardwood echoed lightly in the foyer.

"Yum. Something smells good."

He turned at the sound of Lorelei's voice and bobbled a glass. Only quick reflexes kept the crystal from smashing against the tile floor. Grabbing it mid-air, Mark set it quickly on the counter and slid his eyes leisurely over her. It ought to be illegal for a woman to look that fine, was all he could think.

He grinned and tossed her words back at her. "Yum. Something looks good."

Man, did she ever. He'd had no idea before that cowboy boots could be so frigging sexy. But when Lorelei wore them paired with gorgeous legs, a white top, and a short denim skirt, he decided he'd seriously been missing out. Had missed one vital fact every man should know.

Cowgirls rocked.

She'd even topped off the whole look with a denim jacket, and by piling her dark hair on top of her head in a messy bun, tying it with a red bandana. Just like she'd worn it the other day when he'd watched her hang laundry. He knew she'd done it on purpose just to torment him. Make him remember the hot bout of sex up in her bedroom.

Right. Like he'd ever forget that. She'd rocked his world so damn hard it'd taken him two days to level off afterward. Lorelei Littleton was one dangerous woman.

She tilted her head to the side and smiled. The heat of it kicked his pulse up a notch. Make that *very* dangerous woman. Potent as hell.

"Hey there, Mark. Whatcha cooking?"

Was it his imagination or was there an extra swing in her hips when she walked up to him? Like maybe she was up to something. Like maybe she was thinking about seducing him. God, he hoped so. He wanted to be seduced by Lorelei in the worst way. "I thought I'd make my lemon and dill salmon."

Lorelei stopped when she was less than a foot away and smiled at him through her lashes. "Sounds good. I'm *real* hungry."

So was he. For her. But when he reached for her she sidestepped and laughed.

She shook her head and the ends of her red bandana danced in the air. "No way. You said we were going to talk."

He grinned and leaned his butt into the counter. "All right. We'll talk. Why don't you tell me if you're wearing any panties beneath that sexy little skirt." She laughed and he shook his head. "I'm serious. Are you wearing panties or going commando?"

Lorelei smoothed her slender hands down the faded denim on her curvy hips and asked with a flutter of lashes, "You mean what I'm wearing under this ol' thing?"

His gaze followed her hands and heat pooled in his belly. "Yeah, that ol' thing."

Pure mischief lit her eyes, made them sparkle under the recessed kitchen lights. The brown leather arches of her cowboy boots slid against her tan calves when she put a hand on the counter and shifted her feet. She placed a booted foot behind the other and rubbed it against the back of her leg. He swallowed hard. "I'll tell you what I'm wearing under my skirt," she said with relish, and he knew he was in trouble, "but you have to say please."

Mark raised his eyes from the frayed hem and Lorelei's bare golden skin to see her staring at him with bold challenge in her mossy green eyes, an eyebrow arched. She clearly remembered his comment from a few weeks ago and was trying to see if he still felt the same way.

He didn't. Not in the least, but he was still working on the words and wasn't quite ready to get into the heavy stuff. "I was just being polite. I figured I'd give you the chance to tell me before I stuck my hand under that pitiful excuse for a skirt and found out for myself."

Heat spread across the skin on her chest and up her neck in a pink flush. Turning on the wood-stacked heel of her boots, she scrambled to the fridge and opened it. "Got some white wine chilling or anything?"

Mark knew he'd flustered her and it felt so good to know he had that kind of effect on her that his chest seized up tight. He almost started to get worried when he couldn't breathe after several seconds, but then the air rushed out on a whoosh. It just went to prove his earlier point that Lorelei was a seriously dangerous woman.

"I've got a chardonnay chilling on the top shelf." Something cold was definitely a good idea. Before he spontaneously combusted from staring at the smooth, firm skin on the backs of her thighs. "Why don't you pull the salad out while you're at it?"

For a few more seconds he stared at the backs of her firm legs until his pants began to pull uncomfortably tight from a hard-on. Her head was still in the ice box and she couldn't see, so he reached down and adjusted himself so his fly wouldn't pinch. Then he raked a hand through his hair and sucked in a lungful of air.

"So, I watched the game last night. I still can't believe that John Crispin scored against the Giants star pitcher like that," she said all casual-like, and pulled the wine bottle and salad from the shelf. The door swung shut with a tap of her boot and she shot him a grin. "You looked good out there, too. I just about jumped off the couch when you threw yourself at this outside ball and barely snagged it with your mitt. How do you regain your feet so quick after flinging yourself on the ground like that?"

Intense pleasure swept through Mark and warmed his chest. No wonder they'd won. His good luck charm had watched the game. Lorelei had cared enough to tune in even though she wasn't a baseball fan. The truth of it slammed into him on a burst of happiness.

The timer went off on the stove and he pushed away from the counter. He reached in a drawer for a pot holder and said over his shoulder, "You see the way Drake hammered on the Giants second baseman Javier Martinez during the sixth inning? It took eighteen stitches to close up the gash in his forehead."

She chuckled, and the warm, husky female sound of it slid inside him. "Yeah, I saw that. It was so sweet."

God, what a woman. She'd watched a nasty sports fight and thought it was *sweet*.

No wonder he was crazy about her.

Chapter 24

"PINK," LORELEI SAID as she stared at Mark over the rim of her wineglass. "Every shade from fuchsia to baby. I'm absolutely crazy for all things pink."

Her stomach flip-flopped when he slid his gaze over her face and his mouth cocked up in a crooked smile. A light breeze ruffled the dark blond curls around his right ear. He leaned against the railing that rimmed the huge balcony and crossed one jean-clad leg over the other.

"The ultimate girl color. I should have known." He smirked and took a sip of wine. A drop of chardonnay moistened his lips and he pressed them together, considered the question. "My favorite color? Hmm. I'd have to say I've developed a real fondness for the color green lately. Light mossy green with a tiny hint of blue when it gets heated." He looked pointedly in her eyes and grinned. "Yeah, I'm a sucker for that color, but I gotta say I'm getting a real fondness for pink, too."

Lorelei glanced out at the Denver lights as her insides turned to jelly and she felt, well, flustered. Mark was charming as hell when he wanted to be. Shaking her head with a chuckle she said, "You could charm the habit off a nun if you put your mind to it, you rotten man."

A delighted laugh came from her right and she glanced up to see him smiling down at her. "You think so?" he asked, his deep voice ripe with amusement. "I might just have to test that theory next time I'm around one. But in the meantime I'm still waiting to hear all about your panties."

"You're relentless," she said around a smile, and placed her arms on the metal railing, leaned into it. The thick cream sweater Mark had given her to wear provided a cushiony barrier against the cold steel. "It's my turn for a question. What's your favorite movie?"

"That's easy. *Bull Durham* hands down. The character played by Tim Robbins in that movie slays me. What about you?"

Lorelei thought about it for a minute. What was her favorite movie? "I'd have to say *Sliding Doors*. You've probably never seen it." A siren wail drifted up from the street far below, followed by the blare of a fire engine horn. The sound seemed to echo off all the glass from the huge buildings while she waited for his reply.

Mark surprised her. "That's the one with Gwyneth Paltrow, right?" She nodded. "I've seen it pretty recently, actually. It's not too bad."

"When did you see it?"

"Back in San Francisco at the hotel."

"Are you telling me all you big bad ballplayers sat around eating popcorn and watching chick flicks instead of hitting strip joints?" she asked in disbelief.

"Nah," he said. "After. And I was drinking mochas, not eating popcorn."

He wasn't serious. "Are you serious? You drank a mocha?" She didn't believe him for a minute. He had to be yanking her chain because he didn't drink caffeine.

"Yeah, and those damn things were hell on my system. Gave me a seriously upset stomach, but I'd wanted to see what you were so crazy about, so I gave it a go. I'm just grateful it wasn't game time and I wasn't strapped into my gear. Would have been a real Imodium AD moment for sure."

Lorelei laughed at the visual. "Thanks for that glorious image."

He winked. "Anything for you, baby." He paused as he reached out and flicked the end of her bandana with a finger and said, "I love the cowgirl look, by the way. I never realized that I could get turned on over a pair of cowboy boots before. And now I'm in real danger of getting a woody every time I see a pair, 'cause they'll remind me of your sexy legs tucked into them."

Mark thought her old brown Dingos were hot? Now that was interesting. "When I was eleven my sister, Lucy, got a pair of pink Ropers for Christmas and I got this purple suede coat with tassels. I was so crushed about it that she switched me presents, even though the coat was too small for her. I wore those boots every day for almost a year. Then after she died I couldn't stand to put them on at all. Every time I saw them it reminded me of her and how much I missed her." She sighed and looked out at the Denver night. "I was sixteen before I put on another pair."

The memory of that Christmas used to break her heart, now it made her smile. And she was glad for it. She still missed Lucy, just like she missed her parents and Susan. She'd learned through each loss that the most important thing was remembering the good stuff. The small things that could make her smile. Just like Lucy's pink cowgirl boots.

Mark shifted and laid a big, warm hand on the back of her neck. His thumb caressed the skin below her ear. "Tell me about your sister."

Lorelei figured that if Mark knew about Michelle he might as well know it all, so she nodded and said, "Lucy was only eleven months older than me. One day when I was twelve we went out riding, just us kids. Logan, Lucy, and I. We did it all the time and went out to our usual spot. It's this creek that runs through one of the far pastures. Anyway, Logan and I were splashing around in the water when Lucy screamed. We went running and found that a rattlesnake had bit her left arm right by her elbow. By the time we got her back and to the hospital it was too late. She'd had a fatal reaction to the venom. She was only thirteen when she died."

"God, Lorelei. I'm so sorry," he said quietly.

A breeze ruffled his hair when she turned and looked at him. He looked so wonderful standing there holding his wineglass with the city lights at his back, casting a golden halo around him.

She gave him a small smile and said, "It's all right. I've learned how to endure the grief, mostly. People die. I know that fact better than most. There have been many in my life I've loved and lost. I've dealt with that, but I just can't just sit back and let Michelle die, too. That's why when your ex-wife offered me the money for stealing your good luck charm, I did it. All I could think of was Michelle and that it would pay for the surgery she needs. I didn't think of you, or Dina, or anything else. I thought only of saving her life."

He was silent for a minute as he studied her. The hand dropped from her neck and slid down to cover hers on the railing. "Will you tell me about that, about what's wrong with Michelle? I'd like to understand."

Suddenly she wanted him to understand, to know it all. Even if it meant that she was handing him the key to unlock her past. Vulnerability was only one emotion that she felt with him now. The others were so strong that the tide of them washed a soothing balm over her fears and calmed her. Maybe it would backfire and she'd be rejected once he knew every dirty bone of every skeleton in her closet.

But maybe it wouldn't.

And she found that the time had come that risking rejection was worth it—worth what she stood to gain. He was worth the chance and she finally had the courage.

He made her feel brave.

Lorelei cleared her throat and looked down at their joined hands. "She was born with a congenital heart defect commonly known as AV canal. Basically she has a hole in the middle of her heart that pumps extra blood into her lungs. The defect was too complex to repair when she was a baby so the doctors put a band around her pulmonary artery. It didn't work the way they'd wanted and now she has a severely enlarged heart and needs open heart surgery. If she doesn't get it in the next few months the pressure on her lungs will kill her."

Mark took her glass and his and set them down. "Honey, come here." Then he opened his arms and folded his large frame around her, hugged her to him. She slid into the solid warmth of him as he said, "I won't ask if your brother has medical insurance or if you've looked at payment options because that's just idiotic. You wouldn't be here now if there'd been a choice aside from Dina's offer. Instead, I'll ask what he's doing about getting the money now."

Weight lifted off her shoulders at his words and she felt all the tension she'd been holding release in a rush. Her body sagged in relief. His response was exactly right.

Being on the other side of her fears was freeing.

Lorelei rested the back of her head against the hard muscles of his chest and savored the feeling of his strong arms around her holding her tight. "Logan was a professional bull rider before his wife died. Susan died shortly after giving birth to Michelle so he quit to stay home and raise her with my help. Now he's gone back to riding to get the money and it terrifies me. I don't want to lose anyone else, Mark. I'm not sure I could handle it."

She felt his chin rub against her hair as he murmured, "It'll be all right, sweetheart. Trust me, it'll all be okay."

God, she hoped so. "Yeah, there's always the hope I'll win

the lottery." It felt wonderful to be able to confide in him, to talk about her feelings and what really mattered to her. To know that she could open up and share with him. To trust.

The night wind shifted and swept cool and soft across her bare legs, giving her goose bumps. It felt good to stand out on the dark balcony with a cool wind blowing gently and him pressed against her back. She focused on that, on the moment, and let the other stuff fall away until she was tuned into the man behind her. Took comfort in him.

Mark raised a hand and his fingers closed around a loose strand of her hair, rubbed it gently. Lorelei watched a light flick on in a building window directly across from them. She watched a man in a dark suit drop his keys on a side table. He loosened his tie and shrugged out of his jacket. For a moment he just stood there, the look on his face bleak. Then he strode over and pulled the drapes closed, blocking her view.

It was amazing how people went through their lives. So many of them on autopilot, going through the motions alone. Living without real connections—without reaching out. Scared and empty and hurting. Too afraid to risk the pain, so they ended up living hollow lives that wore them down to nothing.

She didn't want to be one of those people. But she wondered how far away from that she'd really been.

Not that far.

The truth was jarring and she cuddled further into Mark, silent and thinking.

They stood together quietly, soaking up the night,

soaking up each other. She could feel his strong, steady heartbeat pounding in his chest against her back. When she turned her face to his neck she inhaled the clean, male scent of him.

Somewhere deep inside her sighed.

"Lorelei?" he asked quietly after a few minutes.

She kissed the base of his throat, a gentle press of her lips. "What, Mark?" she murmured against him.

"I want to tell you something."

She nuzzled the indentation of his neck, completely lost in the feel of him. "What's that?" she whispered.

He released a slow breath. When he spoke his voice was soft and warm. "You're the most amazing woman I've ever known. Everything about you gets me. It's kind of terrifying. But it's why I have to tell you this. You have the right to know, so you can back out and leave. I have to give you that choice."

She heard him release a shuddering breath and felt his large, strong body tremble. Whatever he was about to tell her was really hard for him. She still felt so open to him, so close that she didn't do what she normally did. She didn't run. She didn't brace herself. She just gave him a reassuring pat with her hand and said, "It's okay, baby."

That seemed to be the response he needed, because he breathed deep and relaxed. "I'm dyslexic," he confessed on a rush of air. "I can barely read and write and it's so hard. It's an awful feeling, you know? Being so limited and having no control. I've been trying like hell to learn to read, but it's just so fucking hard for me. My brain's warped and after all these years of struggling I still barely can."

Instantly she understood what he was saying, what he was sharing. Knew the reasons why he had those books in his library, why his handwriting was so terrible. And he was trusting her enough to tell her.

He'd decided she was worth it.

Suddenly she couldn't fight anymore. His words melted the last of her resistance. She pressed her lips tenderly to his neck and turned in his arms, looked up. Looked deep into his eyes, saw them swimming with emotion, and fell. Tumbled headlong into love with Mark Cutter, the catcher with the fast hands. And it was the best feeling in the world.

He wasn't used to talking about his dyslexia, she knew that. And he probably hated exposing himself, admitting to the slightest vulnerability. But it was their time of honesty.

So even though she was still reeling from the fall and her heart went out to him, Lorelei placed her hands on the sides of his face, pulled his mouth to hers, and gave him a gentle kiss. "Thank you for telling me that. You're a strong, wonderful man."

He blinked, like he wasn't quite sure he'd heard her right. Stared hard into her eyes for several heartbeats. Then he smiled, a slow and beautiful turn of his mouth. "You're a hell of a woman, Lorelei Littleton."

It was good of him to think so. And having him say so did crazy things to her insides, so he was pretty incredible, too. "You're not too bad yourself," she said with a smile of her own as her heart overflowed with love for him. "I'm proud to be your girlfriend."

Big, warm hands slid down her back as he wrapped her up in his arms. Lorelei knew the instant his confidence returned because the vulnerable look faded from his eyes and the tenseness of his body melted away. "Not girlfriend, Lorelei. You're more than that. You're my woman," he said possessively as he lowered his head over hers. His firm, full lips settled warm over hers in a kiss of such tender emotion it brought tears to her eyes.

Never in her life had she been kissed like that. Like she was the most precious thing in the world to him and he'd die if he couldn't hold her. And she kissed him back the same exact way.

With lips and tongue and hands—with every part of her, Lorelei let her love for him show. Told Mark with her body that yes, she was his woman. And that he was her man.

He pulled back with a throaty moan and looked into her eyes. "I need you, sweetheart. Come inside with me so I can show you how much."

They went, and without words he showed her. He told her with slow hands and long kisses. Sensual caresses and gentle demands. He took her high with the most earth-shattering lovemaking she'd ever experienced. When she cried out for him he held her until the tremors subsided. When she came back down he surrounded her with his big body and cradled her in the comfort of his arms.

And when tears slid down her cheeks and fell to his shoulder, he kissed them away and whispered, "I know, baby. I know."

Chapter 25

THEY WERE INVITED to a barbecue at Peter Kowalskin's house. When they got there the driveway was already full of cars and Mark had to park down the street. He pulled his Range Rover over and parallel parked. It was absolutely gorgeous out and he was looking forward to the get-together because he had Lorelei with him. She alone made everything perfect.

"Does Peter tend to throw big bashes at his house during the season? Is this normal? Aren't you guys supposed to be in some zone where you eat, breathe, and think only about your next game?" she asked as they walked hand-in-hand down the tree-lined sidewalk.

He glanced down to see her eyes sparkling up at him and grinned. "Well, the great thing about Kowalskin is that he's a completely screwed-up individual. He never does things like a normal person. He said after the last game he thought we all needed an afternoon to chill, so here we are. Getting ready to *chill*."

She wrinkled her nose in the cutest expression and said with a laugh, "It's *so* not good that he's the team's unofficial leader. He's more likely to get you all into trouble than keep any of you out of it."

Mark tugged on her hand with his and pulled her up against his side. "That's why we like him. Just pray he doesn't have the kegs set out this time. Last time he got the brilliant idea for us all to do beer bongs, and Drake Paulson got so hammered he went swimming in the buff. The sight of his big hairy ass bobbing around on the back of that blow-up crocodile will haunt me till the day I die, I swear."

She laughed over that and it made him smile. *She* made him smile. Every little thing about her.

"I could have lived happily for the rest of my life without that visual," she said.

He regarded her out of the corner of his eye as they walked up the brick paved driveway. "Speaking of visuals, I'm still crushed you wouldn't wear your cowboy boots today. You have to promise to wear them tonight, okay?"

"Okay."

"Naked."

She tripped over the front step and he laughed as he kept her from falling. She sputtered, and just to see her flustered he added, "Then you've got to give me a lap dance in them, Ms. Rodeo. And after that you have to ride me like a bucking bronco so I'll walk bowlegged for a week."

She stopped and stared at him openmouthed. He was referring to the night they'd met. When she found her voice she muttered, "Oh God, I'd forgotten about that."

"I haven't. You were a real naughty girl that first night, Fonda Peters."

"Don't remind me."

Mark didn't knock on the front door. He just pushed it open. "Honey, I plan on reminding you as often as possible. I'm mean that way."

The sound of live music and rowdy voices greeted them when they walked through the door. A crowd was gathered in the huge living room listening and shouting encouragement to Peter as he played a blues number on his acoustic guitar. A female voice began singing the words as Mark slid his hand to the small of Lorelei's back and escorted her down the few steps of the sunken room. Instantly he recognized his sister's voice.

Lorelei caught sight of who the performers were and pulled up short. "Wow. That's a surprise." She glanced up at him. "Leslie's got a great voice."

His sister did have a pretty awesome voice. She used to annoy the hell out of him with it as kids, though. "Yeah, she does."

"Must run in the family," she said.

Mark nodded in greeting to a few of his teammates and leaned down to say, "What do you mean?"

Light green eyes leveled on him and Lorelei smiled. "That you've got a great voice, too. It's so raw and rough, just like a rock star's. I got all gooey inside when I heard it."

Joy flowed warm inside him at her words. "I tell you

what," he said against her ear, "I'll sing for you like a rock star anytime you want if it'll make you look at me like you did that night."

The curve of her neck was calling his name so he kissed her below her ear as she asked, "How did I look at you?" She sounded a little breathless.

He nuzzled that sweet spot just below her ear because he couldn't help himself. When he felt her shiver he grinned. "Like you were falling for me," he said. Opening his mouth, he traced her ear with his tongue and then whispered, "Tell me, Lorelei. Are you?"

She bit her bottom lip and didn't answer. Mark chuckled and slid his tongue over the curve of her ear and nipped. "Chicken," he teased.

The crowd broke into enthusiastic applause and Mark raised his head reluctantly. All he wanted to do was touch Lorelei and if he couldn't restrain himself he'd embarrass them both.

"Pete and Leslie play awesome together," Lorelei murmured.

Kissing her hair, he agreed. "Yeah, they do. My sister's been trying to get him to agree to playing a night at the club this fall after the season's over. So far he's held her off, but she'll get her way. When she wants something she's relentless."

Pete set down his Gibson and strode toward the two of them.

"You and Leslie sounded fantastic, Peter. Have you two played together much?" she said when he reached them.

"Thanks, sweetie. We've jammed a few times before, but not too much. Leslie's got a great voice, though, doesn't she?" Peter said as he started to escort Lorelei down the hall to the back of his house.

Mark watched them go. Actually, he watched her butt go as the two of them chattered on like old chums as they walked down the hall. Releasing a slow breath as his gut tightened, he glanced around Pete's house at the scattering of players and their significant others. Most everyone had plastic cups in their hands, which could only mean one thing: The beer kegs were back.

"Oh hell," he muttered, and began his way down the carpeted hall to the kitchen. If Paulson got shit-faced again and decided to strip in front of Lorelei, Mark was going to have to hurt him. He entered the large, open kitchen and spotted Lorelei through the French doors out on the patio. He started walking toward her when he noticed she was standing next to Leslie and another player's wife, holding a plastic cup of beer in a hand. And that reminded him about the kegs, had him changing direction and heading toward the group out by the pool.

Drake was over there lounging in a plastic chair with his feet propped on an ice chest. Granted, it was a little early in the season for swimming and Paulson was still dressed, but Mark wasn't taking any chances. He wanted to make sure he'd get laid again sometime this century.

"Move your feet, Paulson, so I can grab a beer," he said when he reached the first baseman's side. "Looks like Pete hid the crocodile this time. Actually, he probably threw it away after the way you molested the poor thing."

Paulson slid his feet off the ice chest and grinned. "Nah, he gave it to me and I named her Betty. She's been living in my hot tub since last September."

Mark pulled out a bottle of Guinness and smirked. "Whatever floats your crocodile, man. I just wanted to make sure there wouldn't be a repeat performance. I've got a sweet little thing over there who'd get real embarrassed over seeing you naked." He grabbed a chair nearby and sat down.

"Are you afraid she'd like it, sissy boy?" Drake said and scratched his chest. His Hawaiian shirt was halfway unbuttoned and his chest hair sprang out like a brown afro.

Mark eyed him and drawled, "Yeah, I'm real worried about that." The guy was ugly as a mutt.

A woman he didn't recognize appeared by the veteran's side with a plate full of food. She looked about twenty-two and had a tight little body and huge smile. "Here you go, Drake. I got everything you wanted and I made the burger up just the way you like. Let me know if you want anything else, okay?" She spun to leave and said over her shoulder, "Oh, and I canceled my date tonight so go ahead and pick me up at eight. See you then. Bye boys."

Mark stared after her, his bottle of ale suspended in mid-air. Then he blinked hard and looked at the guy in disbelief. "How in the hell do you do that?"

Paulson grinned over his shoulder at the girl's retreating form and then at Mark, pure male ego in his eyes. "It's a gift, brother. A great big goddamn get-me-laid gift."

Yeah, it was something all right.

"You know, the beginning of this season I'd have given my left nut for that *gift*. Now, I'm cool and you can keep it, 'cause I've found something so much better," he said, and his gaze slid over to it. To Lorelei.

"You ready to admit you're in love yet?" Drake asked and took a pull on his beer.

Lorelei laughed over something one of the women said and the sound floated over to Mark, into him. Curled right around his heart and hugged it tight.

Was he ready to admit he was in love with her?

Maybe.

And he was a little shocked that it didn't terrify the hell out of him. "I'm getting there, man."

Paulson kicked Mark's foot with one of his own to get his attention. His voice was dead serious. "Hey, I want you to listen to me."

He tore his gaze from Lorelei and looked at Drake. "I'm listening."

The first baseman hooked a thumb over his shoulder and said, "That one's a keeper. She's beautiful, funny, and she doesn't take any shit from you. She's not like what we normally date, brother. She's better than that. So do us all a favor and don't screw it up."

HE WAS WATCHING her again. Lorelei knew it because the skin on the back of her neck began to tingle. Turning her head, she scanned the large backyard and the people until she spotted Mark by the huge, peanut-shaped pool.

He was relaxing in a white patio chair with his long, muscular legs stretched out in front of him and crossed at the ankles. When he caught her gaze he raised his bottle of beer in a small salute and grinned.

She could practically feel the heat in his eyes as he stared across the cement patio at her. It melted her insides and began to warm her up degree by degree. In fact, it was getting pretty darn hot outside, period. Raising a hand, she grabbed her loose hair and twisted until she'd created a roll. Then she coiled it like a bun at the nape of her neck and let the breeze wash over the heated skin.

Out of the corner of her eye Lorelei watched him watching her. Tried to understand what that look was in his eyes. Couldn't. So she stared at the rest of him instead. At his black "Big Willie's Hand Jobs—Lubrication and Tire Rotation Specialists" T-shirt and distressed jeans. At his platinum Rolex and gray running shoes, and at the mass of dark blond hair that curled at his neck, framing his smooth-shaven face.

She was so in love with him it was almost pathetic. Lorelei felt like grabbing a notepad and scribbling his name all over it with little hearts. It was all she could do to keep from giggling like a schoolgirl. And if she wasn't so damn thrilled about it she'd be seriously annoyed at her own behavior.

"Earth to Lorelei, hello?" Leslie elbowed her and jolted her back to reality. "Stop drooling over my brother for a moment so I can ask y'all a question."

"When you say 'y'all,' do you mean all of us or just me?" she asked as she tore her gaze from Mark.

Leslie chuckled and tossed her pale blond hair over her shoulder with a feminine swing of her head. "I mean *you*. Do you think Peter is attractive? From a purely platonic standpoint and all since I know you're crazy about Mark, of course."

Lorelei thought about it for a second. "Absolutely. Not in a conventional way or anything, but in a rugged, rough-and-tumble sort of way. Why?"

"I was just wondering, that's all," Leslie said.

Lorelei just stared at her expectantly and waited. If Leslie was asking that kind of question it was because she was interested in the answer. And Lorelei wanted to know why she was interested.

"Oh, all right. I'll give. There was this moment earlier when he was playing his guitar when I thought he looked kind of sexy."

"It was kind of sexy." Actually she had no idea what Leslie was talking about. She'd been too busy playing with Mark. But she figured that probably wasn't what Leslie wanted to hear.

"What was kind of sexy?"

Both women turned at the voice. Mark stood right behind her. Lorelei dropped her hands and her hair spilled over her shoulders. "How do you do that?"

"Do what?" he asked.

"Move without a sound. You're huge."

The rotten man laughed and winked at her. "It does my ego good to hear you say things like that."

Leslie snorted and said, "He's always been the humble sort. Can't you tell?"

He reached out a muscular arm and hooked it around Lorelei's shoulders, pulled her back against him. Lowering his head, he pointed his beer bottle at Leslie and said, "Has my sister been telling lies about me again? She'd lead you to believe that I've got an ego problem."

Leslie looked down at her deep red fingernails and laughed. "You do have an ego problem. You're a diva."

He gave an exaggerated gasp. "I can't believe you just said that." The steel band of his arm tightened around Lorelei's collarbone and he said in her ear, "This coming from a woman who prides herself on using her looks to get out of speeding tickets."

Well, Lorelei thought, *she's beautiful.* And if she looked like a tall, blond Nordic goddess she'd use it, too.

"But I've never been given one now, have I?" Leslie challenged.

"Hey, sis. How long did it take you to get ready today?" Mark teased, and took a pull of his beer.

"A lot less than you, pretty boy."

Lorelei shook her head and laughed at their sibling banter. It sounded like how she and Logan used to be before his wife had died. And she hadn't realized until just that moment how much she missed that ease and lightheartedness between them.

That in turn reminded her that she had to go home tonight. Which in turn reminded her that she'd been neglecting her duties there. And that made her think of sweet little Michelle.

In all the rush of emotions and excitement of falling in love with Mark she'd forgotten to put her family first.

In fact, she'd sort of tossed them aside and pursued her own wants with no regard to them, and that was wrong. Her parents had taught her better than that.

So how did she balance it all?

Mark and Leslie continued to tease each other so she pondered the question. Could she find a way?

Maybe. Family was family, and with it came certain responsibilities. There were things you did no matter how you might feel. But there was also the fact that she deserved a life of her own, too. One full of happiness and enchantment and wonderful, blessed optimism. She wanted to be with Mark.

And that pretty much was that. She'd figure it out.

"Lorelei?"

"Hmm?" she said, tuning back in.

Mark hugged her close with his strong arm and kissed the hair just above her right ear. "What's on your mind? You got pretty quiet there for a while."

"I was thinking about Logan and Michelle and that I should check in. It's been a few days since I've been home and I should see how everything's going." She tilted her head a bit as he kissed the side of her neck. Little tingles of pleasure darted down her throat. He had such a fantastic mouth.

He worked his way up to her ear, and when he spoke, moist breath washed over it, giving her goose bumps. "Your cell phone is in your purse. Here, you can use mine." She felt him shift behind her. "Reach in my pocket and grab it. It's fully charged."

Now that was a loaded one. Lorelei laughed at the

double meaning. Reaching behind her, she felt around for the opening to his pocket and heard his quick intake of breath. "You say the most romantic things, Mark. And those sweet words just capped it." She found the opening, wiggled her fingers inside. "I'm officially in love."

He went rigid behind her.

Too late she realized what she'd said. And it was too late to take it back. So even though her heart jumped up and started racing frantically she kept calm and slid her hand all the way into his pocket. "Ah, got it."

"That's not my cell phone, sweetheart," he said, and his voice sounded strange, hoarse.

"Oops, sorry." No she wasn't. She'd done it on purpose because she was a bad, bad girl. And she'd wanted to divert his attention.

Suddenly her hand was cradling something fully charged in his pocket and it *wasn't* his cell phone. Then his body jerked and he growled hotly against her ear, "You'd better not be screwing with me, Lorelei."

They both knew what he meant.

If her heart beat any faster it could leap right out of her chest and run away. God, could she do it? Did she have the guts to say it? To tell him how she felt even though he probably didn't feel the same way?

Absolutely.

She wasn't ashamed of her feelings for Mark. "I'm not messing with you," she said, and felt his chest expand on a deep breath against her back.

"Say it, then. Let me hear you say it," he demanded.

Lorelei inhaled deep as she pulled the phone from his

pocket, slid it in hers. Then she laced her fingers behind his head and pulled him closer, pressed her cheek to his.

Was this how she was going to declare her love to Mark for the first time?

It was, and her heart leaped at the thrill of it. "I love you, Mark."

His whole big, strong body shuddered against her. Right there on the sun-warmed patio with thirty or so people milling around eating burgers and drinking from plastic cups. Laughing and having a good time. With Drake Paulson eyeing the pool a little too intimately for her comfort and Leslie a few feet away sitting on John Crispin's lap drinking keg beer.

It was perfect. It was exhilarating and oh so right.

"God, Lorelei," he breathed into the crook of her neck. His thick hair tickled the bare skin of her shoulder. "You undo me."

They stood there, deep in the moment, until JP Trudeau walked in front of them near the pool looking like a surfer boy. He even had the bead necklace and baseball cap on backward to complete his look. It was hard to believe he wasn't that much younger than Lorelei. He looked like a teenager. JP stopped and said something in French that Lorelei couldn't understand. But she could tell by the naughty look on his face that it wasn't very polite.

Suddenly Mark was laughing into her shoulder, his whole body releasing tension. He looked up and smiled at JP.

And that's when it occurred to her that Mark had understood. "Hey, you speak French?"

He nodded. "Yep."

She hadn't known that interesting little fact. Maybe he'd talk dirty to her with it later. "What did the little punk say?"

Mark said something back in French to JP that had the rookie shaking his head and laughing. Then he said to her with a chuckle, "He called me a randy bastard and said if he wanted to watch porn he'd rent a video or hit Drake's collection."

Drake had a porn collection? Gross. "Oh yeah? Well, what'd you say back?"

"Didn't you want to call your brother?" Mark said, effectively sidestepping her question.

Oh well, she'd let him have his way for now, but she'd find out later. There were ways to make a man talk. She palmed his phone. The plastic was still warm from his body. "Yes, I did and I do. Is there someplace quiet I can call from?"

He glanced around the patio. When he spotted Peter he called out, "Walskie, come over here for a sec."

Peter looked up from near the grill and strolled over. When he passed the rookie, he grinned wickedly, whipped his arms out, and shoved hard. The kid hollered and went splashing into the pool. Peter just kept right on walking as JP came up shouting curses at him.

Laughing, Peter blew a kiss to the soaking shortstop and then slapped Mark on the back. "What can I do for ya?"

Men. Did they ever grow up? Lorelei stepped away from Mark and asked around a chuckle, "Is there someplace I can make a call from that's quiet?"

Peter looked at her and nodded. She noticed for the first time that he had really awesome pale blue eyes. "Sure. If you go upstairs you'll find a weight room directly on the left. No one should bother you in there. Want me to show you where it is?"

Mark was about to comment, so Lorelei jumped in and cut him off. "No thanks. I'm sure I can find it." She looked at Mark. "I'll be right back."

"I'll be waiting with bells on," he said with a sexy grin.

Lorelei was still laughing when she hit the large staircase at the front of the house and jogged up. When she reached the open landing she turned and went left. Her sandals padded softly against the thick, cream-colored Berber. She found the weight room and stepped through, closed the door behind her.

Baseball posters and pictures of half-naked women decorated the beige walls, and super expensive-looking equipment filled the room. Lorelei took a seat on a black weight bench and dialed home. While waiting for Logan to answer she studied the baseball posters. The chicks in bikinis she skipped.

The answering machine picked up and Lorelei was about to hang up when the message came on. "Lorelei? Lorelei where are you? You're not answering your cell phone. I left messages." It was Logan's voice, panicked and shaky.

Her stomach lurched and she gripped the phone until her knuckles were white. Her heart started beating hard as she listened.

"Michelle stopped breathing. Her lungs are failing

and she's been airlifted to Denver Children's. " His voice cracked and he continued, "Oh God, what do I do? What do I do if she doesn't make it?"

Terror flooded her and she thought she was going to puke. Almost did.

Oh God no, please.

"Where the hell are you, Lorelei? You should be here. She needs you to be here."

Lorelei felt the accusation down to the very core of her, felt it rip her in two. Looking frantically around the room she found a pen on a string by a chart board. But no paper to write on. She shot to her feet and lunged over to an unframed poster and tore off a corner. A sob racked her body as she reached for the pen and her vision blurred as tears pooled in her eyes and spilled over.

This can't be happening. Oh God. Michelle.

With shaking hands she wrote down the directions that Logan left on the answering machine to the Denver Children's Hospital. Then turned and raced from the room in utter panic to find Mark so he could drive.

Her mind went blank with shock and she turned the wrong direction in the huge house and wound up in a bedroom. Letting out a cry she ran back down the hall with the directions crumpling in a hand and a fist to her mouth to hold back the flood.

Pushing past people until she burst out on the patio, Lorelei pulled up short and whipped her gaze around until she found Mark.

He turned from a small group and the smile died on

his face when he saw her. "Lorelei. What's wrong? What's happened?"

The concern in his eyes broke her and she couldn't talk. Could barely see through the tears. But, God, she wanted him to hold her, comfort her. Tell her Michelle would be all right, that she wouldn't die.

But she didn't want him anywhere near her, too. Because all she could think was that it was happening, that her brother's baby was dying and she hadn't been there when she was needed the most. And if she'd loved her family as she should, if they'd have been first, she wouldn't be at some backyard party with Mark.

Logan had left a message on the answering machine because he'd no way to get ahold of her. Because she hadn't left Mark's phone number. She'd been too wrapped up in him to even think about it.

"Lorelei. What's happened? Tell me." Mark took a step toward her and she shook her head, stopping him.

Finding her voice she said, "Here," and held out the wrinkled piece of paper. Biting her bottom lip she waited for him to take the directions. She was very close to losing it.

He took the crumpled paper, looked down at it, and said, "What is this?"

She lost it. She didn't know why, but Mark's question pushed her right over the edge and she lashed out unnecessarily, viciously. "She's going to die and it's your fault!"

He slowly raised his head to look at her, hurt and confusion in his eyes. "What did you just say to me?" he said very quietly.

She hurt so bad inside for Michelle it felt like she was breaking apart. "I never got the money! Don't you understand? You never let me get the money, and now she's going to die." She was being unfair and cruel. She knew it.

Knew it and couldn't stop it.

MARK FELT THE swift lash of pain and thought he'd entered the twilight zone.

Lorelei stood staring at him, defiance in her watery eyes. How could she possibly think this was his fault? Why was she blaming him? Mark looked around at his friends, at his sister, at those who were witnessing his heart getting spit on by the woman who claimed to love him.

"What happened to Michelle?" he demanded, and wadded the paper into a ball. He wanted so much to go to her and give comfort, but the look she threw him was deadly.

He was about to mention the charity he'd founded and his plans when she rounded on him. "I don't have time to explain it to you. You've already taken me away from where I was needed most, and I let you."

That wasn't fair. Didn't she get that he needed her, too? "Lorelei, you didn't do anything wrong."

Mark jerked at the power of her response. She fisted her hands, began shaking, and yelled, "I did everything wrong! I got distracted by you, let you in. I let you be important. And this is my penance. This is what I get for being involved with you."

He didn't know what to say or do. Lorelei wasn't thinking straight. "Why don't you calm down, sweetheart—"

"I can't calm down!" He took a step toward her. "Stay away from me."

At a loss, he raised his hands, palms up, and said, "Lorelei, we didn't do anything wrong. Michelle is just sick. This would have happened whether you were there or not."

Lorelei turned to go and glared at him over her shoulder. "But you made me fall for you and I lost focus on my goal. I had one job to do and I fucked up. I won't make that mistake again."

His throat closed up tight and everything went still. "What do you mean?"

She looked him square in the eyes, hers bright with unshed tears. "I mean that we're through."

He shook his head in denial. It couldn't be. "What about what you told me earlier?"

She didn't even blink. "I lied."

Mark stared down at her as pain lashed through him like a bullwhip. She didn't love him.

And the truth of it nearly killed him.

"Go to hell, Lorelei." She was just like Dina, just like the rest. When was he ever going to learn?

"Leslie, will you take me to my car?" she stood and asked, dismissing him like he was nothing to her.

He was a fool after all.

Chapter 26

LORELEI KNEW EXACTLY what she had to do. And nothing was going to stop her this time. Shutting out everything else, all the hurt and panic, she focused on the only thing that mattered: saving Michelle.

Leslie shoved open the door to Mark's condo and Lorelei slid around her. "Thanks for letting me in. I'll just grab my bag and be right back." Without waiting for a reply, she strode quickly down the hall to the master bedroom. Once inside she found Mark's charm exactly where he'd left it when he'd taken it off the night before and forgot to put back on.

She didn't even hesitate, just grabbed the cross and slipped it in her front pocket as she made her way across the room to her bag. Then she snatched up the small overnight bag she'd brought just in case, threw it over her shoulder, and was back out the door in less than thirty seconds total.

Leslie was still by the front door waiting for her, concern shadowing her beautiful face. "Is there anything I can do, Lorelei? Would you like me to go to the hospital with you?"

She wasn't going to the hospital.

"I appreciate the offer, Leslie. But I think it's best if I go by myself. I'll give you a call later, though, and let you know what's going on." Pushing past her, Lorelei forced a smile and glanced over her shoulder as she made her way to the elevator. "I promise."

But first things first.

They parted ways in the parking garage and Lorelei wasted no time. She'd memorized the address on the scrap of paper Dina had slipped her, knew exactly how to get there. In less than twenty minutes she was pulling into the driveway of Dina Andrews's lavish home. One look at it confirmed what she'd suspected deep down all along: Mark had lied about the lack of money just to shake her.

Impatience and anxiety pawed at her, making her movements stiff and jerky as she climbed the steps to the front door. Lorelei refused to think of the consequences of what she was doing and pushed the doorbell button. She'd deal with whatever happened—later.

After a few tense, long seconds the door swung open. Dina took one look at her, her cold blue eyes assessing, her posture aloof, dripping Chanel. Then she tossed her pearl blond locks and smiled victoriously. "I knew you wouldn't fail me. Come on inside."

Lorelei felt a tremble in the pit of her stomach and

forcefully ignored it. Stepped over the threshold and followed Dina through the decadent foyer. The ex-Mrs. Cutter lived well, that was for sure. The place reeked of expensive, high-maintenance woman.

The frigid sound of Dina's voice grabbed Lorelei's attention, and she turned her head toward Dina. "I take it things fell apart between you and that illiterate bastard. Can't say that I'm sorry about it. I always say that good looks fade over time, but stupidity is forever. You're better off without him."

Lorelei wasn't dumb. She knew exactly what the woman was implying. But she didn't have time to play her catty little games. "Where's the money, Dina?"

The too slender woman smirked. "Touchy, aren't you? Does the truth bother you?"

She bothered her. "I have somewhere to be. So why don't you just get the money and we can be done with this thing." She pulled the charm out of her pocket and dangled it briefly, then put it back. "I showed you mine. Now it's your turn."

Dina pushed past Lorelei and she caught a whiff of expensive perfume. "I've been after that charm of his ever since he walked out. He's so damn attached to it that I'm going to use it to my advantage."

A thought occurred to Lorelei. "Is that why you have the restraining order? Were you stalking him?"

She watched the blond sniff a bouquet of red roses that sat on a side table. Then she straightened and said dismissively, "That and the phone calls and the whole hitting thing. He's such a wuss. Called the cops on me over a little slap. Can you believe it?"

Yeah, actually she could. It was called assault.

The necklace suddenly felt like lead in her pocket. "Look, Dina, I don't care what you're going to do with his good luck charm. But we made a deal and I'm here to collect." Being in Dina's presence was making Lorelei feel slimy and in need of a shower. It was time to go.

The air changed suddenly and the woman spun, hatred plastered across her face. "I'm going to make him pay out his ass. He'll give me twenty million to get his cross back because he's powerless without it. Five million for every year I suffered in that marriage. My best years were wasted on that dumb prick. No matter what I did, he never noticed. Never gave me the attention I deserved. I did everything for him and he didn't give a shit about me." She speared Lorelei with a bitter glance. "You'd better get used to it. Get used to playing second fiddle to a goddamn fucking *sport*."

Lorelei was getting the picture now. In the center of it was a spoiled woman who was used to all the attention and when she didn't get it, she'd become resentful. And that had eventually festered into a need for revenge.

Her heart went out to Mark. Living with Dina must have been a real bitch.

Restless to get a move on, Lorelei opened her mouth to demand payment when a knock sounded at the door. Shifting her feet on the marble floor of the foyer, she glanced out the window and saw two police officers standing there.

Her stomach plummeted to her feet.

Lorelei almost peed herself. There were cops at the door! Oh God. Had she been followed? Were they there to arrest her? Had Mark turned her in after all? What was she supposed to do now? Panic seized her in its white-hot grip.

She looked around frantically for a place to hide as Dina strode toward the door. The small cross poked into her, branding her with its presence. Running on instinct, she whipped it out quickly and slipped it over her head. She was just tucking it under her shirt when the door swung open.

"Hello, Officers," Dina said, all solicitous. "What can I do for you?"

A tall, dark-haired cop responded, his voice a practiced neutral. "Dina Andrews?"

Lorelei's knees shook and her stomach pitched hard. She was going to jail. She just knew it. Michelle was going to die in the hospital while she was arrested for stealing the one thing that was supposed to save her.

This had to be her karmic payback.

Wanting more than anything to melt into the floor and slip under the door, Lorelei frowned instead when Dina tossed her a look over her bony shoulder. What was that supposed to mean? If she wasn't so scared right now, she'd think that look was something close to fear.

Trying to become the wall, she watched as Dina tossed her hair. Then the woman straightened her back, breathed in deep, and said, "That's me."

The tall cop in the slick shades stepped forward,

reaching behind him at the same time. "Dina Andrews, you're under arrest for violation of a restraining order."

Sweet holy God. Relief poured through Lorelei like the Niagara. They weren't after her.

"You're crazy. You can't arrest me!" Dina yanked her arm out of the officer's grasp and tried to walk away. The officers detained her real quick.

"I advise you, Ms. Andrews, to cooperate. Security footage places you two nights ago at the residence parking garage of the party on your order. You are in clear violation. We were also informed by security there that a piece of jewelry is missing from the same party. Know anything about that?"

So much for relief. Lorelei's whole body clenched up tight. The cross under her shirt seemed to throb with life, and the skin beneath the metal cross itched like mad, as if it had suddenly developed an acute allergic response to gold. She felt like she was stuck in an Edgar Allan Poe story. Could anybody else hear the frantic pound of her heartbeat?

Dina began cursing as the officers clamped her wrists in handcuffs. Lorelei watched with wide eyes as Mark's ex jerked a hand free and pointed an accusing finger at her. "I didn't take anything. It's her! She has it, I swear. In her pocket. Check her pocket!" Her voice ended on a shrill note.

Lorelei froze.

The other officer, a balding, middle-aged man with a mustache, gave her a thorough once-over. "Ma'am, do you know what this woman is talking about?"

Like a deer in the headlights, she just stood there, blinking hard. The cop kept his eyes steady on her, waiting for a response. She must have been too slow, because she saw him sigh and begin walking toward her. "I'm going to have to ask you to empty your pockets, ma'am."

Over his bulky shoulder, she saw Dina beam, even as she fought against the cuffs. Blood pounded in her ears as the cop stopped directly in front of her. Finding her voice, she said shakily, "Yes, Officer." Her hands trembled so hard she could barely get them in her pockets. With her stomach flopping and her heart racing, she pulled the cotton liner out from each pocket.

They were empty.

The officer took them both in, stared for long silent moments. They were some of the longest of her life. After what felt like eons, his grizzled mustache twitched and he looked up at her. "Sorry for the inconvenience, ma'am. You can be on your way."

Lorelei wanted to collapse right there on the floor, in a big ol' puddle of relief-filled tears.

Dina yanked against her restraints and yelled, "No! She has it, I swear! Arrest her!" Eyes frosty with loathing pinned Lorelei. "Where did you put it, you lying bitch?"

How she managed to shrug was beyond her, but it pissed Dina off. The blond lurched for her, screaming. It took both officers to restrain her and escort her to the squad car. The woman yelled all kinds of retribution until the door was shut on her. Her outburst had garnered the attention of the neighbors, and several watched the commotion through their front windows.

Lorelei kept at the edges of the cops' periphery and walked as slowly and normally as she could to her car. Once inside, she nodded at the uniformed men and shifted into gear. Fear still skittered just under her skin and pulled at the thread of her composure as she steered down the long drive. Mark's necklace rested between her breasts and she drove away, keenly aware of its presence. She kept glancing in the rearview mirror until Dina's house and the police car were out of view.

Then she released a trembling breath and raked an unsteady hand through her hair. That had been so close! Wanting to give in to the adrenaline letdown, she pushed on instead and headed toward Denver Children's.

There was no money. It was over.

Heartache and acceptance settled over her as she navigated the streets. Her entire family was at the hospital and she wasn't going to waste another minute being away from them.

She hoped to God it wasn't too late.

LORELEI DROVE LIKE a madwoman and made it to the hospital in record time. By the time she hit the ICU doors she was at a dead run. And she dang near plowed her brother over. She *did* spill coffee down his denim shirt, making him swear.

"Damn it, Lorelei." Logan fanned the shirt with his right hand, then took a pull of what coffee was left in the Styrofoam cup. "Watch where you're going."

Bracing her hands on the sides of his rawboned face,

she took a moment to calm her racing heart and studied her brother. For the first time Lorelei noticed the fine lines that had etched prematurely around his deeply tanned face, the worry line between his brows. There were deep circles under his eyes from lack of sleep and worry. But there were no shadows *in* them. She chose to take that as a good sign. "How is your baby, Logan?"

At that question Logan smiled, slowly, devastatingly. It reached all the way to his eyes and lit the dark brown depths. "She's going to be just fine, string bean. She's being prepped for surgery right now. You can thank your baseball player for that."

Her brows pulled down in confusion. "What do you mean? What does Mark have to do with anything?"

Logan put his free hand on her elbow and tried to lead her down the long hallway, but her feet were rooted to the spot. He tugged until she lost balance, then began walking and explaining as he pulled her along. "Your ballplayer has a charity, Lorelei, that gives grants to children suffering from potentially terminal illnesses."

Lorelei stumbled. "He does not."

"Does so." Logan kept on walking, his long stride eating up ground.

She didn't believe it. "What's the name of it?"

They rounded a corner and Logan took another sip of coffee. "Sunny Days Foundation. A representative came to see me a few hours ago with some paperwork and a grant that covers all of Michelle's medical costs. Your baseball player set it all up. Apparently he'd wanted to surprise us, but Michelle was hospitalized before he could tell you about it. He's a right good man, Lorelei. Don't you let him go, you hear?"

After what she'd done today she seriously doubted she'd have a choice in the matter. Once Mark knew the truth he'd want nothing to do with her ever again. She'd stolen something priceless from him. But, much worse than that, she'd hurt a man who'd overcome so much adversity and deserved her respect and admiration. Instead, he'd received anger and nastiness. And after all that he'd still done this for her—for her family. She'd blamed him, and he'd been setting this up all along.

The shame she'd sworn earlier wouldn't get to her suddenly ate a hole through the wall of righteousness she'd built and took a big, fat, guilt-ridden bite.

God, what a day. She needed a drink . . . and a plan. Mark had her love and Lorelei was going to make things right between them. No matter what it took.

Chapter 27

MARK STARED ACROSS the table piled high with the remains of the Rush's victory feast of ribs at Casey's Smokehouse in Houston, Texas. The ancient jukebox kicked on in the corner of the small, dim bar. Good ol' country blues filled the place as George Strait sang about a woman looking so good in love. A red and gold Miller sign flickered on the wall behind the bar.

"You're a real sick individual, Drake, you know that? How many poor cows had to die tonight to feed your sorry ass?" he said to the first baseman next to him.

The veteran raised his arms and looped his fingers together behind his head, grinned. "I'm a growing boy. Gotta get my protein."

Peter leaned down the table and threw a peanut shell. It landed right in his beer glass. Mark raked his gaze over the pitcher and scowled. "All right, asshole. Now you gotta buy me another beer."

"Listen to you, Wall, all pissy like a woman. You've been pitiful since you screwed up last week with my fantasy woman. Why don't you call her and get her back?" Peter said, and signaled to a waitress in a red T-shirt.

Mark frowned down at the table and started ripping a paper napkin to pieces. He was pretending it was Kowalskin's head. "I don't want to talk about it. And stop saying that kind of stuff about her, it's pissing me off. She's *my* woman."

"Really?" Peter challenged. "Seems to me, if I recall right, that she ain't your woman anymore."

If he had any energy he'd get up and kick Pete's ass for that. Hell, he'd deserve it for sticking his nose where it didn't belong. "Watch what you say to me, Peter. I'm not feeling the friendliest lately." That was the understatement of the century. He was downright bitchy, to steal a phrase from Leslie.

JP added a rib to the growing pile of dead animal bones. "I think you need to win her back, Wall. She was great."

Drake nodded in agreement. "Yeah, she's the stuff, all right. If you don't hurry, that woman's gonna get snatched up by some poser and you'll be shit out of luck."

What the hell was this? Dr. Phil night? He didn't have to listen to this crap. "Screw you guys. I'm going to play some pool. And don't anybody follow me."

As Mark pushed through the wooden tables in the small bar, he swore. He didn't need his teammates telling him he should get her back. Hell, no. He already knew that. From the moment she'd left that day with Leslie he'd known it.

But he didn't know how to fix it.

Because the truth was, she'd hurt him. He still felt raw inside from it. That's partly why he hadn't called her back. And because when he did call her back he'd have to explain to her why her words had ripped him open so bad. That her words were an echo from Dina long ago. Blaming him. Accusing him. Saying she didn't love him.

But Drake had been right. Lorelei was a treasure, and if he didn't get his act together someone else was going to come along and steal her. And then he'd have to kill the bastard. Because living without her for a lifetime was impossible.

He knew because he'd been living the past week without her and he missed her so frigging bad it was eating a hole through him.

Mark reached the lone pool table in the far corner and started to rack the balls. Only a single flickering light with a cheap plastic Budweiser lampshade hung over the table. When he stepped the few feet to the wall to grab a stick he was almost surrounded by the dark.

The jukebox shuffled songs, colored lights flashing across its face, and Travis Tritt started singing about smelling T-R-O-U-B-L-E. He grabbed the green chalk and rubbed it over the tip of his cue, blew the excess off, and bent down to the table. His gaze traveled down the length of the pool stick to the white cue ball, across the green felt, over the colored balls, and continued right up to a fantastic pair of breasts pressed together in a plunging red V-neck tank top.

Mark didn't even have to see the face that belonged

to those breasts. He knew it was her. And emotions tore through him with violent force.

Lorelei.

He let his gaze slide up her throat, over her amazing mouth curled in a soft smile, to her beautiful, exotic green eyes. She'd piled her mass of dark hair on top of her head and tied it off with a blue bandana.

Jesus.

The potency of her slammed into his solar plexus and he couldn't breathe. Slowly he straightened and slid his gaze down the rest of her. Over her delicious curves, her short white denim skirt, and her long legs.

Then he saw them and it almost dropped him to his knees. Lorelei was wearing her cowboy boots.

Suddenly he didn't care that she'd hurt him, that she'd shredded him. None of that mattered, not one damn little bit. He needed her, more than he needed anything. And Mark wanted to spill out the truth about himself and that horrible day with Dina, put it all on the table. So that he could let it go and move on with his life. Move on with Lorelei.

Because his life was nothing but shit without her and when she'd left him that day he'd stopped breathing. He needed to breathe again.

Lorelei was his woman. She was his everything. And he needed to find the balls to make things right. He would, too—if she loved him.

"I thought I'd stop by for a little chat, being as there appears to be something wrong with your phone, Mark." She straightened and his gaze dropped to the silky skin of her legs. God, he'd missed that skin. Missed touching it, kissing it. Missed the way it smelled and warmed with desire for him.

But more than that, he missed her. He missed the way her eyes lit up when she laughed, and how her nose wrinkled up like a pug's when she sneezed. He even missed the way she snored when she was pressed up against him sound asleep.

He swallowed hard as his insides started a wicked tug-of-war of emotions. "It's a long way to come for a chat, Lorelei. So I'll make it worth your while. I've got something that needs to be said and I'm going to ask you to not talk until I'm done."

Lorelei tilted her head and eyed him, the ends of her bandana fluttering with the movement. "All right. And when you're done you have to listen to what I have to say."

"That's fair. Here, why don't you grab a stick and we'll play while we talk." That way he'd be able to keep his hands off her, keep from falling to his knees in front of her and begging. Because he didn't know if it would be welcome. He wasn't sure how she felt. But she was here now, all the way down in Texas. And that meant something.

He just hoped she was there for him, for them. Not out of gratitude for Michelle. It might just kill him if she was only there because of that.

Mark motioned for her to break and she bent over the table, lined up, and sent the balls scattering around the table. The orange stripe fell in the corner pocket.

"I'm stripes, you're solids. Now, let's talk," she said, and bent over the table again.

Christ, he wanted to make things right between them. He wanted her back in his life. "Fine, I'll be solids. Now, shoot and listen. Don't talk. This is so goddamn hard for me to talk about, but I have to. I have to let you know why what you said hurt me so bad last week, why I haven't been able to pick up the phone."

Chalking the tip of her stick again, she leveled her eyes on him, raised a delicate brow. "*Mmm-hmm.*" She didn't say a word.

Good. "I married Dina when I was very young. I was an up-and-coming catcher in the major leagues and I was finally getting noticed by women. I was a new man without a past. Nobody knew my secrets, and when Dina pursued me I fell for it. Fell for her. She charmed the hell out of me. We were married three years before she found out I was dyslexic. I'd become damn good about hiding the fact I couldn't read. And I mean at all, Lorelei. I couldn't read *at all* my dyslexia was so bad." Mark bent over and took a shot. He hit the yellow solid in the corner pocket.

Lorelei just raised an eyebrow again when he looked at her. Not a trace of shock or disgust marred her beautiful face. And it gave him the courage to finish the story. "When I finally told her she said she didn't care. But then she started to leave notes all over the house for me. On the mirror, on the fridge, on the counters. And it hurt because I knew deep down she was doing it on purpose." He lined up, sighted the solid green ball, banked it, and sank it into the middle pocket.

"*Mmm-hmm.*"

He felt a smile tug at his mouth and the tight, hot

knot in his gut began to uncoil. "Then I started to see letters left all around the house in handwriting that wasn't hers. When I asked her about them she said they from her family. I believed her, because I wanted to so bad. I didn't want to admit to what I knew in my gut was going on. Then one day I came home from practice a little early and heard her voice in the bedroom along with another man's. I heard her call me a "fucking retard" to that guy, and say how I was so stupid I couldn't read the love letters from him she'd been leaving around the house. They had a good laugh over it."

Lorelei gasped and then a low, feline growl came from her. Her arms crossed over her ample breasts and she started to tap a boot on the floor in a rhythmic tap, tap, tap. "Mmm-hmm." There was way more emphasis this time.

Mark sank another ball. "I confronted her and she went ballistic, blaming me for her cheating. That was the story of our relationship. She was always accusing, threatening, blaming. It wore me down and ate at my confidence. Made me believe that everything pretty much was my fault. Even that it was my fault she'd never loved me. But she went too far when she blamed me for her infidelity. I left that day and have been struggling to read ever since. I swore no other woman would ever have that kind of power to hurt me. And that's why I lashed out at you the way I did at Pete's place. Because you'd hurt me when you told me you'd lied. I'm sorry for it and I apologize. But I don't want to rehash that fight with you, Lorelei. I can't. I forgive you and I hope you can forgive me. I just want to move forward from here with you. I just want to be with you." He straightened and stared across the table at her. Searched her face. "You can talk now."

"I'm taking the first flight back to Denver." Lorelei stated, and set her pool stick on the table.

Mark wasn't sure what to make of the gleam in her eye. "Why would you want to do that?" he asked warily. Maybe she was disgusted by him after all.

Lorelei looked him square in the eye. "So I can go kick her sorry ass, that's why."

God, what a woman.

"Now, sweetheart," he said as the knot is his stomach melted into nothing and his heart started pounding. Hope flared hot behind his ribs.

He started breathing again.

She waved him off. "Oh, all right. Never mind. Knee-jerk reaction." She huffed, bit her bottom lip, and eyed him. "Now it's my turn to admit something. The day Michelle was hospitalized, I took your charm. I would have done anything to save that little girl. I'm sorry for taking it from you again, but I'm not sorry for feeling justified in doing so. Now I'm here to give it back to you and to apologize. I know it might not matter, but I still needed to do it in person."

He watched Lorelei pull his necklace from her skirt pocket and hold it out to him. He didn't want it. He'd learned a while ago that Lorelei was what mattered, not the cross. He made his own luck. It was nothing but a piece of metal and distant memories.

Mark shrugged a shoulder. "I knew you took it, and

told the cops housecleaning had found it. I didn't blame you. I'd have done the same if I was in your shoes. But I don't care about that anymore, so put it away. I only care about you."

She looked at him speculatively for a moment, but he could see the relief practically wash over her as she replaced the cross in her pocket. Her whole body seemed to relax. Then she was rounding the end of the pool table, coming toward him. When she smiled at him through her lashes he almost wept from sight of it. "I've got a confession to make."

"What's that?" he murmured. Damn, but she looked like a woman on a mission. Positively lethal. Grinning, he took a step in retreat and came up against the wall. He couldn't wait to hear her confession.

"I came down here to do more with you than apologize and have a chat," she said, and stopped in front of him. "I just want to be with you, period. Day or night, anytime. Always."

Good God. A strangled sound escaped him and his knees almost gave out. "Really?" That was brilliant. But Lorelei was scrambling his brain and he couldn't think.

She stepped into the shadows with him and placed her hands on his chest, and his heart flopped beneath her palms. "I have another confession."

He didn't know if he could handle another confession like that. "What's that?" he whispered.

"I know what you did for Michelle." Her breath slid moist across his neck as she drew closer. "Thank you."

"It was nothing. But I'm sorry I didn't tell you about it

before she was hurt. Things would have been different between us if I had." Her hands were doing crazy things to his insides and all the blood was draining from his head. He covered them with his own and flattened them to his chest.

"It was much more than that and you know it. But that's not why I'm here." Lorelei placed a warm, soft kiss on the side of his neck and he hissed. "I have another confession."

"What's that, love?" She kissed the underside of his jaw and he felt a shiver dart down his spine.

"I'm so incredibly sorry for the way I treated you. It was inexcusable and I apologize. I admire your strength and determination. And I respect you for having the courage to tell me the truth—even when I don't deserve it. But I lied when I said I was lying. The truth is, I'm crazy for you. Totally, completely, hopelessly in love with you. And I hope you can forgive me."

Thank you, God.

Mark grabbed her waist and spun her around until her back was to the wall and covered her body with his, pressed into her. His heart opened right up and all the pain washed away. It filled back up with Lorelei. Only Lorelei. "I've got a confession for you."

She gasped, "What's that?"

He cupped her face in his hands and lowered his mouth over hers. "I love you, too. And I forgive you. I died inside when you left me last week. I need to be with you. Now, forever. Say you'll never leave me again. Please. I'll get on my knees and beg for you. Just please don't leave me. When you go I can't breathe."

He felt her tremble beneath his hands. "I'll never leave you. *Ever.* I'm your woman. And you're my beautiful, perfect man. My smooth-talking catcher with the fast hands. Now kiss me, show me your moves and make it count."

He smiled against her mouth. "Anything for you, baby." Because she was his woman and she was crazy for him. She was beautiful and she thought he was perfect.

And that made her perfect.

Epilogue

Four Months Later

LORELEI STEPPED OUT the back door of Peter Kowalskin's house and walked across the patio, plastic cup of keg beer in hand. She strode by Leslie, John Crispin, and a dozen other players. She sidled past Drake Paulson floating on a blow-up lobster in the pool—still clothed, thank God—toward the man lounging beneath a green and white striped umbrella table.

There he was, in tan cargo shorts and a navy "Baseball Players Hit It Hard" T-shirt, dark blond hair curling around the edge of a baseball cap. Her husband. Denver Rush's star catcher with the quick moves. Her lover, her best friend. Her heart.

He glanced up and smiled when he spotted her. "Hey, honey, come over here and help me convince this loser that you are officially, seriously off the market." He leaned back in his plastic deck chair and tipped his chin at Kowalskin.

It was September and they'd been married three weeks already. Three wonderful, magical weeks on so many levels. Michelle was getting stronger and healthier every day since she'd had surgery. It still made Lorelei cry when she looked at her sweet, precious niece and knew the little girl was going to live to grow into a woman. That she had a future.

And Logan—he was a new man. A man with hope and happiness. When he smiled and laughed, it reached his eyes. Even now he was in the pool, all bright smiles while he towed Michelle around on a floaty and she giggled and splashed at him. Seeing them together like that made her heart sing a very happy song.

She had that computer chair she'd always dreamed about—the one that cradled her behind like a glove. And she was trying her hand at writing a full-length novel. Oh, she was still writing articles about which organic pesticides were most effective and she still got all excited about it. The tomato plant Mark had given her had been the inspiration for a zinger of an article about natural compost. When it had appeared in last month's *Go Natural* gardening magazine, Mark had bought a copy and practiced reading it to her one night while they'd snuggled on the couch. He'd been mighty impressed to discover horse crap was high in nitrogen.

He said that the Rush would win the World Series for sure because he had the most potent lucky charm a guy could get. *Her.* And yeah, she'd rewarded him good for that one.

Mark raised his hand and slid his arm around her waist when she reached his side. "Tell this bozo you're not interested, sweetheart. That you've got me whipped good and I'm your love slave." He winked at her and caressed her bottom. "And that you're Fonda Peters, my rodeo queen."

Lorelei laughed and slid onto his lap. He had her there. When it came to him she was definitely Fonda Peters— sex goddess.

And why shouldn't she be?

He was Mark Cutter, all-around major league badass. The sweet-talking catcher with the best moves on and off the field. Who she was so deep in love with that she'd never get out. Never want out.

And because he was seriously good with his hands.

Can't wait for the next big game?
Keep reading for a sneak peek
of Jennifer Seasons's
next book in the Diamonds and Dugouts series:

PLAYING THE FIELD

Coming July 2013 from Avon Impulse

JP REACHED OUT an arm to snag her, but she slipped just out of reach—for the moment. Did she really think she could get away from him?

There was a reason he played shortstop in the major leagues. He was damn fast. And now that he'd decided to make Sonny his woman she was about to find out just how quick he could be.

With a devil's grin, he moved and had her back against the old barn wall before she'd finished gasping. "Look me in the eyes right now and tell me I don't affect you, that you're not interested." He traced a lazy path down the side of her neck with his fingertips and felt her shiver. "Because I don't believe that line for an instant, sunshine."

Close enough to feel the heat she was throwing from her deliciously curved body, JP laughed softly when she tried to sidestep and squeeze free. He raised an arm and

blocked her in, his palm flush against the rough, splinter-
ing wood.

Sonny shook back her rose-gold curls and tipped her
chin defiantly. "Believe what you want, you cocky ballplayer. I don't have to prove anything to you." Her denim
blue eyes flashed with emotion. "So why don't you take
your swagger and your over-the-top flirting and go use it
on someone who cares and has the time. I have a business
to run and a son to raise."

JP settled his gaze on her mouth. He wondered what it
would feel like to kiss those juicy lips and decided to find
out. Though she said she wasn't interested, her body said
different. He could feel her pulse, fast and frantic, under
his fingertips.

It made his pulse kick up a notch in anticipation.
"There's a surefire way to end this little disagreement
right now, because I say you're lying." He cupped her chin
with his hand and watched her thick lashes flutter as she
broke eye contact. But she didn't pull away.

JP knew he had her.

Her voice came soft and a little shaky. "What do you
want me to do?"

Lowering his head until he was a whisper away, he
issued the challenge. "Kiss me."

Her gaze flew to his, her eyes wide with shock. "You
want me to do what?"

What he knew they both wanted.

"Kiss me. Prove to me you're not interested and I'll
leave here. You can go back to your business and your son
and never see me again."

As he watched her contemplate, she bit her plump bottom lip and stared at him. It was too much temptation for him to ignore.

He flattened her against the wall and took her mouth in a searing kiss. She whimpered against him and he felt her hands flail helplessly. Her body was taut as a bowstring.

He kept up the seductive assault on her mouth until she sagged against him and her hands fisted in the back of his shirt. Until she was kissing him back with every bit as much desire. When she moaned and slid her tongue over his bottom lip he knew he had her right where he wanted her.

Pulling back, he took in her glazed, passion-drunk expression and tasted the victory. Damn straight, she was interested. "See you next week, sunshine."

About the Author

JENNIFER SEASONS is a Colorado transplant. She lives with her husband and four children along the Front Range, where she enjoys breathtaking views of the mighty Rocky Mountains every day. A dog and two cats keep them company. When she's not writing, she loves spending time with her family outdoors, exploring her beautiful adopted home state.

Visit www.AuthorTracker.com for exclusive information on your favorite HarperCollins authors.

Give in to your impulses . . .
Read on for a sneak peek at a brand-new
e-book original tale of romance from Avon Books.
Available now wherever e-books are sold.

ALL OR NOTHING
A TRUST NO ONE NOVEL
By Dixie Lee Brown

An Excerpt from

ALL OR NOTHING
A Trust No One Novel

by Dixie Lee Brown

Debut author Dixie Lee Brown launches
her *Trust No One* series with this tale of
a hunted woman and the one man who
can save her life . . . if she'll let him.

"Trust me. This is the safest way."

Everything required trust with Joe. So, did she trust him? If she ever got back on the ground, she might be able to answer that question. Cara looked over the edge of the platform. *There's no way!*

"Take your time. Go when you're ready . . . unless you want me to give you a little push."

"You wouldn't dare!" She wrapped her arms around the pole.

"You really don't trust me, do you?" He laughed.

"I was starting to, before you said the word 'push.'"

"There's hope then? If I choose my words more carefully?"

"Maybe . . . if I ever get down from here."

"Let's sit for a minute. Things will look different from that perspective." He sat, dangling his long legs over the side. Cara positioned herself beside him, her hands nervously flexing on the rope that joined her to the zip line.

"Jumping doesn't seem any more reasonable from here." Too bad, since sitting close enough to rub shoulders with him made her nearly as uncomfortable as the stupid zip line.

"We'll just hang out and talk for a while then. That okay?" He gripped the edge of the platform and leaned forward, turning to look at her.

"The last time we talked, it ended badly."

"Now we know which subjects to stay away from."

"Yeah, anything to do with either of our private lives."

"I think it was your ex-husband and my desire to protect you from him that got us crossways with each other."

Cara glanced sideways at him. He was looking at her. Their eyes met. The strangest emotions coursed through her. Somehow, it didn't sound so bad when he said it like that. Who didn't want a knight in shining armor? She was afraid for Joe, but he sounded so confident that he could protect her, and himself, she almost believed it. Recognizing the danger in that, she tore her eyes away from his.

"We're making progress. You didn't rip into me that time." A grin came through in his voice.

"It doesn't do any good to try talking sense into you." She wanted to sound serious, but her heart was no longer in it. She forced her mind back to the task at hand, considering the likelihood that she'd ever be able to *zip* off this ledge. What was the worst that could happen? The cable could break, and she'd plummet thirty feet to the ground. End all of her problems. More likely, it would be a gradual descent, with the jump from the platform the only really exciting part. She could do this.

"We've got unfinished business, you know. We might as well take care of it while we're sitting here."

"What's that?"

"I almost had you talked into dinner that night we met."

"You weren't even close."

"I think you were as intrigued with the idea as I was." He grinned. "I also think we stood a good chance of ending the evening with a kiss."

"That's a stretch. You're making the same mistake you made that night. Going from confident to arrogant in about two seconds flat. There was no chance in hell you were going to get a kiss." Cara smiled at his wounded look.

"Will my chances ever improve?" His eyes met hers again.

She'd forgotten what a good-looking guy he was. The same mesmerizing pull she'd experienced the night she met him overcame her better judgment now. For a moment she wondered what it would feel like, his lips on hers, his arms holding her close, while they lost themselves in each other.

Cara drew herself up short. Was she completely crazy? She was barely free from one dangerous man. Why would she get involved with another? There was an attraction between them she couldn't deny, but nothing could ever come of it.

"Maybe." The word slipped out, almost on its own.